I0634710

IRON

FROM THE

SKY

THE LAST MANUSCRIPT OF THE RICHARDS' TRUST

BY
W.J. CHERF

Foxbat Publishing
ISBN: 978-1-7329779-3-8

The front and back cover's reversing clock image is adapted from
the apple.com time machine logo.

Iron

From The

Sky

ALSO BY W.J. CHERF

The Manuscripts of the Richards' Trust

Bow Tie

Recovery

Children of Ptah

Imhotep

Maat-ka-ra. Memoirs of a Time Traveler

The Adventures of J.J. Stone

The First Soul

The Lictor of Magic

I Am the Storm

Adventures in Paranormal Archaeology

The Magician's Tomb

Netherworld's Gate

Dhampirica

DEDICATION

Every author's first line of defense is made up of editors and brave souls willing to endure the early drafts of a manuscript. They are a patient and hopeful lot, and without them, frankly, any author would be at a total loss. Consequently, I dedicate this manuscript to those gentle beings with deep and heartfelt thanks. Their frank observations were invaluable.

As is always the case, my dear wife, Sweet Sue, did have something to say about this book. Her patient, caring, and always enduring ways support my special form of madness. Bless you, yet again.

EDITOR'S NOTE

My name is Paul Silas. I am the editor and executor of the Richards' Trust. With this last manuscript, I must add to my list of duties that of ghost writer.

For those faithful readers of the first five installments of The Manuscripts of the Richards' Trust, this book falls squarely between book two, *Recovery*, and book three, *The Children of Ptah*. Chronologically, the events described take place before the passing of Peter Borov and John Milson and after the loss—or perhaps better—reacquisition of the Aten space craft by its rightful owners.

The original instructions of the Richards' Trust empowered me to publish three manuscripts. But since Professor Richards' disappearance, the trust directed me to sell his flat and all of its contents. During that liquidation process all went well and according to plan, that is until I got to the contents of his old wooden desk.

That desk turned out to be practically a Russian set of dolls, complete with a hidden recess beneath its lower, left-hand drawer. In it I found a handgun, ammunition, and several gun maintenance items. Beneath it all Richards had squirreled away an oil stained manila envelope. That envelope contained a draft manuscript that became *Imhotep,* the Fourth Manuscript of the Richards' Trust.

That manila envelope also contained a folder of newspaper clippings, academic abstracts, several sensitive government documents, a list of chapters with their contents extensively outlined, and seventy-one pages of text. By their nature alone, I could tell that these documents had nothing at all to do with the *Imhotep* manuscript. Without question, it was another work in progress by Professor Richards.

I fully admit I laid aside these orphaned documents for far too long. As they began to gather dust and yellow on my "to do" shelf, I found myself picking them up to see what, if anything, I could cobble together. Whereas *Imhotep* had required just a clean edit, this effort required the steady hand of a ghost writer in order to bring it to press.

So, as editor, executor, and now ghost writer, you hold the last and final episode of The Manuscripts of the Richards' Trust, which I have entitled, *Iron from the Sky*.

Once again the subject matter of this book cannot be published under our university's house banner. Consequently, I have sought out the good graces of a local publishing house.

All advances and royalties from the publication of this last manuscript will be deposited into the Richards' Trust, where they will be divided among several designated funding instruments. Once the copy write limitation has been reached on this publication, then all instruments are to clear their accounts in one final, lump sum deposit. Thereafter, the Richards' Trust will finally be extinguished.

CHAPTER 1

Preliminaries. Circa 1350 BC

I sat pretending to be busy, engrossed, and fascinated. When in actual fact I was idle, disengaged, and bored, as if once again incubating in an egg cluster. In spite of all of my training, checklists, and psychological profiles, it is my belief that deep space survey work should be the task of thinking machines and not cognitively aware and creative life forms like me. There, I finally said it, and feel better for it.

Fortunately, my survey work will soon end, but nowhere near soon enough. After three hundred and twenty-one cycles of service I will be relieved, transferred out, and sent back home to a world that I will not recognize. The hard and fast rules of space, time, and relativity made sure of that. Frankly, I looked forward to the challenge, to start anew, and discover what my feathered-kind had come up with next.

The troubles began innocently enough. They started with an intermittent dashboard light, a slight wobble in the gravitation gage, and a minor quaver I felt throughout my survey craft. That was when I knew I was in for something special and out of the ordinary, perhaps even something downright dangerous. How exciting!

For the first time in a long time my scalp's crest of colorful plumage ruffled with concern. My large eyes darted over my control console, alert to every detail. Yes, I was in full diagnostic mode and frankly, alarmed. My biometric-package inquired about my physiological condition several times, even suggested a sedative, to the point it too got on my nerves. So I shut it off. Now was definitely *not* the time for a nap.

Then, it happened. As I passed through the outer asteroid-belt of a minor star system, the gravimetric system failed—utterly. Hurtling onward, I was without a hint of guidance or inertial stabilization whatsoever. As my craft began to slowly yaw and tumble, I entered my coordinates and general course. Finished, I then reached for the shrouded button of the emergency beacon. My first clawed talon could not make contact as I became overcome with nausea and lost consciousness. My restraint system took over. My craft spun insanely out-of-control.

* * *

How can a global system failure be attributed to a heavily redundant system? Nevertheless, the failure of Survey Craft Number Four represented a classic example of such a cascading collapse. Fortunately for the pilot, this malfunction did not affect its sensor array. In extremis, the pilot thought the worst had come. Instead, the guidance array located the nearest rock and the emergency jets vectored the crippled craft toward an appropriate landing site. Those sensors then recognized the total hopelessness of a survivable landing.

Put simply, the attitude jets were not up to the task without the assistance of the main engines. This fact initiated the ejection sequence of the pilot's emergency escape pod. A flat area was selected. The pod separated as all twelve of its moorings were explosively sacrificed.

Minus its guidance pod, the survey craft's attitude rapidly deteriorated. Upon atmospheric insertion, the craft's still functional automatic systems took over as it continued to tumble. In a spasm of energy, the gravitron engines accelerated one last time, ensuring a spectacular impact—as designed by its makers. The strict canon of the survey's charter did not allow for the unauthorized transfer of technology. Therefore, Survey Craft Number Four was not allowed to survive. Nonetheless, the ship's sensors merrily recorded its building acceleration right up to impact. Never before in the history of the survey had a machine initiated such an all-consuming death wish … so emphatically executed.

As for the shaped escape pod, given the gravity and atmosphere of the planet, its glide ratio was not ideal. If the pilot had been conscious, then it would have heard the tremendous roaring and felt the atmospheric buffeting of the passage. In the end, the best the pod's automatic controls could manage was a skipped landing followed by a prolonged slide across a silicate surface.

This challenged the restraint system. Yet, somehow, it did not fail nor dissect the unconscious pilot into several pieces.

*   *   *

The goat herder lay exhausted from his day's rounds, as the incessant care of some twenty-two very independent minds required today, and every day for that matter, his total attention. Penned in their desert corral for the night, the herder stretched out upon his meager bedding. He faced the starry night's sky and felt the first cooling breezes that signaled the end of that day's heat. Meanwhile, the herder listened for the stealthy approach of any threats to his personal fortune. For many trails coursed through this region, trails that foreign traders and desert raiders alike frequented.

But man was not his only threat. A hungry pack of desert jackals could strip him of his herd in moments. This night, however, hearing none of either, a satisfied sigh passed the herder's lips. With his stomach swelled from his evening repast of coarse grain and fresh goat's milk, all was right with the world. After all, what could possibly go wrong?

His long, dark eye-lashes fluttered towards sleep. The herder glanced once more across the heavens, reviewing in his mind and naming the many gods and goddesses who occupied that realm aloud, those that his father had taught him. It was his way to remember them all just before sleep overtook him. After all, there would be a time when he would teach his own children—or at least that was his dream.

But this night he caught sight of a new brightness that appeared in the sky, one which he could not name, one which intruded upon his solitude. Startled by the sight, the herder sat up mouth agape in awe as he witnessed one of the immortal gods descend. In what seemed a mere matter of moments, the brightness grew and grew as it neared. The herder, only a young man of sixteen inundations, was mesmerized by the ever-nearing spectacle, which seemed to be afire. A smoky trail traced its passage across the heavens, the very belly of the goddess Nut. His goats also took notice of this celestial manifestation and bleated in alarm.

Memories came and went during this display as the goat herder tried to remember anything from his father's teachings about the heavens that could match what he was seeing. Just before the meteoroid's impact, Sekemka's last thoughts were, *why was the fallen god making such a roaring noise?*

*   *   *

The survey craft's impact obliterated the immediate landscape of the goat pens. Weighing a shade over three tons, it had slammed into the desert at a hyper-velocity in excess of two miles per second, better than ten times the speed of sound.

What followed was a blinding flash of light as the gravitron engines and the ship's fuselage compressed, reached plasma-like temperatures, and for a split second, ignited like a small star. The extraterrestrial visitor cruelly gouged the mostly silicate surface and formed a crater about one hundred and fifty feet across by fifty deep. Ejecta flew over thirty-two hundred feet in the air in a southeastern direction. Multiple seismic tremors transited through the West Saharan limestone plateau. The searing heat of the enormous energy vitrified the surrounding landscape into a molten lake of glass. The atmospheric concussion of the event caused multiple reports of cloudless thunder. Finally, the sheer displacement of sand and rock formed a high altitude mushroom-like debris cloud, which would stain the pristine blue sky for days. Sekemka, and his beloved goats, never had a chance.

*   *   *

When I returned to consciousness, I was greeted by an obnoxious droning background of static, flashing console lights, and general confusion. The more that I blinked in an effort to clear my eyes, the quicker my head ached. Then there were those exploding flashes of light that kept getting into the way of my vision. As for the rest of me, well, I was living a nightmare of pain. While I indeed survived the impact and somehow remained intact, I didn't feel that way. I grudgingly had to admit that my escape pod had done its job. It had prevented me from smearing myself across this god-forsaken landscape like a broken egg.

Those were my first disjointed thoughts after that horrendous impact, and not necessarily in that order. I was concussed, delusional, and in considerable physical agony. Calling up my medical diagnostics with an eye-blink, I gradually came to the realization that my source of pain was from the restraint system itself, and not from any structural damage inflicted upon my delicate form.

A sigh followed by a deep breath. *I guess I will live.*

Only then did I trigger the emergency beacon. With that task done, I blinked at the onboard med-kit for a sedative, felt it take effect, and soon drifted off into what I sincerely hoped would be a restorative sleep.

*   *   *

Just how long I was under that self-induced rejuvenation coma, I calculated out, well, at this point it really doesn't matter. For when I awoke, the exquisite agony had left me, being replaced by several dull and very manageable aches and pains.

Now alert, I felt the urgent need to understand my situation. Engaging my pod's sensors, I found that only two survived. The other four had failed, as well as my emergency beacon. *Well*, I concluded, *that is not very good news.*

It meant I was on my own and with only the barest glimmer of hope for assistance. I supposed I could rely on the dumb luck of a chance scan by one of my kind. But by nature, I was a pragmatic realist. My situation was not good. The odds alone on anyone ever finding me were, well, infinitesimal. After all, imagine finding a near-light craft after who knows how many cycles had passed? My kind's survey teams routinely swept through these outer galactic systems at a brisk pace. By the time my overdue updates were noted, well, that's why I am a pragmatic realist.

What I could rely upon, however, could only be described as the stuff of pure fantasy. My pod's sensors indicated I was surrounded on all sides by life forms. Each individual seemed positioned equidistant from the next and at some agreed upon distance from my pod's hull. I idly mused on this spatial arrangement. *Why were they so egalitarian?*

Relatively short and triangular in structure, their large forward-facing eyes suggested intelligence. Twelve in all, an auspicious number, they seemed to be patiently waiting, perhaps for me to emerge, so that they might communicate with me, perhaps even greet me, maybe even be of some assistance. While those thoughts at first seemed a bit naïve, upon consideration, they also made sense. After all, I was here and they were there. How else am I to make a totally unauthorized first contact?

*   *   *

The pack of jackals did not know what to make of the large, egg-shaped object that had suddenly appeared in their territory. They could not approach close enough to stiff or taste it, as its outer skin was still far too hot from re-entry. So the pack did what all pack animals do. They waited, patiently, for something to happen. Precisely what, they didn't know, just that they were hungry.

CHAPTER 2

Egypt. January 1919

It was an incredible moment, quite electric actually. The desert wastes had again given up one of its secrets. This time it was the discovery of a tight familial cluster of tombs. Within the tomb of Meketre (TT280), the "Overseer of the Seal", "Chief Steward", and "Chancellor" of the Pharaoh Montuhotep I, were two others: Wah, who reported to Meketre initially as a minor scribe, became the later manager of his estate. The other, Intef, was most certainly a close relative.

While robbers had cleared out much from these tombs, they completely missed a secret chamber below it. Within was found many painted funerary models of boats, bakeries, breweries, cattle, and other dioramic scenes from his life. The American Egyptologist Herbert E. Winlock, the principal excavator at the time, was simply ecstatic at the Middle Kingdom find, as was his home institution, the Metropolitan Museum of Art in New York.

Meanwhile, nearby in the same neighborhood, another tomb was located by one of Winlock's men, a promising foreman named Husayn Saeed. Unlike the above mentioned remains, this tomb was far more modest, being a mere shaft grave, and consequently, it barely made it as a note within Winlock's already overflowing field journals. But unlike the above three heavily decorated tombs, the sarcophagus of its owner was found intact. It was almost as if the shaft tomb's security had been predicated upon the ostentation of its surrounding neighbors.

Since this was Saeed's first personal discovery, the Egyptian wanted to take special care in the recording of everything pertinent regarding the shaft tomb's clearance. So Saeed enlisted the help of one of Winlock's many graduate assistants, who was sympathetic to the Egyptian's desires "to get things squared away." In so doing, the pair found out from the coffin's inscription that the tomb's owner was a man named Sebekmose, an astronomer by trade, and *sem*-priest of the Great Hidden One, Amen Re. While no one realized it at the time, hidden within the coffin itself, beneath its fragile mummy, was a cache of hieratic papyri, which once found, would number over two hundred sheets and fragments.

*　　*　　*

When the time came for the "apportionment" of the archaeological material from that season's labors, Winlock, clearly blinded with a museum curator's eye on the many pretty funerary models that were found within the hidden chamber beneath Meketre's tomb, gladly bartered off the unique and intact coffin and modest grave goods of the "stargazer" Sebekmose to the Egyptian Antiquities Service's representative. These were then transported by train to the Cairo National Museum for their inspection, cataloguing, and restoration, if any was deemed needful, while a final judgment was made on their disposition.

At this point in the story, the precise course of events becomes a bit murky. Suffice it to say, the opening of Sebekmose's coffin, while considered an ordinary inspection procedure, fast became one of considerable consequence, when the papyri cache was noted peeking out from beneath the astronomer's mummy bandages.

At that point, the *directeur* of the Egyptian Antiquities Service, *Monsieur* Pierre Lacau, was immediately notified of the discovery. A highly regarded philologist himself, Lacau's first thought was to take the cache under his wing, but when he discovered that the cache was written in hieratic, a very difficult variation of the ancient Egyptian's written language, he did what all good administrators do. He decided to delegate the task.

That person was a French scholar and student of Gaston Maspero—Lacau's predecessor, one Henri Gebbert, who just so happened to be in Cairo at the time—on holiday. But as with every careful administrator, he first had to make sure of the man's competence.

Gebbert, a quiet man in his early thirties, arrived at the director's suite the next day, quite literally with hat-in-hand. After the usual pleasantries and a brief discussion of the situation, the pair made a visit to the restoration department, where the discovery had been made just the day before.

"So *Monsieur* Gebbert," the *directeur* began in French, "this is what my staff has found, a papyrus cache of some kind. I need your assessment of it."

Leading the young papyrologist over to a long wooden laboratory table upon which the open coffin laid, Lacau pointed, "*Monsieur* Gebbert, kindly take a look at one of these fragments and tell me what it is."

At no time did Lacau hint as to the period of the find. He didn't want to influence any assessment that Gebbert might be able to glean from the archive.

Extremely nervous, but also very much up to the intellectual challenge, Gebbert peered into the undisturbed coffin minus its inhabitant and immediately noted the extreme fragility of the papyri within.

"*Directeur* Lacau, these documents are extremely fragile. If I just draw one of them out, I fear that I may damage it."

"*Monsieur* Gebbert, don't be so timid. Just be very careful. That's all I ask."

For the next half hour, Gebbert, now with his overcoat folded next to him and his straw hat sitting atop the neat pile, carefully teased out several manageable papyri with his index and middle fingers and began to assess what he had before him. During this delicate process, Lacau had been good enough to provide him with a stool, a clip-board of paper, and several pencils. Beginning to take notes on the first fragment, Gebbert, stopped, looked up, and said.

"*Directeur* Lacau, this is a list of measurements that specifically refers to the movement of heavenly bodies, in other words, stars. It is dated to late in the reign of Tutankhamen. The author is Sebekmose, a *sem*-priest of Amen Re. And if I interpret this other title correctly, he is an astronomer, which of course makes sense given the content of the document."

Lacau, smiling for the first time, said. "*Monsieur* Gebbert, you seem to understand these documents quite well. Can you plan on staying on in Cairo for the next couple of weeks? My humble museum would be most appreciative to enlist your expertise."

"*Oui Directeur* Lacau, that I can manage."

"Good. Now roll up those pretty silk sleeves of yours and get down to work."

*   *   *

As a result of Henri Gebbert's month and a half in Cairo, the Frenchman had managed to learn quite a bit about museum restoration, procedures, and what it was like to handle a pristine and intact personal archive or *per medjat*. He also gained invaluable philological experience that greatly benefited him during his later career.

To his happy surprise, and in every instance, the many documents found in the cache dated to the Late

Eighteenth Dynasty, specifically the period between the reigns of Amenhotep III and Tutankhamen, or roughly about 1388 through 1323 BC. This fact was crucial, because up until this time, the date of Sebekmose's shaft tomb was suspected to be Middle Kingdom in date on the basis of the neighboring assemblages. As to the content of the personal archive, the documents clearly represented the life-long notes of a scholarly astronomer, named Sebekmose, a fact that nicely dove-tailed with the inscription upon the coffin's lid.

*   *   *

"So, *Monsieur* Gebbert, what am I do to with this astronomer's archive, eh?"

"*Directeur* Lacau, this archive must be studied and published as a unit, for it truly represents the life work of a scientist. To break it up would be criminal. It must be kept intact and studied as a whole. Furthermore, to my best knowledge, very little is known or understood about the ancient Egyptian's notions of formal astronomy. To date, everything that we know is clouded by the shroud of religion and cultic beliefs."

"So, Monsieur Gebbert. Who should undertake such a lifelong task, to study and publish this archive?"

To this crucial question, Gebbert began listing for the director all the men and women that he believed possessed the necessary tools for the task. But then to his complete and total surprise, Lacau, himself Jesuit trained, took apart his argument for each and every name that Gebbert had mentioned. The *directeur* pointed out their current interests, their age, their dispositions, even to mentioning things that quite frankly shocked the young scholar. No, the *directeur* had said. None of them will do. Never once had Gebbert thought about championing himself as a candidate.

"*Monsieur* Gebbert, you are a young scholar, who since your arrival, I have come to trust. With me, trust is a very important thing. So, *Monsieur* Gebbert, I am going to make you an offer. I wish for you to take on the Sebekmose archive and to return to Paris with it. It will provide you with the foundation stone that every scholar needs—research material. What do you say, eh?"

A speechless Gebbert nodded. Then, "But *Monsieur Directeur*, there are so many." He gestured with his hands. "Are you sure that I should take them?"

"*Monsieur* Gebbert, I am quite sure. In fact, I know that you will treat each one with loving care. I have watched you and observed your work. The archive is yours."

And so over the next several decades, Gebbert studied and published much of the hieratic papyri from the Sebekmose archive. At this point in his career, of the archive's several hundred sheets and fragments, he had published close to two-thirds of them, which appeared in seven dense volumes.

Lacau had been correct. Gebbert had became well-known and respected in his field, because of this archive. In fact, his close colleagues had even come to jokingly refer to him as "*Monsieur Astrologue*." Such is the price of established notoriety.

* * *

The passage of time would be extremely kind to Gebbert. He associated well with his domestic and foreign colleagues, and unlike most, was quick to credit them in his footnotes.

Gebbert also had an eye for detail that many did not possess. When he published one of the archive's documents, he approached it in the most rigorous of ways, citing the quality of the papyrus, its grain, texture, color, and even smell. The width and breadth of a document's columns he noted as well as their number. Even the color and quality of the scribe's ink did not miss his comment. No matter how accomplished an ancient scribe was, the subtle slant of the written text betrayed which hand was being used. And as was so very typical of Gebbert, he kept a log on all of these arcane things.

When it came to the hieratic text itself, Gebbert similarly noted any scribal quirks—the misspellings, preferred phrases of address or transition, glyphic usage, and the like. These trends he dared to attribute more to the curriculum of a particular scribal school, rather than an individual's personal preferences or idiosyncrasies.

Later in life, Gebbert began to see dialectical variations emerging that were far less apparent in the formal and ideologically pure official hieroglyphic inscriptions of the royal house, or in such-and-such a temple god's or goddess' temple inscriptions. In fact, and Gebbert himself would often openly admit, his scientific approach to the ancient Egyptian language and the detection of all of its subtleties, was the direct result of his early exposure to the museum's restoration department.

Needless to say, Gebbert's personal research library was itself a philological treasure trove. Not only did it contain multiple grammars, dictionaries, and the usual primary and secondary sources, but also a rich collection of offprints from his colleagues, often inscribed and dated with best wishes and the like.

By far his greatest treasure remained the Sebekmose archive, which over the course of his career he slowly, methodically studied, and published in the various journals devoted to ancient Egyptian philology. As a member of the *Académie des Inscriptions et Belles-Lettres*, he counted among his close colleagues the likes of such greats as Sir Alan Gardiner, Gustave Jéquier, Pierre Lacau, Kurt Sethe, Walter Wreszinski, and Wilhelm Spiegelberg.

CHAPTER 3

Paris. 1940

By the time the German army marched through the Arc d'Triumph on Friday, June 14th, 1940, Henri Gebbert had already retired from his professorial posts at the University of Paris and the Institut d'Art et d'Archéologie.

Living in a third-floor flat with his ever-adoring wife Millie, life had slowed down for this careful scholar. Every day he and Millie would walk for hours together enjoying life. Oftentimes, that would mean a hat store or two would have to be carefully examined, as Millie *did* like her hats. And Henri, so thoroughly, enjoyed buying them for her.

After such adventures, the retired papyrologist devoted time to what he called "his orphans." He continued to publish the occasional article based on the remaining Sebekmose papyri.

It is not widely known, but within the vanguard of the advancing German army, were special elements made up of teams of professors and their graduate students. Their task was the identification of art treasures and antiquities suitable for inclusion in the future *Führermuseum* under construction in Linz, Austria.

Among them was an Egyptologist, a long-time friend and colleague of Gebbert, named Hans Krüger.

When Krüger knocked on Gebbert's door on that Saturday afternoon, it wasn't so much an invasion by an invading foreign soldier, as a surprise visit shared between good friends.

"Hans! What a grand surprise!" Henri said in his guest's native tongue. "What are you doing here? And so elegantly dressed as a military officer to boot? My *God* man, soldiering is for the young ones, and yet here you stand! I'm impressed."

"Henri!" Millie shouted out of eye-shot from within, "My God, let the dear man in!"

"Oh yes, of course, where are my manners." The Frenchman said as he led the German officer into his flat.

Despite Krüger's best efforts, the Gebberts' immediately sat him down, and began to force upon the officer a glass of an excellent red wine, and some bread and cheese that Madam Millie had instantly conjured up.

By the sound of their excitement, Krüger seriously doubted his hosts even knew their fair city had just been occupied. But eventually, the German did explain to them the situation and of a dire dilemma that would eventually come to pass, far sooner than later.

"Henri, Millie," Hans began, looking both in the eyes, "I must tell you the current political situation is not good for you. You must, at your soonest opportunity, flee to Britain."

Two shocked people stared back.

"But why Hans?" Henri whispered. Millie, silent, covered her mouth.

"Please leave no later than tomorrow. Pack light. Pretend," the German waved vaguely in the air, "you have a lecture to give at Oxford or something. Regardless, both of you must get out of Paris and head west as soon as you can."

"But why Hans? This is our home." A confused Henri asked.

Letting out a deep and emotional sigh, Hans admitted the dark truth.

"Because Henri, Millie, you are Jews. And believe it or not, I have already seen the train cars that the *Schutzstaffel*, the *SS*, are preparing for your transport East. It's a one-way trip to hell."

Then Krüger proceeded to explain in rather blunt and graphic terms what he heard and what he himself had seen.

At the end of which, his horrified audience sat numbly with mouths' agape. The German officer flatly begged. "Now *please*, please promise me that you will leave tomorrow, at the very latest."

For the first time in their lives, Henri and Millie, retired homebodies, briefly glanced at one another, and shared a look. There and then they decided to go on holiday to the British Isles. Their snap decision was so unexpected, the couple thought of the entire situation as a frivolous adventure. Packing light per Krüger's suggestion, the soldier assisted the couple into their green Citroën Traction Avant convertible that very evening—much to their visitor's great relief.

As they said their goodbyes for what would be their last time, Krüger thrust a thick wad of confiscated French currency into Gebbert's hand, closing his fingers around it. Gebbert, surprised at his friend's generosity and forethought, took the money and immediately handed it over to Millie, their family's recognized financial accountant. Then, he reached into the back seat, and handed one of Millie's purple hatboxes to Krüger.

"Hans, here. Take care of my orphans. I know you will."

Lifting the virtually weightless package, Krüger wore a confused yet curious look.

As the auto began to pull away, Gebbert called out to his friend through his open side glass. "That box contains the last of my Sebekmose papyri Hans. And as for my library, it's now yours as well." He said with a remarkably cheerful wave of "*Au Revoir!*"

Stunned by Gebbert's carefree generosity, Krüger's heart now soared for his dear friends of some twenty-odd years. He had done his best. Now the rest was up to them. Looking down at the hatbox, he knew he held a treasure. *Well, there goes Monsieur Astrologue!*

As for Gebbert's research collection, the German knew that it would take at least one lorry to move it all, but not to Linz. Openly defying orders, Krüger sent the two loaded down trucks to his home university in

Munich. No, the Egyptologist vowed, none of Gebbert's possessions were going to that Austrian madman.

*   *   *

The academic assistant stood before the long wooden seminar table on the attic level of Munich's Bavarian state library. At its precise center, much like a center piece, sat a faded purple hatbox. Next to the box was a set of terse instructions hastily written in cursive black ink from his *Doktorvater*—his dissertation director.

"Today's task," he grunted to himself. "Now just what has *Herrn* Professor Dr. Hans Gerhard Krüger in store for me?"

Cutting away the yarn that bound the hatbox, the assistant gently lifted off its hexagonal top and closed his eyes. Taking a deep breath, the assistant knew what was inside—papyrus, ancient papyrus. There, among layer upon layer of delicate packing tissue, rested a small private papyrus archive, or *per medjat*. His professor's missive had claimed that it was found within an ancient Egyptian's coffin from Western Thebes.

On the basis of the archive's providence alone, the assistant suspected that the papyri would date from the Egyptian Middle Kingdom. Admittedly, three hundred and fifty years was a long period of time in which to roughly guesstimate a date for the archive before him.

But the assistant knew once he had mounted all the papyri, Professor Dr. Krüger would carefully examine the whole. And, as he had so many times in the past, the dear professor would tease out a detail here, another there, which would allow him to assign a far tighter chronology for the collection.

As for the task before him, the assistant was resigned to the sheer drudgery of the mounting process. In many ways, however, he found it exciting to handle such ancient material. While the assistant really didn't care how the archive had been acquired, he nonetheless did possess a modicum of curiosity and so began to search the exterior of the box for any clues. And sure enough, lifting the hatbox high above his head, there he found what he was looking for. On its bottom the faded printing simply said: "115, Avenue des Champs-Élysées. Paris."

CHAPTER 4

Staying Sharp. Present Day

Allow me to introduce myself, I am Vesna Borisevna Gregorieva, Temporal Field Agent No. 3, of the Russian-American Academies of Sciences. I am quite certain that Joey Richards' identification card reads the opposite—"American-Russian Academies of Sciences." Political one-upmanship remains alive and well between our respective countries.

I was born in 1979 in Belgrade, the capital of old Yugoslavia. My father, Boris Alexandrevich, was a Russian academic in applied engineering at the university. My mother, Ljubica, was a Yugoslav apparatchik within the state's security system. Both were members-in-good-standing within the Communist Party.

As Yugoslavia politically fragmented, our family moved to St. Petersburg, and it was there I first realized how well our lives had been in Yugoslavia. Fortunately, I was a bright child who tested very well. Little did I know how important that simple fact was, because as I was channeled to better schools, so too was my family moved to better accommodations. With such motivation, I excelled in my classes, much to the displeasure of those children of the elite class.

My "perfect" world, however, effectively crumbled in 1995. On January 12th, a Thursday, my parents failed to come home for dinner. Later that evening came a knock at our apartment's door. A kindly woman from the Russian Academy of Sciences stood before me in tears and delivered the terrible news. My parents had been killed in a horrific series of Chechen terrorist bombings in St. Petersburg during the middle of the evening rush hour.

Together, we sat before the television as the news reported no less than five terrorist bombs had been detonated within the city limits, all at the main train stations, killing hundreds and maiming countless more. On that January evening in 1995, my new life began as a ward of the State. I had become an orphan at sixteen.

Unknown to me, my parents had planned for just such a dreadful eventuality. I was to be groomed as an internal security operative under the auspices of the Special Projects Directorate—a relatively unknown branch of the Russian Academy of Sciences. That meant vigorous physical exercise initially as a dancer with my small, flexible, and lithe build. But with later adolescence came an unexpected growth spurt and a consequent shift to track and field, particularly as a middle distant runner. That intense physical curriculum was balanced with an intellectually challenging program in the hard sciences and computer technology. When they got through with me, I was a mean, lean, calculating machine.

It was then that I first met Colonel Alexander Piankoff, also a member of the Directorate, who for whatever reason saw something special in me. In the process, and under the tutelage of a sisterly Russian Egyptologist, I earned an MA in, of all things, Egyptian philology.

Then came dear Sasha's unexpected death and my surprise promotion to take his place as a temporal field agent. Given my academic background in the sciences, time travel was the last thing I thought theoretically possible—much less practical. Yet, here I was, training to take my sponsor's place.

Now, after having successfully completed several operational journeys back to ancient Egypt, I had to keep sharp, both physically and linguistically. I developed into a distance runner, which allowed me personal time, to think, plan, and strategize away from the prying eyes and ears of my minders. Language retention, much like any long muscle, required exercise and conversation drills, which while boring, did serve their purpose. Real time conversation, of course, was the best, but my American colleague resided half a world away. That left me to my many recorded training conversations, made by my Sasha, which I had long-since memorized.

One unfortunate downside to my temporal career, as the Americans like to say, was the lengthy debriefing sessions that took place after each deployment—first with the Americans and then with my colleagues in Moscow. The style and duration of those tedious rehash sessions could not have been more different, but both had their purpose—to wring my brain absolutely dry of any and all information. The Americans were openly encouraging and supportive during this process. Sadly, my colleagues were the direct opposite—being cynical, disbelieving, overly repetitive, and endlessly demoralizing. This grueling exercise was truly not about a frank retelling of events, but rather an intellectually brutal interrogation. At the end of my last such occasion, I buried a good portion of a ballpoint pen into the thigh of my interrogator. I later learned that a pool had been established as to when I would finally "break." Well, now they know and I fully expect that ballpoint pens will no longer be present during the next session.

*　　*　　*

My name is Joseph William Richards and I am Temporal Field Agent No.2 of the American-Russian Academies of Sciences. I was born into an Air Force household that spent most of its time outside of the States. During one of my dad's deployments, this one in Egypt, I fell in love with that ancient culture, its people, and language. So much so, I turned down several lucrative university football scholarships and instead enrolled at a small university in Chicago because of its Near Eastern Institute. During my first semester senior year, Professor John Milson recruited me right out of his graduate class in Egyptian hieroglyphs. After several temporal deployments paired with Colonel Alexander Piankoff, and several solo ones as well, I wrote my PhD dissertation on a topic in Egyptian philology and was subsequently hired as an associate professor of the NEI.

I thoroughly enjoyed teaching ancient Egyptian to my eager undergraduate students in Chicago. In the process, they continuously challenged me to present the material in ever-more interesting ways. That kept me in the game and linguistically on top of things. But I often wondered how my temporal partner, Gregorieva, managed in Moscow. Tough as nails, sharp as a tack, and always with that chip on her shoulder, she was every bit as reliable as Piankoff had been. And upon reflection, I thought her a better teammate, far more spontaneous in difficult situations than the Russian colonel.

When it came to staying in shape between temporal deployments, being a natural gym rat, my biggest problem was bulking up too much. I accidentally did that once and my adopted Egyptian brother Horemheb noticed it. So now I am ever experimenting with lighter weights, higher reps, and even stationary bicycling.

Above all, the temporal debriefs were a hassle, but I understand their purpose and necessity. The key for me getting through them was chronology and clarity. Fortunately, since Doc Allen enhanced my recall, both were relatively straightforward to reproduce.

CHAPTER 5
The Triumvirate

> **Triumvirate**. *n*. In ancient Rome, a group of three men holding power, in particular, the First Triumvirate was the unofficial coalition of Julius Caesar, Pompey, and Crassus in 60 BC and the Second Triumvirate, a coalition formed by Antony, Lepidus, and Octavian in 43 BC.

The three most powerful men in post-Soviet Moscow were not members of the Russian federal government or its military. Instead, they were members of the Russian Academy of Sciences who thought of themselves as curators charged with the preservation of our present reality. According to their own devised creed, called the *RUTI*, or *Rukovodnie Ukazania dlya Temporalnogo Isledovaniya*, which translates roughly as *The Guidelines for Temporal Exploration,* all temporal decisions must occur within the framework of an international, scientific forum outside of, and free from, any religious, political or ideological control. They truly had placed themselves above such noisome considerations.

These three, however, did not shoulder this burden alone. For in the West, a similar panel of academics, representing the American Academy of Sciences, participated with their colleagues in all their decisions. Needless to say, their teleconferences discussed weighty matters of extreme secrecy and delicacy.

Consequently, the security that guarded those deliberations was paramount.

The government buildings of post-Soviet Moscow were riddled with secret warrens within, beneath, and between them. Perhaps the most infamous example was the Neo-Baroque, yellow-bricked building of the former KGB headquarters on Lubyanka Square. It included an extensive prison complex beneath it. But the most secure vault within the city was located deep within the Russian Ministry of Science. There, the triumvirate held their closely-held discussions and their international teleconferences with their American colleagues.

This vault, this hidden niche, even by former-Soviet standards, was considered a dreary one. Its stale air tinged with acrid cigarette smoke never cleared, no matter how the chamber's overworked ventilators worked. The room itself was a visual wasteland with no windows and no artwork on its dirty tan walls. Only several ghosted shadows remained where former party memorabilia used to hang.

At its center stood a round table surrounded by five generously padded chairs. There had once been six, but a former triumvir, Academician Nikolai Fedorov, had ruined it because of a head wound to his temple inflicted by an errant fountain pen.

The first to arrive, an elderly but fit man who possessed an unremarkable Slavic face, carried a thick purple file that indicated its ultra-level security status.

Dropping his burden on the table-top with a muffled thud, his body language seemed to carry a still heavier weight that could not be so easily shrugged off. Folding his gnarled and arthritic hands before him in an overhand clasp, he then waited for the others to arrive.

In the dull and all consuming silence of the vault, Karlov Drazinzka, Head of the Special Projects Directorate, had been granted a rare opportunity of vagrant time to consider what he had accomplished, what he had failed to do, and why he was here. In many ways, it was the closest thing to a Christian examination of conscience that the avowed atheist had ever experienced.

My dear Karly, he began. *You have done much. About that there is no question. You built the directorate literally with your own hands. You nurtured it with the sweat of your own brow. You advanced its causes sometimes with your own blood, sometimes with the blood of others.*

At this point the mechanical sound of the arriving elevator allowed Drazinzka the opportunity to pull himself together before the others arrived. As had always happened in the past, that transformation was successful.

"Ah, Karlov, it's so good to see you," beamed the older of the two new arrivals. "May I introduce you to Academician Stefan Rosovec? Academician Rosovec, Academician Karlov Drazinzka, Head of the Special Projects Directorate."

Slight bows, formal gestures of accommodation, and efficient handshakes followed the exchange of cagey and measuring eye contact.

The presenter, Academician Vasily Ostrogorsky, the Director of the prestigious Institute of Theoretical Biology, then seated himself next to Karlov. Rosovec, taking the hint, took a seat opposite them with the conference table between. Given this arrangement, the newcomer realized he was in for yet another interview that pitted members of the old Cold War Guard against a Young Turk. Decades of ideological doctrine divided them.

Ostrogorsky continued. "Karlov, as you are already aware, Academician Nikolai Fedorov has recently retired due to an unfortunate cranial aneurism. To take his place on this committee, and at his strongest recommendation, is Rosovec here, the new Director of Advanced and Theoretical Technological Research."

Ostrogorsky then went on to describe Rosovec's impressive academic and administrative credentials in detail, all of which Karlov had already read and reread several times. The man, in Karlov's mind, had never once made a personal sacrifice for anything during his meteoric career. Nonetheless, Karlov paid a respectful attention to the entirety of his old colleague's oration.

So, thought Karlov, *this is what the new pup looks like! He's more Hollywood glamour-boy than intellectual warrior in my mind. But Karly, be careful, appearances can be deceiving.*

As impressive as Rosovec's resume was, his jet-black curly hair, olive-colored skin, and chiseled appearance was, Karlov had to admit, just as impressive.

Ostrogorsky, having ended his presentation, let out a sigh, and then asked Karlov if he had any questions for the director and prospective new member of their close clutch.

Theatrically opening his hands and slightly shrugging his shoulders, Karlov began his grilling. "Frankly, my dear Vasily, I do not know which to be more impressed by, Academician Rosovec's resume or his good looks."

Rosovec allowed a careful, closed-lip smile that his eyes did not participate in. Instinctually, he knew something was surely coming and he wasn't disappointed.

"I am curious, Academician Rosovec. Have you ever spent any time in the military?"

"No, Academician Drazinzka, my course of study did not allow for it."

"Ah, I see." Karlov paused to reflect as he studied his hands. "Well then, do you have any problem with taking precise orders, being told what to do, even if personally distasteful?"

"An interesting question, Academician. It would have to depend on the circumstances surrounding such a request."

With gritty steel in his voice, Karlov restated his

question. "Academician Rosovec, I am not discussing a 'request.' What I need to know from you is, if ordered to do something, are you capable of carrying out that command to the best of your ability?"

The question figuratively slapped Rosovec across the face.

Blushing slightly as his blood-pressure began to rise, Rosovec sat back and replied with equal parts of sangfroid. "An order from my superiors is an order to be obeyed and followed through upon."

"Yes. Good textbook answer," Karlov answered with a chilling smile. "But since the world is a place that is never quite what it seems, allow me to ask you this. Have you ever ordered the death of a close colleague?"

Ostrogorsky then broke in as planned.

"Karlov!"

Raising one hand, open-palmed toward his generational twin in a sign of truce, Karlov then pressed, "Your answer please, Academician Rosovec."

Now with an ashen face and suddenly moist palms, Rosovec, beginning to feel his composure melting, answered perhaps a bit too strongly. "Why, of course not! Never!"

"I see," Karlov softly replied. "Well, Academician Rosovec, I must inform you that my colleague next to me and I have had to, how shall I say, make some rather grim decisions in the past. Rather permanent decisions that sometimes, unfortunately, 'impacted' some of our very close colleagues. Given your pretty credentials and even prettier face, are you prepared to make such difficult decisions, Academician Rosovec?"

Pole-axed by Karlov's directness, Rosovec then counterpunched to buy some time to collect his thoughts.

"Academician Drazinzka, you are of course referring to the case of Academician Sasel, are you not?"

Immediately recognizing the ploy, Karlov inwardly smiled. *He's stalling for time. He really needs to think about that one. Good. Very good!*

"Of course. But again I must ask, can this inner circle depend on you and your directorate to carry out an order no matter how *nikulturny* an act it may seem?"

Karlov's goad in using the highly-charged Russian euphemism, which best can be translated as "totally barbaric," was calculated for its shock value.

Now angry, Rosovec growled back, "Yes, you son of a bitch! I would eat my own mother's liver if I had to!"

During this heated exchange, Ostrogorsky remained silent, but quite alert.

Karlov, now smiling at Rosovec's reply, thought before he spoke his mind. *Ah, a bit of colorful savagery does exist behind that pretty exterior. Well, perhaps this one does possess the needed ruthlessness, the steel required.*

"My dear Academician Rosovec. I thank you for

your most colorful affirmative. As for me being a son of a bitch, you are absolutely correct. I am. As for you, however, I believe that we have successfully established you will allow nothing to get in the way of your own ambitions. I believe on that basis we have begun to forge a common ground, a common understanding. May I welcome you then to join our inner circle?"

"Thank you, Academician Drazinzka, for that is indeed my wish."

"In that case, my dear colleague, you may call me Karlov."

"Karlov it is," Rosovec said with a nod. "You may then call me Stefan."

Ostrogorsky simply beamed. With Rosovec's acceptance by Drazinzka the process of their inner circle's generational transition had successfully begun.

CHAPTER 6
Horizon Pass

Every nowhere must be somewhere.

In this case Horizon Pass, located west-northwest of Holloman AFB and the New Mexican town of Alamogordo, it concealed itself in a high-altitude open-scrub desert populated with roadrunners, scorpions, buzzards, and the stray coyote. It can be reached by helicopter in twenty to twenty-five minutes from the airbase or overland by truck in two-and-a-half hours along a dusty dirt track "road."

This top secret facility is situated beneath a curious, split-fingered, two-hundred-foot rock outcropping that dominated a desert plain surrounded by rugged mountains. On its northern side, a fresh spring afforded the harsh landscape a rare dash of green. To the south, an old and dilapidated wooden shack leaned against a rock face. By the look of it, a stiff wind could blow it down. To the east a concrete helicopter pad lay hidden, complete with inset landing lights alongside a masterfully camouflaged loading dock cut into another sheer rock face. Such measures were deemed necessary to foil the notice of transiting spy satellites and unauthorized curiosity seekers.

As with many US government facilities in the American southwest, Horizon Pass was a subterranean complex that took advantage of native rock formations.

In many ways, the facility was much like a medieval castle that used nature for its walls, battlements, towers, and keep. Access into the complex began by entering the door of the rickety lean-to shack of weathered silver pine. Once inside, a gray, featureless, and hardened steel door greeted the visitor. The shack itself, really a sophisticated detection booth, scanned all who stood before the steel door's frame.

In many ways, a visit to Horizon Pass is reminiscent of a villain's underground lair right out of a James Bond movie. This impression was a function of its 1960s construction of concrete walls painted bright reflective white, exposed HVAC conduits, piping and tubes of all shapes and colors that ran along the ceiling and walls of every room, corridor, and tunnel. Safety underground was held foremost as everywhere one could find emergency phones and lighting fixtures, fire extinguishers every one-hundred feet, and convex traffic mirrors at every intersection. Last, but hardly least, the many twenty-foot-wide corridors and connecting tunnels were painted with bright yellow painted stripes running down their centers.

Navigating Horizon Pass' layout would have been very confusing if it were not that each corridor, intersection, and tunnel was clearly named in large stenciled letters on the floor. As with so many things, Dr. Peter Borov—the facility's founder, builder, and chief researcher, allowed his humorous imprint to run wild—Yellow Brick Road, Penny Lane, Trafalgar

Square, Times Square, Appian Way, and the like. These accesses interconnected the underground complex named "The Swamp" in honor of the scientist's favorite television series *M.A.S.H.*—a particular favorite of Borov's. The mess hall, bakery, and kitchen was "Betty Crocker's," the gym "Venice Beach," the main lab complex was originally "Frankenstein's Castle," but over time, was shortened to just "Frank's."

The high security area devoted to research and testing of the temporal device was a serious place, and its name reflected that fact—Tomb Stone. Its entranceway was a circular double door that looked like a bank vault—complete with a short, low ramp leading up to it.

What lurked beyond those massive steel doors always held visitors with a mixture of awe and wide-eyed shock. Stepping through the massive doorway, a steel grated landing spiraled down to the interior's floor level some fifty feet below. The sheer volume of the cavity, once a fair-sized cavern, had been transformed into a massive engineering bay with a workshop, climate-controlled computer room, and generator area. In the center of it all, connected by thick power cables, stood a most curious-looking collection of devices.

Descending down the long and continuously curving ramp to the Tombstone's floor level, the visitor received a slowly revolving look at that most strange and marvelous creation of man—the Mark VI Soap Bubble. The latest and greatest of a revolutionary series of temporal machines, it proudly proved the theoretical basis of time travel through cutting-edge engineering and advanced materials research. The Mark VI provided the very essence of wonder itself.

Four black rectangular pylons, each about six feet tall, were arranged symmetrically and outlined a circle about twenty feet in diameter. Each pylon had its own thick power cable and attached at their tops were short, horn-like devices that oriented inward, which also had their own power cables. In the center of this circle of pylons and horns, a thick, white, Hula-Hoop-like object about four feet in diameter floated horizontally and absolutely still about five feet off the ground.

*   *   *

The workings of this contraption represented decades of research on the part of Dr. Peter Borov. On one occasion, specifically Gregorieva's first tour, she and Richards were treated to its marvels.

"Well Joey, do you remember what I told you about the Standard Model?" Borov quizzed.

"Some," was the Egyptian philologist's monosyllabic response.

"Well, scientists have described the building blocks of the known universe and the forces that influence these building blocks, really atomic and subatomic particles, with what is called the Standard Model. But as with all such neat models, it possesses one mathematical flaw. That flaw is the thing or stuff that describes a particle's mass.

"Mass imparts to a particle the qualities of color, size, hardness, softness, not to mention its chemical and electrical properties. In fact, mass, or *masslessness*, determines a particle's terminal speed as being just short of the speed of light. But to go to faster than the speed of light, for instance, one would need to lose one's mass—in essence to become *massless*. But to do that would mean we understood what this remarkable quality is in the first place. What mass is.

"The truth is that we have yet to discover the mass particle. Not that scientists from around the world haven't tried. But it was finally the folks at Fermi who actually proved the existence of the Higg's boson, and when they did, they discovered that the mass particle itself was composed of several more subatomic particles.

"With that discovery Joey, my life's work has now been made complete, for up until that momentous discovery, the quantum mechanics behind the workings of the Soap Bubble, despite all of its sophistication, remained poorly understood. We now know how a particle, or for that matter a living organism, can be in two places at the same time.

"My point folks is that the Soap Bubble's technology is subtly changing, evolving, getting better, and becoming more energy efficient. Our ability to temporally calibrate is improving as well. But you still have to climb a tower, drop through the drop-ring, and for an infinitesimally brief moment in time, be in two places at once. Your physiology has and will continue to react to that brief temporal event. After all, our bodies are nothing more than sensitive biochemical electrical engines.

"Joseph, Doc Allen's suspicion is that your physiology may change over time, as it did with Piankoff. In fact, Doc Allen suspects Piankoff's physiology may have been affected by those earlier drops he made. The good doctor even went so far as to say Piankoff may have briefly blacked out on the insertion that he broke his foot. I mention this because I know you already have had two visits with Doc Allen about the lengthening of your post-drop recovery."

CHAPTER 7
Several Observations

The Philology Annex is housed within a corner brownstone nestled in the idyllic serenity of a heavily-treed and well-trimmed university campus on Chicago's South Side. Open to the general campus population, the annex, devoted to the ancient languages of northeast Africa and western Asia, represented one man's dream of what a modern academic monastery should be.

The Annex, however, did not exist in a vacuum, but was the necessary extension of another facility located in the deep desert of New Mexico—Horizon Pass. While it was a highly secretive scientific research and development facility, the Annex was its very public front for linguistic research and training.

Dr. Peter Borov was the genius mastermind behind both the Horizon Pass and the Philology Annex facilities. The latter he designed around three floors of cozy book stacks and softly lit study rooms. These last were dominated by sturdy wooden writing tables. Their comfortable and slightly sloped upper surfaces invited a scholar to take a seat and then stay forever. All that was missing from this monastic setting were the heavy bees' wax candles. In their place, the theoretical physicist installed shaded lamps, which directed their glare-free soft lumens down upon an open page.

Dr. Borov also stipulated that only soft slippers

should tread upon the annex's waxed wooden floors. Street shoes should be left within an assigned cubby hole at the entrance foyer. Why the slipper rule? Because Dr. Borov believed places of serious scholarship should be quiet out of courtesy for another's deep thoughts. In his mind, the loud click-clacking of street shoes on the Annex's wooden floors just wouldn't do.

In part to enforce the slipper rule, a welcoming receptionist was stationed within the Annex's foyer, seated behind a substantial wooden desk and two flat screens. Several lush orchid plants tried to take over one corner of her desk with all of their seeking green tendrils and broad spear-shaped leaves.

The receptionist, Jennifer Ann Kelly, was a lean and mean, thirty-something knockout with green eyes, and a splattering of freckles across her nose and cheek bones. Her preference in attire trended toward flattering yet conservative earth-toned silk blouses and comfortable knee-length skirts. Her secretarial skills were as exceptional as her technological savvy.

This natural strawberry blonde welcomed one and all to the Annex. Quick to unleash her devastating and incapacitating grin upon anyone who crossed her threshold, so was Borov's slipper rule ruthlessly enforced. And if you lacked a pair, of slippers that is, disposable blue hospital booties were available for fifty cents—no exceptions.

Ms. Kelly reported directly to the Annex's head

librarian, whose milky glassed doorway stood directly behind her. Currently, the head librarian position was open, as its former resident, Alexander Piankoff, disappeared from the face of the earth without so much as a two-week notice. While Kelly would have nothing to say about the selection of the Annex's next head librarian, she hoped that the next one would retainer her as she really needed to keep her job.

Why? Her real employer, a very curious and black organization based in Maryland, had gone through great pains to place Kelly at the Philology Annex in the first place. There were no two ways about it. Kelly's unofficial boss wanted in on whatever that facility was up to. While they had their suspicions, they now wanted names, places, and in short, the whole enchilada.

So who was this jaw-dropping cougar of a receptionist? Her real name was Jennifer Ann Borgensen, who was born and raised in central Minnesota to a middle-class Presbyterian family. The middle kid, and only girl of six, Jenny was raised more by her competitive and sports-drunk brothers than her loving parents. Being the brightest bulb of the Borgensen pack, Kelly earned a full ride to a private regional college. However, the fact that Jenny was also the first girl on her high school's varsity hockey team hadn't hurt her application either in that frozen Nordic state.

During college Kelly excelled in her classes. By her sophomore year, the spring job fair had caught her interest. Jenny, thinking ahead, aggressive as ever, was trying to find her place in the world and an opportunity to make a contribution. As she wandered about, quickly passing over the gaudy displays and marketing hype of several well-known Minnesota corporations, Kelly noted a young man in a plain blue suit and red tie seated behind a bare card table.

Kelly wondered. *Why was he here?* He offered no literature or had any signage, just an empty folding visitor's chair. More out of sheer curiosity than anything else, Jenny walked over and sat down. In so doing, this inquisitive Nordic goddess surprised the young man, who had been deeply engrossed in a paperback by somebody named Clausewitz. Its title, *On War*.

"Hi," she brightly began, "my name is Jennifer Borgensen. I'm curious. Which company do you work for?"

The shyly smiling young man answered.

"Well, hello there yourself, Jennifer Borgensen. My name is Paul Browner and I do not represent a company. I am looking for individuals who love our country, our way of life, and who want to protect it."

That succinct and softly spoken reply completely encapsulated what Kelly had been looking for. Refreshing in its simplicity, he had said so much.

"Wow, that's a clear and straight-forward answer. So, Mr. Browner, tell me more."

That first contact forever changed Kelly's life. She

now had a purpose, a career, and an employer, who appreciated and respected who she was at a root level. After several well-paid summer internships under her belt in the Maryland-Virginia corridor, Kelly graduated a semester early, earning a *magnum cum laude* in psychology and computer science.

*   *   *

On her first day as the receptionist of the Philology Annex, Kelly created a partitioned and encrypted space on her hard drive. She thought of it as a "Z-Drive," but this modification was special in that it would not show up anywhere on her computer's screen on any of its internal menus. Consequently, only she knew about the drive's existence and so this is where Kelly squirreled away all of her observational notes about the Annex, and of course, her weekly status reports. With her special drive, Kelly didn't need e-mail. Instead, if she wished to send something to her secret employer, all she needed to do was to go to the DOS prompt and type in a particular file name that resided on her Z: Drive. When she hit the ENTER key, the file would go directly to another that was linked to it. This other drive, needless to say, resided in Maryland.

*   *   *

Kelly's first challenge was learning to endure the boredom of her job. For the star high school hockey forward and later college field hockey winger, just *sitting* from nine to five was excruciating. So immediately after Jenny got her flat all squared away she joined the local health club, where she worked out like a demon nearly every evening. Every drop of sweat expended removed an equal dram of boredom, or so she calculated. Besides the physical benefits of her grueling self-imposed regime, she quickly discovered some social ones as well.

As the weeks passed, Jenny found herself surrendering to the rhythm of the job. Physically, it was definitely low impact. Intellectually, she performed her tasks quickly and efficiently: sorting the daily mail, monitoring the comings and goings of the Annex's odd academic faculty and bookish student patrons, receiving and purchasing books, balancing the book budget, and juggling the Annex's many bits of correspondence. But what actually pleased Kelly was the occasional compliment she received from her former boss Alexander Piankoff. He was one of those men who actually appreciated what she was doing, how well she was doing it, and said so to her face. But in the end, it was Piankoff's wry smile that she worked so hard for. It seemed to promise so much.

Compliments aside, what an odd duck Piankoff was. With that shaved and highly polished chrome-dome of his, the man's scalp line clearly indicated that he had a full head of hair. Kelly also noted that he kept extremely peculiar hours and came and went with no particular schedule. The man was even absent for days, sometimes even weeks on end, without giving any warning or hint as to his whereabouts. The only clue was the marvelously smooth and deep tans he often wore upon his return.

But what a marvelously sexy British accent he had, and whenever Piankoff moved, it was like watching a cat. Clearly, from the gaunt look of his face and from the hang of his tailored suits, the man did not have an extra ounce of fat on him. And it was then and there that Kelly began to wonder. Was he former military? There was the crispness in his expression, the rigid expectation of immediate compliance, which one does not see anywhere, but in the military.

After her first month, Kelly decided that Piankoff was born and bred military, pure and simple. His general psychological profile absolutely screamed it. Yes, he had expertly rubbed off most of the rough edges, but personal mannerisms are far more difficult to change, much less hide. The real question now was— who's military? While "Piankoff" is clearly a Slavic, if not overtly Russian last name, then why the British accent? If he was a Russian spook, then why hadn't he changed his last name to a "Henry," or a "Blanchard," or a "Smith"? Why hadn't he learned English with an American dialect? No, Alexander Piankoff was a mystery, and now that he was no longer employed by the Annex, he forever remained one.

CHAPTER 8

Gone Missing

Losing a team member is perhaps the greatest fear that any principal survey investigator could experience. Be it in the wilds of a Central African jungle, the tenements of an East Indian megalopolis, the endless depths of the Marina Trench, or, for that matter, the void of deep space, turning up missing was more than unfortunate. For everyone, not only the lost individual, were impacted. First Investigator Doog was such a concerned administrator as one of his brood had gone missing.

Whenever great distances are traversed in space at near-light velocities, a discussion of relativity always dominated the conversation. It just can't be avoided as time aboard a near-light vessel slows to almost a heartbeat, while planet-side time continued apace as sweet as you please. And if, God forbid, you turned up missing at a way point, then any rescue attempt worth its salt must try to retrace your steps. A formidable task, given celestial navigation being what it is, that will only work if the missing one was prescient enough to have left a bread crumb trail. Such was not the case, as there was no trace or hint of an emergency beacon pulse. So the funerary chime pealed for Survey Craft Number Four, all the more so given the constantly moving universe.

"Survey Craft Number Four did not rejoin the survey mission's agreed upon coordinates and is currently thirty-six cycles late," reported the project's navigational coordinator, PIMA, a nagging, prickly, and recalcitrant artificial intelligence, which ignored the loss of the Survey Craft Number Four's pilot. The sole role and purpose of the Proximal Input Matrix Algorithm, or PIMA, was to strategize, plot, assign search parameters, and coordinate the data retrieved from multiple survey craft into a central storage matrix.

"Scheduled data retrieval did not occur. A two by one parsec deficiency has been identified that threatens the precision of this survey. Such deficiencies should not be allowed to occur. Recommendation: retask Survey Craft Numbers Eight and Nine's current objectives in order to properly overlap Survey Craft Number Four's original survey track. Recovery of Survey Craft Number Four may then be possible."

Without a PIMA, accurate intra-galactic surveys could never get off the ground as there were too many computational variables, at any given time, for a sentient being to properly manipulate. Space was by definition a dangerous place. It contained within its endless reaches equally endless challenges that could threaten even the most mundane of tasks—like survey work. On top of that, Investigator Doog never before had one of his own fail to return. And that really troubled this being devoted to scientific endeavor. Quite suddenly, its priorities shifted their focus.

What to do?

Doog considered, as the scientist trundled his way, bird-like, down the central access tunnel of his command ship. What PIMA recommended supported the survey's mandate, and the over-arching and rigorous adherence to completeness and accuracy.

To halt the survey, and wait for Eight and Nine to follow up on Four's survey path, to re-gather its survey data, and in so doing perhaps find Four ... what are the relativistic odds that Four would be located?

That was what Doog wanted to know, full-knowing that the question was unknowable. So the investigator did what it thought was the responsible thing.

Yes, even if this was a relatively vacant arm of the galaxy. What of it? Completeness and accuracy must rule the day. And just perhaps by some blessed hatching Four will be found.

So Doog dispatched Eight and Nine, while the rest of the survey team of seventeen loitered at the rally point.

"Completeness and accuracy" were crucial for the four dimensional charts produced by the intra-galactic survey. For instance, all Level Three charts of normal space, in addition to the basic four dimensions—x, y, z, and time, also had to take into consideration the expansion and rotation of the known universe, a given galaxy, and a specific system within that galaxy.

Only Level Four surveys gathered the mechanics of a specific system's satellites. Usually such surveys were only made whenever an anomalous or unique feature was identified that did not already appear in the Universal Codex of Astronomical Elements, or UCAE.

Whereas, Level Five surveys, while extremely rare, did occur whenever sentient life was detected. Such situations called for near-space observation initially. Only with subsequently approved authorization were atmospheric and eventually planet-side surveys undertaken with the specific purpose of initiating first contact. Such first contacts were undertaken only after certain, codified procedures and specific parameters were satisfied. Otherwise, examples abounded of well-meaning failures, if not outright disasters.

*   *   *

All twenty of First Investigator Doog's survey fleet were massively constructed, heavily redundant craft, which were built to withstand and survive the vagaries of extended, deep-space, survey work. Propelled by voracious gravitational engines that consumed vast amounts of dark matter, these near-light behemoths were designed to protect only one life-form—the pilot. Shaped like gigantic sugar cones, only the very tip was devoted to the needs and comforts of its master, as the rest of survey ship was devoted to its massive gravitron engines.

As chance ordained, by the time Survey Craft Number Eight arrived in the vicinity, its sensors were overwhelmed by a virtual waterfall of single source, discrete, electromagnetic emissions across a wide spectrum of frequencies. The protocol for such an encounter the pilot of Survey Craft Number Eight immediately engaged. Several minutes later, Investigator Doog was informed and the entire survey was placed on standby. Meanwhile, Survey Craft Number Eight was informed to hold position and await further instructions.

Per established procedure, Investigator Doog sent a flash transmission to the survey's central administration. Three hours later, he was authorized to proceed with all due care with the entire survey mission, to Survey Craft Number Eight's current stationary position. If at all possible, the retrieval of Survey Craft Number Four was to be made. However, atmospheric and terrestrial first contact procedures were not authorized at this time, and to expect further instructions.

Resigned to that instruction, Investigator Doog gathered together his remaining brood of surveyors and transited to Survey Craft Number Eight's position outside a minor solar system from where the electromagnetic emissions originated. By the time that he and his brood arrived, Survey Craft Number Nine had joined up with Eight, and was waiting for them as well.

*   *   *

The task of the Air Force Space Command, or AFSPC, at Peterson Air Force Base in Colorado Springs, was to monitor and catalogue any object within Earth's immediate near-space neighborhood. Up and running since 1985, AFSPC employed powerful radars and optical sensors that tracked everything within our planet's orbit.

Fine. That description anyone can find on the Internet.

On the other hand, just how far out into near-space did the AFSPC consider its domain of inquiry remained an open question. However, during the recent near-Earth asteroid miss and asteroid collisions on September 29, 2012 of the Poliahu and Toutatis bodies, the AFSPC was interrogating with their many assets those heavenly bodies for a long time and from a considerable distance—often quite far beyond the near-Earth neighborhood. This they accomplished easily with the massive radar observatories that the AFSPC employed, which included NASA's Deep Space Network at Goldstone, California, and the Arecibo Observatory in Puerto Rico.

In direct response to the events surrounding September 29, 2012, the AFSPC established in only six-month's time, an array of twelve satellites parked in equidistant equatorial orbits. The Deep Space Defense Grid (DSDG)'s primary purpose was to passively scan the immediate neighborhood and star field with optical sensors. Their secondary task was to illuminate with their onboard radars any object for the purposes of establishing its range and composition. To accomplish this, both narrow-band and wide-band radars provided metric information, and space-object identification (SOI), which can resolve the pivotal question: "What is it?" With each satellite responsible for approximately forty-two degrees of the heavens, the DSDG constantly compared every thirty seconds the state of Earth's near-space region.

*　　*　　*

Major Charles M. Perry, US Air Force, ran the Deep Space Defense Grid along with his wife, Dr. Becky Hildebrand. Both with PhDs in astronomy, this brain-trust were perfect for the job because they were the first ones on top of the Poliahu and Toutatis asteroid event of September 29, 2012. In fact, Hildebrand first identified Poliahu while it was still a distant speck and subsequently named it after a Hawaiian goddess. Why? Because she first observed it from the Keck Observatory atop Mauna Kea. With their staff stationed at Peterson Air Force Base in Colorado Springs, DSDG was connected at the hip with AFSPC.

"Major Perry. DSDG Nine has identified something of interest." Senior Airman (E4) Doug Cooper reported from his dedicated and numbered console. This matter-of-fact statement caused the rest of his surrounding colleagues to prick up their ears.

"*Something of interest*" was the DSDG's internal euphemism for anything unique or out-of-the-ordinary.

"Be right there, Doug." Perry replied, and he was, as his office was only twenty paces from The Pit, where twelve technicians sat in a circle before their screens.

"This just showed up." Cooper said pointing to his screen. "It's a non-reflective object that moments ago just wasn't there."

Perry bent over to examine the object in question.

"Interesting ... " was all that Perry had time to get out of his mouth before, right before his very eyes, now there were two dark objects, parked side-by-side. The second bogey had just glided into position.

"Now that is downright odd." Cooper interjected at the appearance of the second dark unknown.

"Indeed it is Doug. Do you have your tape running?"

"Yes sir. Absolutely."

Now on one knee next to the airman. "Good. How far out are they?"

"I haven't bounced any radars off of them, sir."

"Okay, then give me your best guess before we light them up. A case of beer is riding on this senior airman."

Now with the pressure really on, Cooper began his mental calculations and finally came up with, "Well, major, my best guess is at least two astronomical units, maybe more."

"So you're shooting for about 186,000,000 million

miles plus—twice the distance between us and the sun."

"Yes sir." Cooper said with conviction. "My money says they'll drift toward the shadow of our moon. And if they stay behind it, then we'll have two for real bogeys out there."

"Now that would be really interesting," Perry murmured. "Imagine what a job that would be to keep our moon between us, especially from that distance. That would mean serious capability."

"Yes sir. No doubt about it."

At that, Perry stood up and declared to The Pit. "Okay people, Airman Cooper here has himself a pair of bogeys. Keep your eyes peeled. We just might have some more pop up in our vicinity."

CHAPTER 9
Odd Job

Early on Kelly sensed that something wasn't right at the Annex. Someone called a meeting of some sort. Thirteen academics appeared between four forty-five and five in the afternoon. But after fifty-seven minutes, *fourteen* left the Annex and one had street shoes on. That was when Kelly realized the Annex had a second entrance, one that she was not aware of. That was a really big surprise, as Kelly had made it her business to visit every nook and cranny of that brownstone. Apparently, however, she hadn't found *absolutely* every one.

So the receptionist decided to do some further investigation. During her lunch hour the next day, the intrepid receptionist inspected the building's perimeter, beginning this time from the alley side. Besides the locked backdoor that provided access to a meager fenced-in backyard and the trash dumpster, there was precious else to see. Even the narrow gangway, which provided a public access between the Annex and its neighbor to the east, was a dark and dreary canyon of sheer brick walls with only a few upstairs' windows.

Looking down at her watch, Kelly realized she did not have the time to return to the alley. So she circled around to the Annex's front entrance and instead took the short cut through the gangway. While doing so she noted a small, smudged chalk mark on the narrow concrete walkway. It was once clearly a 'V' or 'arrow' symbol that pointed towards the Annex's blank brick surface. Stopping to examine the wall, Jenny didn't see anything at first, but just before she moved on, she did notice that one brick, at shoulder height, was different. It was worn on one end, or perhaps better said, cleaner than the rest of the bricks, but only by a shade or two in color. Not daring to touch it, she moved on thinking what would be her next, best move.

After some thought, the receptionist ruled out a video camera to monitor the gangway. Given the passage's straight and uniform lines, she knew that any new addition would only stand out in stark relief. So she decided on patience, and snow.

*   *   *

The next clue that caught Kelly's attention was an offer made to her by a member of the Philology Annex, a certain professor from the Department of Linguistics.

"Ms. Kelly, my specialty is in linguistic psychology and language learning. Currently, I wish to conduct an experiment upon a subject in a most unusual way. What I have in mind, and I know that this is most unorthodox, is first to mildly sedate the subject, and then, in a controlled environment of intense sexual stimuli, record which language first passes his lips as he regains consciousness.

"Ah, I wish to enlist your assistance in this highly unusual experiment. I fully realize the, ah, delicate and confidential nature of this request, but I wish to test just how deeply my experimental language implantation process truly is. I am approaching you directly, because I highly doubt that I could receive proper authorization to perform such an experiment on a human subject through the usual means. If anyone at the university ever heard about such a non-sanctioned undertaking, well, my career would be ruined. Nonetheless, certain governmental agencies, which I am not at liberty to name, are pressuring me to produce data upon which they can base their evaluations of my research and future funding. Since you yourself have a background in psychology, you know well enough how basal, rudimentary, and powerful the sexual act truly is. In fact, some believe that the sexual orgasm is stronger than prayer evoked during times of extreme stress and crisis. As to why these governmental agencies want this research data, I can only surmise.

"So Ms. Kelly, if you would like to participate in this experiment, you must first sign a non-disclosure statement, not only to protect yourself, but all parties involved. Additionally, I must insist upon a full medical examination, both before and after. These will be provided at no expense to yourself. Needless to say, I can assure you that the honorarium, if you indeed did choose to participate, would be most generous."

Feeling adventurous, Kelly allowed herself to be

recruited into a very bizarre investigation into the language preference of one man's mind. Secretly, Kelly already knew what this was really all about—to test the conditioning of an individual. But to Kelly's surprise, she discovered that the human subject was a student who visited the Philology Annex quite often, and a very hunky one at that. She also found out that once on camera, she performed quite brilliantly, several times. As for the hunky test subject, he did not speak a word of English during any of the climactic events, but rather spoke another language, one that Kelly could not make heads or tails of. But from his very manner and intonation, the poetic-sounding words were clearly ones of begged physical release.

*   *   *

Kelly's third bit of evidence was the test subject himself, Joseph Richards, a rugged specimen if she ever saw one. Still and all, during the "experiment" this individual had shown her a gentle and tender side that frankly she had not seen in quite a while.

Then the thought hit her right between the eyes—this guy is being conditioned to be a deep undercover agent of some sort! Given the general philological subject matter of the Annex, he's probably targeted for Iraq or Iran or someplace similar. At this point, Kelly's mind really began to cook when she realized that Richards' hair color, eyes, and general build, even if it was so deliciously ripped, could easily blend into any Islamic city.

Then another thought came to her. Is it possible that the Philology Annex really is an intensive language training site for one of the black agencies of the DC beltway? If so, am I in danger of reporting something to my masters, something that should not be exposed?

At this point, Kelly nearly panicked. She really did not know what she could prove and what she couldn't. So, calming herself as best she could, she counseled patience.

"Okay girl, now gather some hard evidence to prove your thesis. Figure out how they secretly meet here. And come to think of it, just where can thirteen, no fourteen, people meet in this building? Nowhere comfortably, that's for sure, much less for fifty-odd minutes. And where does Richards' fit into this picture?

Not twenty minutes later, the answer to Kelly's questions walked in. There was Richards all smiles, wearing this drop-dead gorgeously deep tan and a shiny bald head to match! And breathlessly, she noted as well, there was that deadly looking, cat-like gait as well.

Trying very hard not to let her jaw shatter on the floor, Jenny now had it all, or at least a good part of it. First Piankoff, and now Richards, had been absent for some time. Both had tans. Both had their heads shaved for a long enough time so that they were deliciously browned as well.

So girl, she furiously thought while she typed out her weekly report, just where is a tanned, bald head an undercover requirement?

*　*　*

It was late and already long past rush hour. A gray-haired man with his sleeves rolled up sat puzzled over a densely written, two-page report. With his head in his hands and his grey-flannel suit coat hanging from the back of his high tech chair, he occasionally spoke to himself as he read and reread what was before him. In his right hand he held a yellow, No.2 pencil. The pages before him, laid out side-by-side, were covered with wispy notes, question and exclamation marks decorated their margins. He closed his eyes, sighed, and said quietly aloud.

"Oh shit Kelly, just what have you stumbled upon?"

Then came a polite knock on the door. Looking up, Colonel Richard "Rick" Black, USAF retired, motioned for the visitor to come in.

"Ah, I see that you got Kelly's latest. Still think she's just an over-imaginative blonde?" asked Troy Sullivan.

While Kelly's immediate supervisor, Sullivan was Black's right hand man, who at that moment let out a mild grunt as he straightened up in his over-priced and ergonomically designed chair. Sullivan clearly heard, when his boss did so, several snaps, two crackles, and a pop. So much for ergonomic.

"Well, I certainly will say this for that nymphomaniac. She's innovative. And no, I don't think that she is 'over imaginative' either.

"Two months ago we got a copy of a supposedly secure satellite teleconference from the satellite jockeys over at Patterson. The video was between a four-man panel at the Philology Annex in Chicago and three old farts in Moscow. I have been since informed that these three Russians are absolute ghosts from the Soviet past.

"It seems that Patterson, in their infinite wisdom, decided to loan our friends in Chicago an Air Force communications satellite complete with the latest state-of-the-art English-Russian translation software. Now those same jokers are shopping the teleconference around the Belt Way. It seems that they are looking for additional ways to fund their Deep Space Command initiatives."

"So what's so special about this teleconference?" Sullivan asked.

"Well first off, for what it's worth, the ex-Soviet panelists were three totally faceless enigmas until this video. I'm told that the psych-experts over at Langley had an absolute field day analyzing their body language. But as for the Chicago group, there was a Greek bio-geneticist, an American Egyptologist, an unknown quantum physicist, and a Brit economist. Now that is one heck of a duke's mixture."

"An unknown physicist?" Sullivan asked.

"Yep. It's like he just appeared out of nowhere."

"Is that even possible in this day and age?"

"Well, this guy's proof positive that it can be done."

"Soooo, what's this teleconference all about?" Sully probed.

"An excellent question. From all appearances, it seemed to be an inaugural feeling out session between some very select members of the Russian Academy of Sciences and our side's toss salad. As you might expect, whenever one listens in cold on a conversation, some things have no context, but others are clear enough.

"However, what they discussed at some length, were some genetic laboratory results, and what they found was something clearly troubling. Then there was mention made of field operatives, and of the telepathic and telekinetic abilities of some children. Concern was even expressed about the future of the human genome and fears of an alien colonization effort."

"You're shitting me! What is this? *The X-Files*?"

"Nope. And then it got even better. The Russians proposed that the 'target,' their words, 'should be eliminated' immediately.' Then the Chicago panel, and the Greek bio-geneticist in particular, poised a question that caused the Russians to briefly go offline. Something about our current human species not evolving. But when the Russians returned, they agreed to consider the Greek's point-of-view."

"And then?"

"Dunno. I haven't seen the second teleconference."

Silence for several moments.

"Okay," Sullivan began, "the Greek bio-geneticist I can understand, given all the discussion of genetics and genomes. But where does an economist, a physicist, and above all, an Egyptologist, fit into that conversation?"

"I've been thinking along those lines as well, Sully."

Now lifting Kelly's latest report before him.

"Your girl Kelly has just mentioned tanned faces, bald heads, and queried, I quote, 'Just where is a tanned, bald head, an undercover requirement?' Sully, she's on to something."

Sullivan eyes took on a dreamy aspect and then his jaw sagged and face turned white as a ghost. Black, seeing this reaction from his sidekick whispered with concern in his eyes.

"Okay Sully, I know that look. Now what's got you so spooked?"

"Boss, have you ever seen the movie, *Star Gate*?"

CHAPTER 10

"Peek-a-Boo, I See You..."

Senior Airman Doug Cooper could not believe his eyes. Sure enough, his two bogeys disappeared behind the moon's shadow and did not reappear, but not before he received authorization to illuminate them with his satellite's narrow- and wide-band radars. Their returns were both satisfying and troubling. Satisfying in that the relative distance to target was 2.13 astronomical units; troubling because both were hollow constructs.

"Looks like I owe you a case of beer, senior airman," Perry kibitzed. "That doesn't happen often. Savor the moment."

"Oh, I will major, like for the next couple of weekends."

Now getting back to business. "So our bogeys are hollow. How intriguing."

"Yes sir."

"Let's play a game with them.

"DSDG Six and Twelve," Perry commanded. "Immediately retask your satellites to range on DSDG Four's corridor. Do not, I repeat, do not illuminate your radars. Let me know when your retasking is complete."

Cooper smiled.

"So major, you're trying to peek around the moon aren't you?"

"Yep. Two can play this game."

*   *   *

The pilot aboard the Survey Craft Number Eight was startled into alertness when his onboard sensors registered a powerful narrow band radar pulse that almost clanged off his craft's bulkhead. Right then and there the surveyor panicked, convinced that he was under attack. As for the far more subtle second wide band bounce, that one passed his attention. Meanwhile the surveyor on Survey Craft Number Nine, who had received only the second wide band energy pulse, remained blissfully unaware of what had happened to his colleague.

"That's it! I've had it! I'm moving into the satellite's shadow," communicated the pilot of Survey Craft Number Eight to his oblivious colleague.

"Why all the distress?" came back the reply.

"I'm under attack and so I'm moving to safety!" The frantic voice said.

"I will comply. The rest of the survey mission will be here shortly. Then, perhaps, we'll receive some useful direction."

*   *   *

Thirty-odd minutes later both DSDG Six and Twelve were in position and both independently confirmed the presence of the two bogeys hiding in the moon's shadow, relative to DSDG Nine. Significantly, the two bogeys had maintained their position in relation to the moon's shadow at a distance of approximately 2.13 astronomical units.

"Well," Perry thought out loud, "either they are content to observe us from afar, or, they're waiting for some reason. Any ideas, Doug?"

"Maybe, they're waiting for the cavalry." The senior airman quipped sarcastically.

"And, Doug, if the cavalry does show up, what do you think we should do?"

"Don't piss 'em off any further."

"Sage advice. In the meantime, get me a line to the folks across the street. I think that they deserve to know about this development. Besides, they might have an idea of what to do *if* indeed the cavalry arrives."

"Major?"

"Yes, senior airman?"

"What if these guys are the same ones who raided Wright-Patterson?"

"Good thought. I'll mention that as well."

*   *   *

The brass at AFSPC ordered a high planetary alert when DSDG reported to them the current situation. They took the notion of the cavalry arriving extremely seriously, which caused them to rush into immediate operation four ground-based laser systems and three massive rail guns. Russians and Chinese acknowledged the alert as well, but as to what they intended to do, AFSPC did not know. All the American assets were based in various parts of the western deserts and so really didn't provide planet-wide defensive coverage. But it was the best that they could do given the warning received.

Why this knee-jerk bellicosity? Because AFSPC command was more than well aware of the heist of the extraterrestrial craft from Wright-Patterson AFB on September 29, 2012, presumably by their rightful owners. The question now on the table was: "Is this a retaliatory mission?" Frankly, after the daring recovery at Wright-Patterson, AFSPC was not taking any chances. After all, they might be coming to fetch the remains of their pilot. No one knew what was going to happen next. Hence, the planetary alert status.

*   *   *

The rail gun crew located out in the desert wilds near Los Alamos, New Mexico, dutifully began powering up the rail's thirty-two magnets. For them, this was just another exercise. Maybe this time, they joked, an authorization would come through to discharge this forty-foot beast.

Then the crew learned that this was not a drill. They had received authorization to prime and load up the rail with a half kiloton neutron projectile in an aluminum pig. Suddenly, the atmosphere got serious.

Originally designed for ship-to-ship warfare by the Navy, this particularly massive application was envisioned to take out a swarm of inbound MIRV warheads high up in the atmosphere prior to re-entry.

Meanwhile, fourteen miles out of Sparks, Nevada, another crew, this time a laser battery, were powering up their instrumentation and warming up the laser's superconductors. Rated at six megajoules, the laser's impact pulse on target was estimated at a little over six sticks of high explosive. Due to atmospheric blooming, the realistic estimate of the laser's punch was reduced to only about two megajoules, or a little over two sticks of dynamite. That's still a lot of bang.

What was nice about the laser was its rapid cycling time, which made it perfect for detecting and destroying multiple instances of inbound missiles or warheads within the atmosphere, or, striking the same target multiple times. At least that was the case during field testing.

*   *   *

The pilot of Survey Craft Number Eight was greatly relieved when the rest of the survey mission arrived, all seventeen of them. Their ships, identical in their cone-like form, could, in times of emergency link up to form a defensive sphere.

Contrary to the usual Hollywood hype, intra- and intergalactic warfare was not the norm in open space.

While far less sexy, exploration and commerce took pride of place. As a consequence, this survey brood possessed no offensive weaponry, just a passive, defensive means of survival. In many respects, their first instinct at any sign of aggression was to form their defensive sphere and withdraw at best speed.

In this instance, that is precisely what Investigator Doog instructed his brood to do. Confronted with the perceived threat, Doog had them form up into a sphere. Once that was accomplished, he then sent a second message off to the survey's central administration, informed them of the bellicose nature of one of this minor system's planets, and then awaited their predictable reply and project-centric, risk-adverse recommendation. Nonetheless, Doog was affected by the experience.

I regret the loss of Survey Craft Number Four, but that, sadly, is the high price of deep space exploration.

*　　*　　*

While Senior Airman Cooper's view of the situation was blinded by the moon's shadow, observation Consoles Six and Twelve were not, for almost in unison both operators announced the arrival of a swarm of bogeys, which, amazingly, immediately oriented themselves into a tight ball.

That well-orchestrated maneuver alone, Perry thought to himself, *is well-worth the price of admission.*

"Range?" Perry requested.

"Holding steady at 2.134 astronomical units, sir." The operator of Console One crisply reported.

"General Stark, are you seeing this?" Perry deferred.

"Yes, I am major. Interesting. It looks like they're taking a defensive posture. Much like a box turtle or a circling of wagons. They haven't moved any, have they, other than following the moon's shadow?"

"No sir. They are clearly maintaining their distance. If I had to guess, I'd say that our two radar pings really got their attention, sir."

"I concur. The question is, what are they waiting for?"

"Again, my guess sir is that they might be waiting on further instructions."

"Major, are you saying that those folks have a bureaucracy as bad as ours?"

"No telling general."

"Good answer major. You'll go far."

* * *

Console Seven was the first to see it.

"Major! The bogeys are bugging out, sir."

"I concur." Added Console Six. "They boogied like bat shit fast." Then she remembered to say, "Sir." As the slowly tumbling ball faded away into the dark distance.

CHAPTER 11
Release the Hounds!

Within the hour Sullivan summoned his team of wizards to his cramped office. The three of them were polar opposites, but when teamed together to crack down on a project, they were unbeatable in Sullivan's eyes. It was then that their differences became a real advantage, much like having a can of WD-40, a set of standard and metric wrenches, plus an oxy-acetylene torch, to attack to a frozen bolt. Apply all three and that bolt isn't going to be frozen for long.

"Okay gang, here's the deal. There's this academic institution, department, facility, what have you, in Chicago, that we believe is a front for something far greater. Here's the cast of characters I believe will help us figure out just what that front is hiding." Sullivan said while he passed out the list of thirteen names that Kelly had provided him.

"The front's name is called the Philology Annex and it is located on Chicago's South Side. Somehow, it's associated with the university there, but, and this is key, it is not *actually* part of the university. Instead, it bills itself as a semi-private research institution that is available to the university's faculty and student body."

A hand raised. "What do you mean by semi-private?"

"Good question Larry. It means that it's not open

to the general public. But if you are a member of the permanent faculty, or are a student at the university, you can pay fifty cents and buy yourself a semester pass. And, get this, all members must wear slippers. No street shoes are allowed in the place. No exceptions."

That answer raised three sets of eyebrows in total disbelief.

"What is this Philology Annex? A slumber party?" queried Jerry.

"Clever, but no. Actually, it's a deadly serious place where the super-intense go to study and research ancient languages like Egyptian, Hittite, Sumerian, Phoenician, and God only knows what else."

More raised eyebrows.

"So, what I propose is that you guys work as a unit, figure out your strategy and approach, and then take this Philology Annex apart. What I want to know is 'who is funding it.'"

Pete then asked the inevitable question.

"When do you want this budget number?"

"Three days ago. Black himself made this request."

*   *   *

In addition to their widely differing personalities and resultant quirks, one must mention that a part of their natural competitiveness had a lot to do with their alma maters. Pete was from MIT, Larry CalTech, while Jerry matriculated with high honors from Carnegie Mellon.

These three tech-savvy terrors, now loose in a vacant conference room with plentiful whiteboard space, went at it with machinegun-like rapidity.

Sitting around the conference table and perched before their laptops like expectant vultures, it began.

"*Wiki*'s only reference to the Philology Annex is worthless. It reads like a travelogue description of a dust bin," Jerry announced.

"Yep, I concur," Larry agreed.

"Looking at the 'cast of characters' that Sully gave us, the economist Young turns out to be that university's Dean of Humanities! That suggests to me a guy in the know." Pete said with slit eyes. "You guys want to hit on him?"

"Sure. How deep?" Larry and Jerry chimed together.

"How about we copy as many e-mail headers as we can. Then analyze. Sound doable?"

"Absolutely."

As one the terrible trio went heads down as they individually raced each other to hack into a certain university's e-mail server.

At thirty-one minutes into the game, Larry, with his arms stretched overhead signifying touchdown as if he were an NFL referee, announced. "Damn, I'm good. Just copied out some three and a half years of the man's e-mail headers. Pay up dudes!"

Grudgingly, two quarters flipped in his direction.

"Yes!" Larry exclaimed with a fist-pump.

"Alright already Larry, now share your take," Pete grumbled.

The "take," all told, was 13,398 e-mail headers. That multiplied by the oftentimes multiple e-mail addresses present, expanded that total to well over sixty thousand recipients. Quickly realizing this, the terrible trio decided to divide and conquer. Larry was tasked with a mass collation of the addresses to come up with a total number minus duplications. Pete took on a hierarchical frequency analysis of address usage. Jerry, on the other hand, performed a similar frequency analysis, but on when the e-mails were sent.

After about seventeen minutes of numbers crunching, the trio discovered, minus duplications, the universe of unique e-mail addresses had collapsed to a far more manageable number—only 349. The frequency of any one e-mail address' use indicated that 212 were one-time unique correspondences, while only three took the lion's share. Remarkably, the dean's use of his e-mail remained steady throughout the year, and in fact, actually picked up a bit during the summer months when one would have thought, given a typical school year, that a decline should have set in. Wrong.

"Have you guys noticed some really odd e-mail address formats?" Larry asked.

"Yep, and guess what, my top three are all with the same odd ball address: @67240759311. All the rest have typical .edu formats. It looks like these three all work at the same place. Wherever that is?" Pete added.

"Okay," Jerry queried, "who are your top three names Pete?"

"'pborov', 'cacartwright', and 'jhallen', respectively."

"Okay, now just who are these guys? I'll take 'pborov'," said Pete.

"'Cacartwright' is mine," Larry piped in.

Miffed at himself more than anything else that he was so slow on the trigger, Jerry caved and said, "that leaves 'jhallen.'" *Christ, there must be a million folks named "allen" out there.* He groused.

* * *

It took Larry some thirty-two minutes before he crowed, "Pay up bitches!" Two more reluctantly dug out quarters flipped his way.

"Damn, thank you gentlemen! I can now get myself a Twix! I'll be right back, while you two losers finish up."

Seven minutes later Larry returned with his half-eaten candy bar. What he found was Jerry sitting back with a smile on his face and his hands behind his head. But Pete's face wore a deep frown as he continued to type into his laptop. The unwritten rule was to remain respectfully quiet until either all were finished, or until one finally conceded. And with these three, conceding was never a healthy option as the downstream ramifications were just too great.

After another twelve minutes of furious activity, Pete, with a really puzzled look on his face, shook his head once, sighed deeply, and declared.

"Guys, I quit. This 'pborov' guy is an absolute ghost. That's not to say that there aren't any in the States, but certainly no one that even looks mildly like a match. He has no social. He's not in the IRS databank. He has no credit rating. He not military. There is no birth certificate. Ditto no passport. In short, zero, zip, nada. In fact, this guy could well be an alias. And what really bothers me now, is that this guy is Dean Young's favorite correspondent by a large margin. And, if I was a betting man, I would put down a quarter that this guy, this *ghost*, is as important to the Philology Annex as is Dean Young. And if that is so, then he must be an awfully powerful ghost."

Thoughtful silence. Then Larry asked his colleagues.

"Is it even possible in this day and age to have an e-mail and still be a ghost?"

"Apparently so," said an introspective Jerry.

After several more moments while the crew considered just how hard it would be to exist totally off the grid, Pete took a deep breath and said.

"So, 'pborov' is a bust. What else do we have?"

Larry took this as his queue to tell his cronies about 'cacartwright.'

"Okay, it turns out that 'cacartwright' stands for Charles Abraham Cartwright, a graduate of Annapolis, who hails from a long and distinguished Army family. His great-grandfather fought and survived the Battle of Antietam Creek during the Civil War. His grandfather was a cavalryman, a member of the Rough Riders, and saw action in Cuba. His father, also an Annapolis grad, went into the mechanized cavalry and was a staff officer assigned to General George S. Patton, Jr.

"Charles Abraham was born in 1940 and graduated from Annapolis in 1961. He majored in security and languages. Thereafter, he became a ghost as his personnel jacket was earmarked 'Top Secret' by the Pentagon. On Cartwright's scanned jacket cover I could make out the words: 'SOAP BUBBLE.' Whatever that means. His current residence is in Lamkin, Louisiana, which is titled in his wife's name only. They hold no mortgages or liens. They have no kids. He doesn't have a credit card. Instead, the wife holds all the cards and has a spotless credit rating. Their most recent IRS filling indicates that she is the bread winner of the family. She's big into real estate."

More thoughtful silence, which was finally broken by Jerry. "So, in other words, some more big blanks in the picture.

"Well what I have to say about 'jhallen' is going to sound pretty much like a broken record. James Henry Allen was born in Stillwater, Oklahoma in 1946. Went to Stillwater High School and graduated in 1964. He attended OU and graduated in 1968 with degrees in biology and psychology. Then he attended the Baylor

Medical School and graduated in 1974 in internal medicine. He then inexplicably joins the US Army and receives his Honorable Discharge in 1982. Hereafter he practically falls off the grid. He has no credit rating. His postage goes to a post office box in Alamogordo, New Mexico. The only thing that indicates that he is still alive is that he is current with his IRS fillings."

More silence.

"So," Jerry continued, "what that leaves us with is three odd dudes."

"No!" interjected Pete, "two dudes with IRS statements. Sully asked us to follow the money trail, so let's do that. Let's pull the latest W2s on Cartwright and Allen and see who is paying them."

After some furious typing and several pencil scribbles later, Pete chortled. "I don't believe it!"

Two quarters were flipped his way.

"Okay Pete, whatcha got?" Jerry sullenly asked.

"Both Cartwright and Allen are paid by the same government agency, the Department of Energy in Washington, D.C. And now get this, they're both paid by the same account number! How cool is that?"

"Okay jackass, what's the number?" Jerry aksed.

It turned out to be a twelve-digit number, and again, the contest was on to discover who owned that number within the DOE.

A mere seven minutes later Jerry triumphantly stood up with arms outstretched and declared.

"I can't believe it!"

Two quarters rolled to the side of his laptop.

"Listen to this. The account number is a single budget line item tied to the Oak Ridge National Laboratory in Tennessee. I found it under the heading—Material Sciences Category. And best of all, right next to the number is supplied an identifier—Horizon Pass, New Mexico."

Immediately, the other two tech-heads began looking for Horizon Pass, New Mexico, but Jerry didn't move a muscle as he already knew. It didn't exist.

*　*　*

"Guys, I'm telling you, Horizon Pass, New Mexico, is a black budget operation. *Period*," Jerry pleaded. "On top of that, Alamogordo, New Mexico, is Dr. Allen's postal address. My money says Horizon Pass must be nearby."

"Okay, I'll buy that," Larry said, "but what kind of numbers are we talking about anyways? Whadda' ya' say?"

And the terrible trio was off again, now with a budget number, a department, and an identifier in hand. It was only a matter of time and Larry won quarters for the third time.

"Okay, here's the deal. The online budgetary files only go back to 1972. Nonetheless, for 1972 the funds associated with this account number were $7,984,000. That number steadily declined over the years to $4,012,000 in 1996. Then in 1997, the funding spiked to $10,546,000, and since then, has fluctuated between nine and ten million dollars per annum. Anything earlier than 1972 would have to be dug out of paper files—if they even exist."

"That's not that much for a black budget line item," Pete observed. "Especially for what B-2 bombers go for today. Just how big can this outfit be anyways?

"Hold on guys," Jerry interjected. "What we're looking at is most likely only an annual operating budget, for stuff like salaries, pensions, and the like. That means they must have quite a staff to burn through ten mil a year.

"What we have no idea about was their original capital budget, for stuff like building construction and other infrastructure items. All of that must have occurred prior to 1972."

"So that means," continued Larry, "that since we have operational budgetary evidence from *at least* 1972, when did Cartwright go off the grid?"

"Sometime after 1961," offered Larry.

"And Allen?"

"1982."

"Okay then, just for argument's sake, let's establish 1962 for the physical foundation of Horizon Pass, New Mexico. Now the question becomes, when was the Philology Annex established?"

Jerry blurted out, "1997."

"And," Pete continued, "When was the operational budgetary upturn?"

"1997," Larry confirmed.

"Therefore gentlemen, I surmise that the budget line item marked Horizon Pass, New Mexico, applies also to the Philology Annex. And, that makes both Horizon Pass, New Mexico, and the Philology Annex in Chicago, two separate locations funded by the same source—the DOE.

"Now the real question is—just what the heck is the Philology Annex fronting? Are they fronting for Horizon Pass, New Mexico? Possibly. But if that's the case, then what does Horizon Pass, New Mexico, do?

"Does anyone want to ping one of those e-mail addresses to find out? Just for giggles."

"I *sure as hell* do," said Jerry.

And so in an odd moment of non-competitiveness, where their intense curiosity took hold, both Pete and Larry got up and stood behind their colleague as he did his thing. And what they found was most revealing. Using the pborov@67240759311 e-mail address, Jerry pinged the source and found himself trying to interrogate a heavily defended and encrypted virtual server. The best that he could do was locate it, somewhere near Alamogordo, New Mexico. But for the terrible trio that was proof enough.

"There you go guys," Jerry said. "Horizon Pass, New Mexico, is indeed in New Mexico. Dr. Allen's postal address and this ping prove it!"

"Isn't Alamogordo near White Sands?" Larry asked.

"Yes it is," confirmed Pete. "In fact, there is a big ass Air Force facility there as well—Holloman AFB. And as we all know, absolutely nothing of a secret nature has ever occurred in New Mexico or with the Air Force."

*   *   *

Sullivan heard a tentative knock at his door, and upon looking up, saw three grinning faces.

"Come on in guys," he said as he waved them into his office. Then looking at his watch, he grimaced. "Jesus, it's late. So, okay, what do you have?"

The download took a full ten minutes by Sullivan's wall clock and after it was over, he said, "Do you have all of this in writing?"

Pete just handed him a thumb drive and three pages of densely typed text.

"Excellent work men.

"Now, who won the quarters' contest?"

Blushing, Larry said, "I did."

*   *   *

After the trio had left, Sullivan read through their investigative report and sighed. *Jesus, I have to kick this upstairs immediately.*

Five minutes later, he was again sitting before Black, who at this ungodly hour looked really beat. He should be. It was almost ten in the evening.

"Sir, I have my team's preliminary analysis on the Philology Annex's budget account. Here it is."

Now sitting back deep into his chair with his hands rubbing his eye sockets, Black said, "Leave the hardcopy with me. Just give me the short version, Sully."

And Sullivan did.

Afterwards, Sullivan asked. "Should we pull the content of Young's e-mails? The analysis will be numbing, but potentially quite enlightening."

After some consideration, Black replied.

"No, not yet Sully. This entire investigation is going places I didn't expect. While that's a good idea, let's just sit on this for a while."

Sigh.

"Damn Sully, I would never have thought the DOE was behind all of this."

*   *   *

Black was conflicted. His fair-haired girl had come through big time. His boys had successfully followed up on her observations, but now what would he do with the information? A glance at the available budget numbers for Horizon Pass, New Mexico, revealed little, as they were practically speaking insignificant, in this town of nine-digit annual black budgets. The only way to know what the Philology Annex did would be to copy out the contents of one to perhaps a half-dozen people's e-mails for the past couple of years. To do that, crossed a line that Black didn't want any part of. That line required a judge's signed warrant. But what could he muster as justification for such a hack? With only a handful of circumstantial and disconnected events and the stolen transcript of a secret teleconference to go on. Not much, and surely not admissible to a judge. In short, Black was stuck. He needed something firm to act upon, because at the moment his hands were tied. All he had was Kelly.

CHAPTER 12
Munich. 2003

The attic reading room of Munich's main library was rumored to be so dry that it caused nose bleeds, so noted one foreign papyrologist. Ever wishing to please, the library's administration thoughtfully provided each carrel with a box of tissues.

Such dryness was necessary, however, for the collection's extremely fragile contents would not have survived otherwise. Delicate beyond imagination, the unrolled papyrus scrolls, separate pages, and assorted fragments had all been catalogued using an extremely arcane system, and then mounted and sandwiched between panes of plate glass. Only so, could the precious relics be safely handled, read, and studied. Each pane in turn bore the signs of faint etching, which divided its surface into precise squares—a coordinate system. So could a reference to a particular passage, word, or sign be exactly found or cited. Such is the world of a papyrologist—part conservator, reader of ancient texts, jig-saw puzzle master, and oftentimes an expert of several very dead languages.

The man that hovered over Exhibit 43 wore extremely thick eye glasses secured in equally heavy tortoise-shell frames. Shaggy salt and pepper hair half-covered his ears. His heavily tanned and weathered skin seemed to actually crack as he squinted over the exhibit. On the table, to his left because he was left-handed, a yellow legal pad lay covered with lightly and carefully penciled characters, some in German, others in Egyptian hieratic. Slightly smudging the surface of the exhibit with the forefinger of his right hand, the scholar followed the barely readable text from right to left, all the while murmuring out its sounds, stopping only to pencil in another brief note.

It was a veritable miracle, the scholar thought, that these heavy panes survived the war intact, all the while those mad Nazis burnt books and the allies continuously fire-bombed. Nature itself, through deterioration, should have long ago consumed these fragile and delicate windows into mankind's past.

It is well-known the Gebberts had fled Paris during the Second World War and had successfully made it to Britain. It is also well known that his seven published volumes were not complete. *So does that make this papyrus the remainder of the Sebekmose archive?*

Then, shifting gears, the papyrologist made another note on his pad and whispered to himself.

"Krüger was right. This document cannot be Middle Kingdom in date. The orthography is suspect. It's written in a direct, reportage style that employs a later dialect and idiom, almost like an entry from a military or campaign diary. This chronological datum absolutely proves it, as "*Ipip*" is a New Kingdom neologism for the third month of the harvest season. Exhibit 43, therefore, must be of New Kingdom date, but when? My God Frantz! That period spanned some four hundred years, spread across three full dynasties of Egyptian kings."

Ending his personal rant, Professor Dr. Franz Horst von Staufen, professor of Egyptology at *Ludwigs Maximillans Universität München*, sat back. His vertebra cracked. His wooden chair creaked. He rubbed tired eyes for the hundredth time, then sighed deeply. He reread his translation, hoping he finally captured the essence of the ancient papyrus before him.

Column A

> Regnal year nine, the third month of the harvest season, day twenty. I, Heketemankh, astronomer of the house of the Great God Amen Re, write this.
> On this day was recorded a strange movement among the eternal ones of Nut's belly. One of the most ancient myriads fell towards the Red Desert.

Column B

> Since this happened after the evening meal, its bright passage was recorded by the priestly astronomers at *Per-Wadjet*, *Iunu*, *Men-nefer*, *Khmun*, *Menthu*, and *Nekhen*, and was seen by myriads of Black Land's inhabitants as they prepared for their evening rest.

Column C

> Their reports say the eternal one fell in the direction of the Red Desert in a straight line, and that the eternal one finally came to rest in the desert beyond the southern oasis.
> This place is sure, as a great bright light appeared,

as if Ra himself at dawn, transforming the evening darkness into the light of day for many moments.

Column D

This wonder was followed by a loud crack of thunder in a cloudless sky, and the earth moved several times. Great winds blew, scattering sand everywhere, and the sun was clouded for two days. All men and beasts were greatly frightened by these events.

"Regnal year nine," grimaced the scholar, "that does present a problem, because I know, just off the top of my head, of over twenty New Kingdom pharaohs who reigned at least that long. That means most of the kings of the Eighteenth, Nineteenth, and Twentieth Dynasties. So, I have no way of cogently narrowing down the date of Exhibit 43.

"Verdamnt!"

The scholar swore and pounded the table with his right hand.

Then with a tone of resignation, "At the very least the papyrus is clearly of New Kingdom date and not that of the Middle Kingdom. I suppose that's a good beginning, at least for now."

CHAPTER 13
Rhodes. May, 2008

"In conclusion, and based upon the fragmentary nature of this papyrus, it appears, given all the available internal evidence, that this papyrus provides a description of a meteor impact and its immediate aftermath. When?" The speaker gave a theatrical shrug. "Sometime during the New Kingdom. Where? Somewhere in the vicinity of the Nile Valley, most likely located in the southern Western Desert of Upper Egypt. It is up to those who understand satellite imagery to provide us with its precise location.

"Thank you for your attention." The speaker concluded.

Among the patch work audience at the Xth International Congress of Egyptologists, made up of scholars, graduate students, and other interested parties, sat an American who was extremely interested, no fascinated, by the German Egyptologist's paper. This American also knew who to talk to about that much-needed satellite imagery. And while the Google Earth platform was officially launched in 2001, it still was working out its bugs and coverage in 2008.

Very intriguing indeed, the American wondered. *But what kind of meteorite was it? Stone, iron, or, perhaps, something else? Or perhaps was it a comet?* He mused.

The American thought the topic might be well-worth looking into back home. But the vague New Kingdom date still represented quite a broad expanse of time. His first thought was how to narrow down this extraordinary event's chronology.

I just wonder...

Then John Milson, professor emeritus of Egyptology, unconsciously raised his hand signaling a query to the speaker. Recognizing Milson's face and his shock of white hair, the speaker, Professor Dr. Franz Horst von Staufen, smiled and immediately selected him over several other raised hands, much to their displeasure, not to mention easily bruised egos.

"Herr Professor Dr. von Staufen," Milson posed his question in flawless German, "Where and approximately when will this important paper appear in print?"

"Herr Professor Dr. Milson," von Staufen replied in equally flawless English, "the galleys are in final proof as we speak. The article will appear shortly in the *Zeitschrift für Ägyptologische Sprache und Altertumskunde*. May I send you an offprint to your university address?"

Milson just smiled broadly at the positive response to his question and indicated a simple thumbs up in silent reply. Von Staufen, for his part, made a note to do so on the margin of his notes while still at the lectern.

Milson busied himself with gathering up his plastic bag of publications that he bought earlier that day, one in particular by his good friend Bill Petty. The title said it all, *Ahmose. An Egyptian's Soldier's Story*. That was sufficient. Meanwhile, further questions were fielded and answered by the speaker. While doing so, a good portion of the audience, including Milson, began to silently leave the auditorium en route to other lectures, meetings, or liaisons.

*   *   *

Back at the Near Eastern Institute in Chicago, Milson applied himself to an unpublished acquisition on loan to the institute from a reputable source. As Egyptian hieratic writing was not his forte, he transcribed the cursive characters first into their hieroglyphic form before he tackled the papyrus' translation.

NEI-P No. 73.1962
Hieratic papyrus. Late Eighteen Dynasty. 23 x 54 cm. Provenance: The Fortress of Buhen. House D. NW quadrant. Level 7, Pass 2. Upper Egypt. Acquisition date: 1962. Unpublished. On loan from the W. B. Emery Archaeological Trust (Cambridge) via the Egyptian Exploration Society (London).

Column A

> Ninth regnal year, the fourth month of the harvest season, 29th day.

I, Sobekptah, Greatest of Fifty, of the frontier army at the fort of Buhen at second white waters, write of a remarkable event.

Thirty-nine days ago, one wick past the evening meal, the sky of the Red Desert was marked by the passage of a bright light.

Column B

The sky turned into day with a splendid brightness like Re's first appearance. Then a great sound came forth like that of a wounded hippopotamus. Next followed a trembling of the ground like that of a passing chariot squadron. Finally, a great sand wind from the south blew forth, hiding the sun for two days. Plots of land were buried. Their crops turned to dust.

Column C

Three days later, my garrison commander, Thutmose, received a command from the vizier of Upper Egypt Nebamen, that the King of Upper and Lower Egypt, Nebkheperure Tutankhamen, may he be granted life, prosperity, and health forever, demanded a full accounting of these strange events.

I was ordered by my garrison commander, Thutmose, to make my troop of fifty spear men and prepare for a great journey into the Red Desert to discover what had occurred.

Column D

With fifty donkeys laden with water and provisions, we did this, and after twenty days' journey, we came to a strange place.

Whereas before we marched on the packed sand and rock of the Red Desert, now before us stood a much-blacken and still smoking mound, streaked with white lines down its sides and upon the ground near it.

Column E

These lines were like the spokes of a chariot's wheels as they did not meet. Instead, they extended outwards and in all directions from the smoking mound.

As we neared the smoking mound, we dared not for three reasons. First, the sand and rock all around had been greatly burned and appeared as if melted wax.

Column F

Walking upon this ground one clearly left the sign of one's passage, as if treading upon many colorful pot shards of yellow and green, making much noise with every step. Then, several loud shouts rang out, as the ground breaking beneath our feet began cutting through the men's sandals, injuring their feet with terrible and bloody wounds.

Column G

Fearful, since so many were so afflicted, I called a halt to our examination of the smoking mound in order to attend to the many wounded. Nearly one third of my retinue had been so injured.

The second reason that we halted before reaching the smoking mound, was the great heat that poured forth from it. The heat was like that of a potter's kiln.

Column H

> The third reason we halted was because the smoke
> rising from the mound so offended our eyes and
> noses, that it caused great tears and choking.
> We collected pieces of this very sharp ground
> along with many dark stones, which littered the
> ground. I was told upon my return that these
> strange rocks were ore from the heavens, being
> most similar to those from Hatti.

Column I

> When placed near one another, these stones
> sometimes moved of their own accord! Other
> times, these strange stones could not be easily
> pulled apart, as if they were bound in some
> manner.

"As best as I can tell," Milson murmured over his
fresh translation, "this word in the papyrus' Column H
is a New Kingdom neologism. *Bi3-n-p.t*, or 'ore from
the heavens,' is best understood to mean 'iron,' or so
says the *Ägyptische Wörterbuch*, which generically
dates that expression to the New Kingdom. That
assignment conveniently dovetails with the dative
qualifier 'of Hatti' that also appears in Column H, a
well-known terrestrial source of iron during this period.
And given the chronological information from the first
paragraph, I think that we can tighten up the chronology
on this word's first usage quite a bit. Given the
chronological information from its first paragraph,
again New Kingdom in date, and specifically to

Tutankhamen's reign in particular, I think that we can tighten up the chronology on the origin of the phrase 'ore from the heavens'. It actually seems that the term 'ore from the heavens' was coined during the reign of Tutankhamen. Quite literally, this is hard evidence of a celestial event of sufficient magnitude that actually affected a culture's vocabulary!"

*   *   *

Dear John:

I trust your health is better.

I heard via Ulli Schachermeyr that you are, or were, struggling quite a bit. Needless to say, our prayers are with you.

Enclosed you will find my promised offprint on the papyrus I equated with a meteor strike in the Egyptian southern desert.

Hope you find it of interest.

--Frantz

Oh, Frantz, my friend. Your timing could not have been better! Milson beamed.

CHAPTER 14

Bingo!

With a dreary battleship gray skyline over Chicago, the forecast predicted non-stop snow starting around noon. Then almost like clockwork, beginning around 4:45 pm, they began arriving. Thirteen of them in all. As Kelly greeted each, she ticked their names off in her head and the departments that each represented: Jennings–Philosophy, Hartung–History, Milson–Egyptology, Grace–Classical Studies, Benjamin–Geology, Junkers–Near Eastern Studies, Brown–Biology, Shaw–Linguistics, Philips–Economics, Young–Dean of Humanities, Porter–Hittitology, Johnson–Near Eastern Studies, and Gregg–Classical Studies.

Eager as a sprinter poised at the starting line, Kelly somehow managed to contain herself for a full five minutes. When she could stand it no longer, the receptionist was jumping out of her skin. The Minnesotan kicked off her soft Minnetonka moccasins, and jumped into her fleece lined boots and ski parka. Slipping out the front door, Kelly cut across the Annex's snowy lawn and looked around the corner of the gangway's entrance. And sure enough, there they were. Easily six or more sets of foot-prints entered the gangway from the front and rear of the passage. All ended at that chalk-marked telltale. Then a hunched over figure suddenly appeared at the opposite end of the gangway coming from the alley! Quickly ducking back around the building's corner, Kelly's heart really began to pound in the early winter's near darkness.

Another one! Her mind screamed. *That makes at least twenty-one in all! Where are they all going?*

Now very carefully she slowly peeked from around the corner and was rewarded with actually seeing the figure disappearing *through* the brick wall!

Bingo! She thought with considerable satisfaction. *This calls for a special transmission!*

*   *   *

Before Black could answer Sully's question about his total lack of a real life, much less the last time he saw a movie, his laptop chimed. Glancing over his reading glasses more out of habit than anything else, he saw the FLASH TRAFFIC designation.

"Just a minute Sully. Your girl just sent us an urgent message."

After several moments of intense scrutiny, Black announced. "Sully, get this. 'Secret side entrance to Annex confirmed. Multiple footprints in the snow and one intruder seen in the act.'"

Silence.

Then Sullivan piped up. "Do you think that they're having another one of those teleconferences, boss?"

"Perhaps, but I don't think so. This sounds like

more a meeting of the minds to me. Something's up. Something important. Enough that adults are sneaking around and walking through brick walls."

Pause.

"By the way, next month bump up Kelly's pay grade to a GS 12. Get me the paperwork tomorrow and I'll sign it."

"Boss, for Kelly a GS 12 is a double-bump!"

"Yeah, and do you know what? She's more than earned it."

Pause.

"As for your technical crew Sully, I want them to do some deeper digging as well. I want to know whose black budget within the DOE is responsible for the funding of the Philology Annex. Maybe that will give us some insights into just what is going on during those secret meetings."

"Do you want me to get a search warrant?"

"No, but I *do* want you to put the argument together—just in case."

CHAPTER 15

Chicago. September, 2008

"Joseph, if it is convenient, would you be so kind and join me in my office?" John Milson politely asked his colleague, who resided four doors down the hallway.

"Sure, John. Just give me a minute to shut down my computer."

Almost to the second, a respectful knock was heard by Milson on his wooden doorframe. Even with his door open, Richards had remained at its threshold, while he waited for his mentor to acknowledge his presence.

Remarkable, thought the emeritus Egyptologist. *Such fine manners and respectful reserve, no doubt the result of his military upbringing. If only some of the other faculty would practice such!*

"Enter my good man," Milson softly said. "Kindly close the door, take a seat, and make yourself comfortable. This might take some time to skull out."

Even though the younger colleague carefully sat down, the old wooden chair creaked in loud protest nonetheless.

"John, you should really get yourself another guest chair. This one seems to be on its last legs."

Glancing up from a much dog-eared offprint on his desk, Milson only smiled, and then sighed as he took in the well-muscled and compact figure before him.

"Ah, youth," he moaned.

Drumming the desk's pad with his right hand, Milson debated with himself as to how to begin.

Richards, noting his colleague's pensiveness, just sat in patient anticipation. Ten seconds later, Milson announced.

"Joseph, something has come to my attention that *may* require a bit of special investigation. The kind that would require the help of our good friends in New Mexico."

Instantaneously, Milson noted that Richards had moved to the edge of his chair so quickly that he had not even witnessed the act.

"Really?" Was Richards' quick reply.

"Yes Joseph. Maybe," he said with an upraised finger. "But I am going to recommend that you are not to participate on this junket."

"Why not?" the younger man asked with undisguised disappointment in his voice.

"Well, for several reasons actually." The professor stated, now with his hands folded on the desk before him.

"The first is your recurring post-drop syndrome. Doc Allen says that it's not getting any better. On an investigation this small, I would rather hold you in reserve, allow Gregorieva to finally earn her solo spurs, and in the process get some more experience. Further, the temporal coordinates will place her in a period that she is not only familiar with, but is already known as your sister and assistant. Those facts carry a lot of clout."

With his arms tightly crossed, Richards, who had listened carefully to his mentor, pursed his lips in thought as he took in the bad news. Then, after several moments of silence, he said.

"John, believe it or not, I totally understand. The PDS has indeed been a bitch, but as best Doc Allen knows, it all has to do with an electrolytic imbalance. I guess, to date, I've been extremely lucky. But that said, since when is any investigation so minor that the use of the temporal device is being seriously considered? And given all the inherent risks involved, are we now chucking the buddy system out the window as well? I'm sorry John. I can't follow that line of reasoning. It would be far better to recruit and train another temporal field agent altogether and then deploy as a pair. Perhaps even another woman."

Pleased, and also quite surprised by his young colleague's reaction to the bad news, not to mention his proffered recommendation, Milson sat back deeply into his leather chair with a squeak. His hands steepled before him.

"Yes Joseph, you are absolutely correct. Nothing minor or insignificant should be the subject of a temporal insertion. And yes, the buddy system should be strictly followed. But I ask you, do you not remember your solo deployments? How well you performed? How rapidly you developed as a temporal field agent as a consequence? Eventually to the point of even becoming an Egyptologist?"

"Yes, John, I do remember those deployments, in fact, perhaps even too vividly given all of Doc Allen's psychic enhancements. But again, remember John, I went on all of those solo deployments before the PDS kicked in. As I remember those days, there was a certain urgency in the air as well.

"Now, I'll be the first to admit that Gregorieva did marvelously on her first drop, but who's to say that she will not develop similar symptoms without a buddy to spot her?" And now with his hands up in surrender, Richards concluded. "I'm just saying. Now what is this minor investigation all about in the first place? Fess up, John."

"Well, Joseph, it is all very intriguing, really. A colleague of mine in Munich read a paper at the Rhodian congress back in May about a papyrus he thinks refers to a meteor strike in Egypt. Time frame— sometime during the New Kingdom. I have his offprint right here. But what von Staufen does not know is that we have an eye-witness account in our basement's vault of most likely the very same meteor fall, its aftermath, and its location in southwestern Egypt, deep in the Western Desert, somewhere due west of the Second Cataract. That places the impact near the Egyptian-Sudanese border, which now-a-days, is nothing short of the Wild West.

"As far as the papyrus is concerned, it was found during one of Walter Emery's archaeological expeditions at the frontier fort of Buhen. What is so important about this unpublished papyrus is that it gives us a precise date for the impact: Tutankhamen's ninth regnal year, third month of the harvest season, twentieth day. So, it gives Gregorieva a conveniently narrow window to work with."

Still with his arms crossed, but with now an interested tilt to his head, Richards surmised. "So, this minor investigation is to reconnoiter the impact site. Perhaps even bag some samples. Is that it?"

"In essence, yes."

"So, to summarize John, you propose to drop Vesna solo into the holy of holies at Karnak. She then procures a boat that takes her south to the Nubian frontier. Once there, she disembarks, treks inland across the open desert, somehow finds the impact site, and then treks out with some goodies. Only then does she return to Thebes and her eventual recovery by Tuna Cartwright's security team.

"Yep, you're right John. It's a piece of cake, a real cream puff of a deployment, and it'll give her lots of opportunities to think on her feet. If, that is, she isn't eaten by lions first, or second, is killed or captured by one of the desert tribes, or third, sold into slavery or skinned alive by some disaffected Nubians."

Clearly hearing the not-so-veiled sarcasm in his colleague's voice, Milson could only nod his head in acknowledgement.

"When you put it in those terms, Joseph, I agree, this is a very ambitious mission for a solo deployment, which has its fair share of potential pitfalls. Nonetheless, I believe that Gregorieva is ready for it."

"Fine, John. But don't you think that she should, at the very least, be granted the opportunity to visit the site first?"

With a furrowed brow, Milson queried.

"Visit the site?"

"Yeah, let's recon the place. As in first locating and then visiting the current meteor crater by trekking in from the Nile Valley. Heck, we both could do it together. Basically, trace the trail in the present, so that she isn't surprised in the past. I don't believe I'm saying this, but a present-day recon may suffice."

*　　*　　*

"Out of curiosity, Dr. Gundersen, what sort of heat would be required to glaze over a stretch of open desert? Basically, to reduce the sand into a glass-like sheet of green and yellow vitrified material?"

With his bushy gray and unruly eyebrows raised high, the geologist was extremely surprised by such a question from an Egyptologist, but by the look on the face of the question's source, he knew it was seriously asked.

Pinching his lower lip in thought, Gundersen grunted twice, shook his head once, and then said. "Well, Professor Milson, it would have to be both a very hot and a very intense heat to produce such a condition, certainly not something a terrestrial desert could normally produce. You see silica melts around 3,300 degrees Fahrenheit. So, figure that temperature, plus or minus several hundred degrees, but intensely applied, as in an industrial electric furnace.

"But you said that an entire open stretch of desert was so affected, turned into sheets of green and yellow glass. Now that would really take the expenditure of some serious energy. Yep, if we rule out a modern nuclear blast, it would have to be something extraterrestrial. Something like a meteor or comet impact, to produce what you have just described. Now John, where is the location of this vitrified field? You have really have piqued my interest."

"Dr. Gundersen, you probably would not believe me if I told you."

"Try me."

"Southwestern Egypt."

"Gad! You don't say!"

CHAPTER 16

Suspicions

Ty Lawson, the university's database administrator, had an odd, scratchy feeling that something wasn't just quite right. Usually when he performed an evening backup on the university's e-mail servers, the CPUs ran at warp speed, but not tonight. It was as if something was dragging them down, like somehow a tangible element of friction had been added to their hard drives. While the unusual phenomenon had lasted only about thirty seconds tops, Lawson logged it anyways, and even made an external copy of the last half of the event.

This, he thought, *I am going to look into.*

The next day, Lawson scrounged some spare time to investigate the past evening's anomalous slow down of his maintenance backup routine. Plugging the flash drive into his laptop, he began casually scanning through the code, looking for anything out of the ordinary. The backup process appeared to be proceeding normally, until the technician saw and *blinked* in surprise, that near the end of the process, there was a line of code that he didn't recognize. Easily understanding the meaning of the code, Lawson's blood pressure spiked as his territorial and highly protective instincts took hold.

"Holy shit!" he whispered to himself. "My e-mail server has been hacked. But what did *they* copy?"

Scrolling back and forth several times, his fears were somewhat lessened as the intrusion was very specific. In actual fact, it messed with only one e-mail user, and then, only that user's e-mail headers. Now breathing easier, Lawson's blood pressure then spiked again when he confirmed just who had been so affected: payoung@usc.edu—Dr. Paul Allister Young, the Dean of Humanities.

*   *   *

Getting a mid-day audience with any university dean at the drop of a hat, and without offering a specific reason for the need of such urgency, is a rare event. For Ty Lawson, at wits end with Young's officious secretary, he just hung up the phone in disgust and decided to act.

Eight minutes later he entered the dean's outside office chambers and presented himself before his secretary's desk. There, hiding behind her fortification of computer monitor, appropriate reference books, and weeping tendril plants, she disdainfully looked up over her golden chained half-glasses through a sprig of salt and pepper hair.

Eventually she acknowledged Lawson's impatient presence. "May I help you?"

"No, but Dr. Young certainly can. Is he in?"

Mildly ruffled by the evasion, "Do you have an appointment with Dr. Young?" the secretary enunciated with a heavy emphasis on the word "Doctor."

"No, I do not." Lawson carefully enunciated as if to a simpleton. "I am Ty Lawson. I just got off the phone with you. I need to see Young immediately. Is he in?" he purposely repeated.

"Yes, he is in, but is extremely busy. I am sorry sir, but you really do have to make an appointment."

"No, Madam, I don't." Lawson said with considerable exasperation. Because with those words, Lawson turned on his heel, strode purposefully across the lush Persian floor covering, passed the elegant mahogany paneling, and entered Young's office unannounced.

As he did so, Lawson closed the dean's door behind him, stole a peek over his shoulder, and saw the secretary's enraged beet-red face, who already had her phone to her ear.

Dean Young's office, as with all high administrative dignitaries of established universities, was a splendid example of aged woodwork, paneling, tasteful period furniture, bookshelves, and their luscious smell. The desk, the sacred altar of university status, was center stage and Young was comfortably ensconced behind his. Lawson ignored all of this as his mind was totally focused on far weightier matters.

Young, who knew of Lawson and his importance to the university at large, looked up from his green felt blotter in mild surprise. Putting down his black Mount Blanc fountain pen, he smiled, folded his hands, then observed.

"Ah yes, Mr. Lawson, I can tell that you ram-rodded your way in past my secretary Miss Andersen. Congratulations to you, sir. I'll wage you a dollar that campus security are on their way."

*   *   *

"So Mr. Lawson, to summarize, you are seeking an emergency authorization to better secure our university's e-mail servers. Do I understand you correctly?"

"Yes sir. That is precisely what I need. And, I have already have taken the liberty of sourcing precisely what we need to address this particular issue. But sir, I am telling you now, today, that this fix will only be a temporary one, as what this university really needs is a far more ambitious solution for its database security."

All was silence while Young steepled his hands and gathered his thoughts.

"Well then, Mr. Lawson, I thank you for acting so swiftly on this matter. I find it shocking that our e-mail servers were so exposed. Do go ahead on this 'patch' solution as you call it. Expect the authorization for that to be in your mailbox later today. As for this 'far more ambitious solution' for our server security, the one that you just have championed, kindly put together a request for funding and submit it directly to me within the week, so that we can get some immediate traction on it. Again, thank you for acting so quickly on this issue."

As Lawson turned to leave, Young stopped him.

"Mr. Lawson, here's that dollar I wagered. Apparently, campus security has figured out my secretary's overzealousness."

Surprised, Lawson took the dean's proffered bill.

"Why, thank you sir," he managed.

* * *

"Campus Security. This is Officer Davis. How may I help you?

"Oh, hello Miss Andersen.

"Who?

"Ty Lawson?

"Okay ma'am, slow down, so what's the problem again?

"Ma'am, I know Ty Lawson. Heck, I know his father as well. He doesn't represent a threat to Dean Young. He's just a computer geek."

Pause.

"Yes … yes … I understand.

"Miss Andersen, have you heard any screams yet from the dean's office?

"No? Okay then, Miss Andersen, here's what I'm going to do. I am going to dispatch Officer Robertson to check out the situation.

"No, I do not think the Campus SWAT Team will be necessary this time.

"Thank you again for calling.

"Have a nice day."

Holy shit, Officer Davis thought. *What a psycho! I will never forget when she called us in to defend Young from that evil Egyptologist Milson.*

What a joke that was!

Now where's Robertson?

Thumbing his radio, "Robo, you out there somewhere with your ears on?"

"Robertson, here. What's up boss?"

"I drew straws and you get to visit Dean Young's office today. It seems that his secretary, Ms. Andersen, is once again on the warpath. So your mission Robo, is to go over there and cool her down."

"Aw, gee thanks, boss. You're the best."

CHAPTER 17
The Stone Cutter

Nakhti was the son of a stone mason and occasional carver of private, family shrines. His name, which means "the strong one", was given to him in the sincere hope that he would follow in his father's footsteps.

Born in Thebes during the twentieth year of the Pharaoh Amenhotep III, his earliest childhood memories were of following his father about, picking up limestone fragments and sweeping away all the debris left behind. And there was always a lot of it as his father's projects always tended to start big and end small, as volume, the established rules of proportion, the application of a grid, and its precise measurements, were totally beyond the illiterate man.

Yet, in order to make ends meet for his family, Nakhti's father, a stone cutter by trade, did take on the occasional artistic commission, and in doing so, blurred together two typically separate professions—that of a stone cutter and sculptor. Nonetheless, and early on, Nakhti's keen eye helped his father's lack of artistic sense when it came to space and perspective, to the point that by age seven, the youngster painted the roughing lines, having already learned how to take full advantage of a stone's structure, texture and form.

They made a great team, Nakhti planning and designing, his father providing the initial muscle in roughing out the stone's general form. Then, together, they would apply themselves until completion. Throughout, his ever-smiling father was very proud of his son.

Nakhti's first commission came during the middle of his eighth inundation. The noble lady, Inhapi, who had recently lost a child, wished a life-sized memorial made for her beloved daughter, who had gone West. Having heard in the marketplace of this creative father and son team, she approached them, and was surprised that it was the son, and not the father, who asked all the questions and answered all of hers.

"Most noble Inhapi, what sort of stone do you wish? What size? Do you wish a standing or seated figure? Would an offering table for your beloved daughter's *ka* be desired as well?"

The noble woman was totally surprised and taken by the young boy's demeanor, his sensitivity to her needs, and his gentle politeness. All of these things naturally reflected directly upon his father, who just stood silently next to him.

* * *

Little did Nakhti realize that this very commission, so beautifully rendered in flawless white limestone, became a showcase of the young man's innate abilities. Both stone carver and sculptor, Nakhti represented a rare hybrid of practicality and aesthetic—qualities that would become extremely advantageous. Needless to say, Inhapi's memorial to her daughter created a sensation throughout the royal court, as the word had spread like wildfire of its lifelike naturalism. One said, "Such a sensitively carved statue." Another, "Truly, it seems almost to breathe."

As word spread among the Theban court and its attending circle of nobility, the fortunes of the young apprentice stone cutter and his family took a turn for the better, as commission after commission kept the talented pair of father and son continuously busy. But one individual at court, the royal Prince Amenhotep, found a deep kinship with Nakhti's relaxed artistic style and his subtle manner of naturalistic presentation, which had so deftly drifted away from the usually staid, Egyptian canons of artistic expression. The young prince, after having seen the monument dedicated to the young daughter of the noble lady, Inhapi, had no less than two personal portraits commissioned, all to be carved in common red sandstone.

Young Nakhti and his father, flattered beyond words and quite intimidated as well by their royal client, nonetheless set to work on the prince's bust, which were to be gifts for his parents. Beginning with a mockup that they could later use as their guide in stone, the pair rapidly worked the plaster into shape before the sitting prince. The first attempt was rejected as "too sterile and formal." The second was deemed "too conservative in its rendering." But the third, hand formed according to what Nakhti actually saw, finally won the prince's favor.

While carrying away the dried bust to their workshop, father and son spoke quietly and quite frankly among themselves. They wondered why the prince wished to be so memorialized in stone, with his gaunt look, large eyes, and head so captured. But, as they finally agreed, a royal's gold was as good as a noble's.

After the passing of one cycle of the moon, the two royal busts were completed in their raw red sandstone, smoothed to perfection, and delivered as promised. As for Prince Amenhotep, he was overjoyed and paid the stone carvers triple of their agreed upon fee. With the proceeds of that boon, Nakhti's father, after much consideration, decided to invest in the construction of a modest, single-chambered family tomb, which he and his son planned to bring to final completion. The smoothing of the tomb's rough rock walls and the plastering throughout in preparation for the painters was a wearisome task. Nonetheless it was a new process for Nakhti to master, one which would provide the young stone cutter with valuable practical experience in the medium on a massive scale. Then, after three painters from the royal craftsmen's village had performed their own brand of "magic," all was in readiness. For Nakhti, the tomb's completion represented the fulfillment of a son's ultimate duty to his parents. In this particular case, Nakhti not only contributed to the tomb's construction, but also to its preparation.

*   *   *

Up until the passing of King Amenhotep III during his thirty-fifth year, the family's stone carving business had remained steady and profitable. Even during the first years of his successor and son Amenhotep IV, the very prince that Nakhti and his father had made the sandstone busts for, work had remained plentiful.

No longer a gawky adolescent of all arms and legs, but now a fully formed man with ruggedly handsome features, Nakhti sported a neatly trimmed moustache, a roguish affection that he had adopted as young men often do.

Young, strong, fit, and walking with a bit of swagger, Nakhti's place and responsibilities within his family had matured as well. His father, now suffering from arthritis, seldom accompanied his son during the agreement process of this or that commission. Instead, the father remained at home, while Nakhti's clear eyes, sound judgment, and sense of fairness had never failed either the welfare of the family or of their clientele. In fact, oftentimes during such negotiations, Nakhti appeared older as the limestone dust often grayed his shock black hair, so granting him an appearance of wisdom and thereby some additional negotiating leverage.

After the passage of one season word had spread that confirmed the truth of the rumors. The king wished to construct a new city to the north. Encouraging news of the generous incentives for skilled labor caused Nakhti to move to the site.

When he arrived two days later by boat, Nakhti found a barren and undeveloped half-moon shaped wasteland bordered on the east by high cliffs and mountains. During those first months, he lived in a simple mud brick structure, more a crude hut than a house, and was fed mostly by the largess of the river. Fortunately, the king's wages, while one month late, were very good, which were supplemented with daily food rations and sweetened with the promise of permanent housing—complete with a private well and toilet.

Such were the advantages of signing on early to the royal construction project for skilled workers and laborers. More remarkable was that Nakhti could easily see that the king's promises were being kept as the architects drew their lines in the sand, the laborers dug their foundation trenches, and the brick layers began building row upon row, street after street, of a well-planned, spacious, and hygienically progressive housing community.

In many respects, the building of this northern city from scratch was a daring and unheard of act that broke with all Egyptian tradition. But for the stone mason Nakhti, it had been a godsend. While a very capable stone mason and artisan, he was not yet a master craftsman. The calculations needed to grid out a work in cubits consistently confounded him as they had his father, but he was learning the skill quickly under these unprecedented conditions. Better still, because of Nakhti's remarkable sense of space and proportion; he could better eyeball the needed dimensions far quicker than calculating them. He knew instinctively where to precisely snap the caulk-dusted string. And given the rapidity of the new city's construction, his natural skills were quickly noted by several of the managing architects, as well as his strides in calculation.

So when the city construction project took off at a breakneck pace, Nakhti found himself in an extremely advantageous position. Speed was everything as mud brick, small limestone blocks that one man could easily carry, and the liberal use of plaster were the primary construction materials of the day.

Armed with his practiced eye for proportion, Nakhti did well in an environment that had totally abandoned the traditional Egyptian canon of art, for one that was more free-flowing in its execution and tendency towards outright naturalism. Discarded was the idealism of perfectly proportioned human forms. Banished were the stereotypical poses of husband and wife, of king and queen. All were replaced with scenes best described as "in the moment": a king bouncing his daughter on his knee; a queen bending over to kiss her consort; wild colors in profusion; flocks of birds fighting for space within a fleeing flock.

Within such an environment, the management of space and the filling of it took artistic license and imagination, qualities that Nakhti understood. The stone cutter excelled, so much so that the king himself, recognizing him from his earlier portraiture, singled him out from the masonry ranks. The king then instructed him in what he had in mind for a series of inscribed stones which would mark the limits of this ancient city.

"Nakhti, you have done well. My architects tried to hide you from My eyes as you make their surveys straight and true. My royal artisans similarly covet your natural-born talents. My laborers trust you because of your fairness of heart and clearness of eye. I like you because of your ability to make stone breathe. Thus, I command you Nakhti, to undertake a great task, the construction of sixteen boundary markers that will surround my city. My architects will show you where each boundary marker is to appear as their locations hold for me a magical and protective meaning. My chief architect will provide you with plans for each. My chief scribe will provide you with My words that I wish inscribed and so made eternal. You may choose the members of your work gang. I wish all to be completed within two years time."

Needless to say, such a royal commission Nakhti could not refuse. He began planning his work and enlisting those whom he trusted in this great endeavor.

These massive markers were to delimit the extent of the city of Akhetaten and to proclaim to all the greatness of the king and of his god the Aten.

Each *stela* was to have a specific orientation that the chief architect provided, an orientation that would relate to the city's divinely inspired plan. What Nakhti marveled at the most was the absolute clarity of vision that the god-king possessed as to how he wanted the boundary markers to appear, what they were to contain, and how they were to be adorned with the royal images of the king and queen beneath the life-giving rays of the Aten itself.

The supreme confidence that he had felt emanating from his king in his personal ability to complete such an ambitious task had filled Nakhti's heart with overflowing joy and zeal. It had even permeated his crew. No longer were they just the laborers of the king. They had become the makers of a magical region, all defined by the monuments made with their own hands. While it was the eighth month of Year Four of the king's reign, all must be completed by the same month of Year Six. Despite the brief time frame, the stone mason knew that he could do it, as did his crew.

*   *   *

Over the course of the next two years, Nakhti's forearms, shoulders, and torso became as hard as beaten bronze. His body bled freely from the flying stone chips and became as heavily scarred as a veteran warrior's, who would not turn away from his foe. His artistic eye and intuitive knack for proportion became better and better and much progress was made.

The king often made visits to his far-flung work sites, where the city's boundary markers were being cut, shaped, carved, and painted all according to the god-king's wishes. At first, his royal presence had caused quite a commotion among Nakhti's work gang, but over time they had become almost expected, even welcomed. Such royal interest in their labors only seemed to spur them on to greater and greater feats of exertion, creativity, and production.

On the occasion of one such royal visit, the king brought along one of his sons, a young boy-prince named Tutankhaten. The royal pair found Nakhti and his crew toiling long into the heat of the day over a massive *stela* that faced the northern end of Akhetaten. Pleased with what he saw and amazed by Nakhti and his crew's diligence, the king rewarded them with extra rations of beer, onions, garlic and bread. As for Nakhti, the head stone mason was acknowledged with a smile and a slight bow of the royal's head. The impact of that simple act threw Nakhti into elation, for never before had the king granted him such praise, much less before his work crew.

Besides the surprise inspections by the king, no less than four times young Prince Tutankhaten had driven out to inspect Nakhti's work. Curious about the entire process of stone cutting, carving, shaping, and the like, the head stone mason recognized that this scion of the royal household was just being a boy—out adventuring, exploring, and looking for potential mischief. So Nakhti asked him if he could shoot a bow or throw a spear. To all of these things young Tutankhaten had proudly, with a puffed out chest, answered in the affirmative. So, the stone mason handed the royal youth his wooden mallet.

"This is not so heavy," said the boy. "It is big, but not so heavy."

Then Nakhti passed over his favorite bronze chisel.

"But this is," came the quick reply that was immediately followed with, "but how can you then cut stone?"

To this Nakhti smiled and explained that while the mallet is reasonably light and easily controlled, it is the heavy thing that does all the work.

"Why is this?" the youth continued.

Nakhti replied, "Because that which is heavy, like the chisel, is a thing that must be carefully controlled." The boy ruminated on this as Nakhti demonstrated the use of his tools, which produced smooth, regular, and clean paths in the soft, white limestone, as the stone cutter seemed to be shaving away the stone's surface.

Then the royal crossed his arms and declared, "Your words, stone cutter, are wise ones that I can see have many lessons and many meanings. So, are you a philosopher too?"

To this observation Nakhti smiled, "Perhaps royal prince. Sometimes when my hands are busy at a task, my mind is freer to think about other things, sometimes deep thoughts. Would you like to try a few cuts at the stone?"

And cuts Tutankhaten did make, small chips at first, then once he understood how to correctly hold the chisel, smooth and shallow flakes began to fall at his feet.

"Stone cutter, I now better understand what you meant by taking care of that which is heavy. This was a good lesson. I will visit you again."

Bowing deeply to the boy-prince, Nakhti said, "As I am your father's servant, so am I yours. Your presence would be much appreciated anytime."

*   *   *

In his later years, Nakhti could easily recall each of the sixteen boundary *stelae* that he had been commissioned to create. The earlier ones contained small and minor imperfections in their design, which he later improved upon with each subsequent effort. But he did have a favorite marker, the one that guarded the entrance pass to The Most Select of Places of the Aten. Yes, its limestone had been simply superb to work with, being almost as soft as alabaster, and without flaw. Yes, its color and grain were remarkably consistent. Even its text was slightly different from the others. Nakhti, now literate enough to read what he had carved, had even memorized that boundary stone's message.

But the real reason for his favorite choice were the four visits made by the young royal, Tutankhaten, who like a bolt of dry fine linen had absorbed many of the tasks involved in its creation, and who possessed an extraordinary eye for snapping the leveling string true. And there was one thing more. Nakhti was convinced that the experience taught the boy something he could not have learned at court—the value of effort, skill, and control.

CHAPTER 18
Southwestern Desert, Egypt

To Richards' delight, Milson agreed that scouting out the meteor crater's present location would be a grand idea. Gregorieva's people made sure of her availability, as they were more than curious themselves about any Egyptian excursion into the deep desert.

In order to best replicate the journey, Gregorieva and Richards departed from Luxor on a common, wind-powered felucca boat. About the only thing that both had absolutely insisted upon was its prior inspection, specifically for fleas and lice. Finding none, they were off, sailing with the prevailing wind and against the current en route to modern Aswan, the First Cataract, and the Aswan High Dam. Once there, they procured another boat to ply the waters of modern Lake Nasser south, where they continued on to the vicinity of ancient site of Buhen, sited just north of the river's Second Cataract, now long submerged by the waters of Lake Nasser.

* * *

It was still dusky dark when the pair arrived at the agreed upon location on the western bank of the lake.

"Alright, here are our GPS coordinates," Colonel Cartwright announced to his two charges.

"From here, it's all slog into the desert and back. Out there is absolutely no water. Consequently, there will be strict personal water rationing. Each of you is to carry eight liters on your back, plus some personal items. And oh by the way, because of current state of Egyptian-Sudanese relations, common sense broke out. You get to cheat going overland."

He paused to take a breath.

"Now I know all that extra weight will be a real burden for you panty-waists, but I'll be damned if I'd have one of my fine troopers carry any of it for you. After all, they are responsible for their own sixty pound packs, plus ammo, and their weapons.

"Have I made myself clear?"

"Crystal." Richards said with a quick nod.

"Understood," cooed Gregorieva with such a disarming smile that it caused the veteran security commander of Horizon Pass to do a double-take.

That damn Russian is one hell of a handful! I don't know how Joey there can handle it. Then Cartwright quickly reconsidered with a hidden smirk. *That must be some really tough duty.*

"Okay everybody, *load up,*" the cantankerous commander bellowed. "Our Humvees have four hundred miles of desert terrain to cross and four hundred getting back. Fortunately, we don't have any serious obstacles in the way. So people it's open desert running. Let's make the best of it! I can hear my wife already bitchn' that I'm late for supper."

Four minutes later, the six heavily armed vehicles, loaded down with spare fuel, water, and their personnel, disappeared into the Western Desert. All they left behind was a quickly fading telltale of dust in the first rays of dawn's light.

*   *   *

True to Cartwright's directive, the column made good time, clocking by the colonel's GPS, a steady double-nickel. At this rate, even with a thirty minute halt thrown in midway to unkink and provide a bio-break, Tuna calculated eight hours to target. Piece of cake for his men, but for the two civilians, he had no clue, except that they would just have to gut it out and put up with the brutal pace and its physical pounding.

Given the nearness of the Sudanese border to the Kamil Crater, he had strict orders from on high to get in and out with two hours max on site. Period. No arguments. Then it would a mad dash back to the C-130H Hercules heavy transport aircraft parked at the Abu Simbel Airport. Why? Because Tuna didn't want to miss his wife's supper.

"Yep. Absolutely no lolly-gagging on-site. We go in hot and come out slicker than snot," the veteran commander loudly declared.

*   *   *

For me, never before had I been so hot, dusty, shook up, and disoriented in my entire life. Just the simple act of slipping water from a plastic liter bottle became a challenge. The idea, after all, was to drink it, not wear it. Meanwhile, the passing terrain, a fast-moving and dusty blur, only seemed to reinforce the totally surreal nature of the trip. Add to that, the constant pounding of the armored Humvee across the open desert. It was quickly threatening to jack-hammer my spine into jelly.

Taking in my immediate surroundings, the vehicle's dust laden interior, I simply marveled at my two accompanying soldiers, who seemed to float in their seats, despite their harnesses, their heads on a constant swivel, one driving, the other pointing and talking into his mate through his helmet-mounted stalk mike. On and on they went, relentlessly, as I floated in and out of a foggy, heat-soaked consciousness. It was then that I remembered what Joey had told me about the Iraqi War, how men such as these had driven three days straight, day and night, only to be stopped by Nature itself in the form of a sandstorm of gargantuan proportions.

At the midway point, I finally came to. Somehow, I had drifted off into some kind of catatonic state only vaguely related to sleep. At first a bit confused, I then realized I was not being perpetually jarred and banged around. The vehicle was actually stationary! My driver and his sidekick were not in the Humvee, so I unbuckled my harness, levered myself out, and fell flat on the ground as my knees had totally buckled under me. Here I was, God knows where, on my hands and knees in two inches of the finest, pumice-like sand, that instantly stuck to me nearly everywhere. Shaking my head in disbelief at my situation, two strong hands suddenly grabbed me from behind and lifted me to my feet.

"Are you okay?" Joey helpfully asked.

"I think so." I replied.

"Pretty shocked-out from the ride, aren't you?"

"I think so."

"Same with me. Fell flat on my face. I'm still spitting grit and drinking water doesn't seem to help one bit. How about you? When was the last time you drank your ration?"

And that's really about all that I remember of the midway stop, as we immediately mounted up again.

We arrived at the crater during the heat of the day. The sun's full force was out and it was devastating in its effect. Add to that, the entire team looked like a bunch of dusty tan zombies. Movement threatened to create an unwanted cloud of tan. Any surface that had been left uncovered was now smothered with a thick layer of that god-awful fine, pumice-like, powdery sand. Fortunately, all concerned had been issued desert goggles.

As for the meteor impact itself, I saw it immediately. A low mound with rayed whitish lines that emanated from it as if they were the parallel spokes of a bicycle. Everywhere around it were weathered ruddy-red fragments of iron and a strange greenish and yellowish glass-like material. In some instances it was over an inch thick, very sharp, and very jagged. One soldier, perhaps not thinking, actually cut his foot on this material as it had sliced right through the side wedding of his boot. What a bloody mess that was.

Per Milson's request, Joey and I collected several representative samples of any iron or vitreous material that we encountered. Why? I don't precisely know, except that he wanted them analyzed in a proper laboratory.

Personally, I was looking forward to the trip back to civilization, a long cool shower, and several gallons of heavily iced tea. This mound, its eroded crater, and its dangerously sharp surroundings were not for me. But then I heard Joey excitedly call me over from the opposite side of the crater. He was waving his arms like he was on fire, or, had he actually managed to find something extraordinary?

Now what? I thought dreamily at the time.

What Joey had stumbled upon was embedded in the crater's upthrust southeastern bedrock, or perhaps better said, looked like it was melted into it. The object was long, rectangular looking, clearly artificial, and needed to be removed. Somehow, we had to get it back to the lab along with the rest of the samples. The real question was how? We didn't have a jack hammer. Fortunately, Colonel Cartwright's team had several rather canny sappers, talented explosive types, who quickly were put on the case. Fifteen minutes and one muffled explosion later, the object was extricated intact within a rough limestone casing. Weighing about sixty pounds, two soldiers quickly hefted the prize over to one of the Humvees and dumped it rather unceremoniously into its rear cargo bay.

Then, right on time, per Cartwright's own wristwatch, he declared it high time to get underway. Looking down to my own watch, we had been on site for only thirty-five minutes. Clearly, I sensed, something had the colonel spooked. Moments later, I buckled myself in and was ready to go. The colonel's troops too had caught their colonel's nervous vibe and before I knew it, we were roaring off back towards the Nile Valley, my cool shower, and that several gallons of iced tea. No, at second thought, make it a pitcher of that deliciously sweetened, and frothy lime-mint drink the Egyptian's call a lemonana.

*　　*　　*

Five hundred meters to the south, straddling the border behind a low dune, two Sudanese border guards swaddled in desert camouflage watched the American detachment with considerable curiosity. Their five-power Russian military binoculars, panned back and forth over the scene, while they continuously chattered among themselves. It was all so curious. What were those foreigners doing? What was that woman doing there? Was she their whore? What were they gathering from the ground? But when the explosive plume suddenly appeared and the concussion of its detonation reached them, they reflexively jerked down for cover, and the once calm conversation became quite animated.

"Bakri!" one said in shock. "Those infidels must have found something very valuable!"

"Yes, yes, you are right my brother. Look Tahir! Two of them are now carrying something over to one of their vehicles. It looks very heavy. What could it be?"

"Do you think they found treasure? Maybe gold?"

"Absolutely, you ignorant camel! Why else would anyone visit this desolated hell hole? Quickly now. Inform Command of what we have seen and ask for further orders."

*   *   *

Cartwright, sitting in the passenger's seat of the lead Humvee, had this really bad feeling. In fact, he had this itchy, twitchy feeling almost as soon as they arrived at the crater. Having long learned through hard experience to listen to his witchy sixth sense, he pulled out his secure satellite phone, and called his support detachment, who were waiting back at the Abu Simbel Airport.

"Rabbit Hole. This is Wiley Fox. Over."

After a moment of silence came back the clear reply.

"Rabbit Hole reads you in the clear. If you're already en route back, then you're early. What's your Status. Over."

"Rabbit Hole, we are indeed early and Wiley Fox is really nervous. Spool up the Bambino and have it cover us on our way inbound. Over."

"Read you, Wiley Fox. Bambino will be up in five. Over."

Now sitting back into his seat, Cartwright's mind remained a blur as he continued to strategize his situation.

"Joshua," the colonel said to his driver through his stalk mike, "drop us back to the caboose. "Riley." He said next. "Wake up, you lard ass. Get up in your chair, prime the Dragon, and stay real sharp. I've got a real bad feeling."

"Roger Colonel. On it." Said the third man in the Humvee as he climbed into his firing position and charged his weapon, an electric M-134D-H mini-gun mounted on a three-hundred-and-sixty degree roof swivel.

"Petterson, this is Wiley Fox. Do you read? Over."

After a scant moment of silence.

"I read you, Wiley Fox. Am I now lead? Over."

"Affirmative, Petterson. You are now lead. Just don't get us lost. Over."

"All vehicles, this is Wiley Fox. Go to alert status. Over."

Richards, seeing the lead vehicle suddenly dropping back with its gunner climbing into position, sensed that something must be amiss. The dead giveaway and confirmation was the glance and nod that his driver and his sidekick shared. Apparently, they had just gotten the word over their tactical radios, as had the other vehicles.

Oh, boy. Richards thought. *What's got 'em all so excited now?*

Meanwhile, Gregorieva just noticed the same thing that Richards had, and so asked the soldier in the passenger seat. "Corporal, what's up?"

Over the roar of the motor and wind, he yelled back. "The Colonel has his ears on! Ma'am, that cat is an absolute witch! He can tell when an attack is coming, or smell out an ambush, ninety-nine percent of the time!"

*   *   *

Back at Abu-Simbel Airport, Sergeant Callahan, Cartwright's second in command, had his men readying an oddly shaped aircraft for takeoff. A carbon-fiber marvel, the Bambino had the radar signature of a hummingbird, a twenty-foot wingspan, and a hushed pusher turboprop motor. With a range of seven-hundred miles, fully loaded, and a top speed of three-hundred miles-an-hour, the Bambino was every field officer's wet dream, in the realm of personalized stealth and aerial ground support. For this deployment, the Bambino was armed with two shrouded Hellfire missiles located near its wing roots. For reconnaissance purposes and target acquisition, the nose was loaded up with an infrared and laser targeting receptacle and a real-time, high-dev camera. Nowhere near as sophisticated as the usual drones flown in Afghanistan and Pakistan, the Bambino was light, easy to maintain, and highly portable, as in tiny, within the cargo bay of a C-130 Hercules airframe.

True to his word, Callahan's men had the Bambino airborne in five. It reached five-thousand feet a minute later and was already four miles down range. The drone was now fast closing on the GPS signature of the tiny, east-bound convoy.

* * *

"By my rough reckoning, Petterson, I figure that if we keep to the double-nickel, we're going to be naked for about an hour. After that, the Bambino will be on station overhead. That answer your question corporal?"

"Yes, sir," the lead vehicle driver responded, as he ever so gently began to press his accelerator pedal deeper into the floor.

* * *

It took nearly two hours and twenty-five minutes for the Sudanese chain-of-command to deploy one of its Mi-24D Hind attack helicopters, from the nearby provincial Wadi El Halfa Airport, to investigate the reported territorial intrusion.

Nicknamed the flying tank by Russian pilots, the Hind could fly just a tad over two hundred miles an hour on a good day. But this particular airframe was only marginally maintained and practically had to grunt itself off the ground and into the air.

Manned by a crew of three and sporting a ten soldier compliment, the helicopter was a formidable foe, armed as it was with missile pods and several heavy machine guns. But the Hind did not have much in the way of range, and knowing this, the airframe was dispatched directly north to the Egyptian-Sudanese border, a mere sixteen miles, where they had strict orders to loiter near the frontier village of Argeen. Once there, they were to wait and look for the dust plume of the fleeing infidels. Why there? Because the obvious destination of that truck convoy had to be the Abu Simbel Airport. A mere twenty-mile incursion across the Egyptian-Sudanese border, a strafing run in the open desert, followed up with a quick snatch and grab, was deemed an acceptable risk by the Sudanese frontier command. Frankly, nothing less could satisfy the avaricious machinations of a certain enterprising Sudanese commanding officer.

*   *   *

Almost immediately the Bambino's infrared targeting module picked up the ferocious heat signatures of the Hind's twin turbofan engines, as it lazily race-tracked counter-clockwise over a miserable looking collection of structures. The drone's operator, Lieutenant Ken Hassig, a young airman from Kansas City, immediately identified the bogey for what it was, and then noted its rather suspicious presence within easy striking distance of his colonel's egress route.

"Calli! We have some company!"

Now looking over the man's shoulder in order to get a better look at his flight monitor, the former basketball player from Indiana drawled.

"Well, lookie there! The colonel was right on! Well, I'll be! It's true! He is a witch! What's that heat signature of, anyways?"

"It's a Russian Hind, sir."

"Well, you don't say. Well, lieutenant, why don't you overwatch that bogie, and be sure not to let him know that you're there. Got that? We're not shadowing the recon column any more. Just stick like glue to that Hind."

"Absolutely sir! But what's the drill if the Hind crosses the border and attempts an intercept?"

"Lieutenant, as soon as he crosses that border, drill him into the ground. Absolutely drill him. Got that?"

"I hear you loud and clear sir. He'll be a grease spot."

*   *   *

"Rabbit Hole to Wiley Fox. Come in Wiley Fox. Over."

After a brief moment, Callahan got his reply over the recon team's secure satellite radio.

"Wiley Fox here, Rabbit Hole. What's the good word? Over."

"The good word is that Bambino is up and is shadowing a threat to your south. Please advise, Wiley Fox. Over."

"Where's the threat? Over."

"From your position, about one hundred out. A Russian Hind. Over."

"Sudanese? Over."

"Yes sir. Most likely. Over."

Silence, then Cartwright asked.

"Which side of the border? Over."

"Loitering just inside the Sudanese border. Over."

"Nail him, Rabbit Hole, if he crosses the border. In the meantime, we will vector north and away from his location. Maybe that will make him think twice. Out."

Now with the situation clearly before him, Cartwright could understand why he hadn't seen hide or hair of the Bambino in his sector. Calli had wisely held it back to shadow the threat. Now, he just hoped that there wouldn't be another bogie out there, lurking somewhere.

* * *

In mid-turn towards the southwest the Hind's copilot spotted the recon column's dust plume at his two-o'clock. Just like that, what had been a numbing flying exercise for the pilot had turned into the real thing. It was about time too, as his fuel and patience were running low. Immediately, he began calling out orders to his crew to prepare for a strafing run, and the troops in the hold to ready themselves for a ground assault.

* * *

"Sir," Hassig alerted Callahan in total disbelief. "That damn Hind is one really dumb mother. It just broke its loiter pattern and looks to be ready to cross the border."

"Gently now, Hassig. I want you to nail him once he's a full five-hundred meters inside Egyptian territory. Understood? And not one meter farther."

"Yes sir. Crispy toast at five-hundred and one meters."

* * *

The near-invisible Bambino had been loitering over its prey at five thousand feet for quite some time. When the order to launch had been finally received, the craft's

Hellfire missiles ignited. The launch was beautiful in a way, two fluffy billows of propellant that quickly arched downward directly upon the Hind's two red hot engines. Their impact could only be described as awesomely spectacular, as in Fourth of July finale spectacular, as the helicopter's remaining fuel, hot hydraulic fluids, and armaments cooked off, creating a brilliant funeral pyre. Fatally stricken, the Sudanese helicopter augured deeply into Egyptian soil, leaving absolutely no question of its illegal presence.

"Damnation!" Hassig exclaimed at the pyrotechnic result.

"Fine shooting!" Callahan said as he slapped the airman on the shoulder.

Then Callahan keyed his satellite radio.

"Rabbit Hole to Wiley Fox. Come in Wiley Fox. Over."

"Wiley Fox here. Yeah Rabbit Hole, we saw all the fireworks. Many thanks! Over."

*　　*　　*

I felt the concussion in my chest first, and when I opened my eyes I followed the energetic pointing from the front of the Humvee. A burning cloud of fire seemed to have suddenly erupted from the desert floor to the south. Excited fist pumps were shared between the soldiers. Naturally, I just had asked why.

"Ma'am, that there is a for-real drone kill! And a quite spe-tac-u-lar one at that!"

Stunned, I then followed up.

"But what did the drone kill?"

"Apparently, a Sudanese attack helicopter was fixen' to grease us all!"

Quite frankly, you must believe me when I say this. When I finally realized I had been the target of some unknown attacker, I was at first stunned, then shocked, and finally very angry. All the nervous energy that had been stored up in me released in one huge gush of emotion. I remember quite distinctly screaming at the top of my lungs.

"Those damn terrorists!

"You fuckers took my parents, but that wasn't good enough!

"Now was it!

"No! Now you want to send me to hell as well!

"Well, you better not get in my way, because I will kill every last one of you!

"All of you!" I absolutely shrieked.

During this sudden outburst, this classic temper tantrum of corded neck muscles and blue-white fists, I had not realized the Humvee had come to a sliding, skidding halt. Both soldiers were fully turned around in their seats, staring, totally dumb-founded, at me in the back seat.

With tears bursting from my eyes and my fists still insanely clenched, I vented again with emphasis.

"Nobody!

"Absolutely nobody, fucks with me!

"You guys got that!"

After a few moments of dead silence, my driver then quietly said. "Yes ma'am, we read you loud and clear."

Turning back around and getting the vehicle back underway once more, the driver, using his in-cab radio channel, whispered to his colleague.

"Damn, that is one tight lady. She'd just as likely scratch out your eyes as rip your balls right off."

In response and glancing over to his driver, "Homey, you got that dead right."

CHAPTER 19

Wright-Patterson AFB. Dayton, Ohio

On Tuesday morning, at nine o'clock, Dr. Roy Allen Peters, the Director of the Materials Technology Department and Laboratory, really needed a diversion, a project, some real stimulation, as his current duties had become purely administrative—again. Since the repossession of the Aten space craft over a year ago, he was practically sitting on his hands.

This hurt, as Roy always was a very hands-on materials scientist. Sure, he admitted, the organic remains taken from the Aten space crate continued to be an endless source of wonder for the life sciences types. Sure, they still had the SNOWMAN, but that had already been fully dissected, its charred remains well understood, and even its preserved last message in that downright pretty Light Language deciphered. Only an extensive digital record now remained of the space craft that on September 29, 2012 was taken from the base. Every time the Hoosier reviewed those, as fascinating as they are, his ulcer began acting up.

With a bowed head, he quietly said. "Roy, my boy, it's time to finally admit it, that the really big one just, flat, got away." His sole audience, his desk's green blotter, remained blessedly silent and without comment.

Thirty seconds later Peter's phone rang. His secretary apologized for the intrusion and then said a

John Milson from Chicago wished to speak with him.

"Maggie, put the good man through," Peters said while simultaneously thinking, *now why does the good professor want to talk to me?*

"Good morning John, what can I do for you?"

"Actually Roy, we really need your help."

"Okay, that's simple, you got it. So what's up?"

"In eleven hours a corporate-looking Gulfstream V is going to land at your airfield. The flight is coming in direct from Egypt. Aboard the aircraft are samples taken from Egypt's Western Desert that I want you and your folks to take a look at. Are you okay with that?"

"Well, I just don't know, it's been real busy around here lately, John, but for you, I will clear off my desk. What color is the plane?"

"I don't know."

"You're kidding."

"Nope. It can change color."

"You're joking?"

"Nope."

"What's its tail number?"

"Again, I don't know. It can change that as well."

This time the materials scientist just took that information for what it was.

"Okay then, can you at least give me a hint as to what I will be looking at?"

Brief silence.

"Not on this phone Roy. I think you know what I mean."

Roy, now genuinely smiled for the first time in quite a while, answered. "Professor, I completely understand. Has your plane been cleared to land?"

"Indeed it has Roy. Just meet it with two push carts. You'll need them."

*   *   *

Roy was so jazzed about all the cloak and dagger stuff that he hung around to meet the corporate jet personally. Being that it was nearly eight o'clock in the evening, the glistening white bird seemed to appear as if by magic out of the dark sky. The plane then taxied over to the open hanger where he stood with two laboratory push carts, along with a young assistant. Remarkably, only Jonathan Grisom of his core team had heeded his call for help at that late hour. As for the head materials scientist, he was just simply jumping out of his skin in excitement.

Finally coming to a stop, the plane's access hatch opened and its stairs lowered. Then, this familiar looking young fellow with dark hair exited with what looked like a large blue plastic storage bin, the kind that one so often sees on sale at Walmart. He noted that its lid was sealed with gray duct tape.

Smiling, the visitor said. "Good to see you again, Dr. Peters. I'm Joey Richards. Remember me? The Egyptologist who opened up the Aten?" With that introduction, he plopped his burden on one of the carts with a jarring thump.

"By the way, this bin is taped shut just to keep in its contents. It's not a biohazard. We got one more for you. But that one is one heavy mother."

And off scampered the Egyptologist up the stairs and into the plane. After a couple of minutes, Richards reappeared cradling in his clearly well-muscled arms, a longish object that was wrapped in clear plastic bubble wrap. Taking one stair step at a time on his descent, the weight of the object must be considerable, Peters noted, as the stairs sagged with each of his steps. Placing it on the second cart, which now teetered awkwardly under its mass, Richards wiped off his sweat-streaming brow, shook Roy's hand, and said goodbye.

Throughout the entire transfer, the plane had never fully shut down, and even now it was slowly taxiing away. Peters, a bit jarred by the experience, looked to his young assistant and said.

"Well, Jonathan, that was a bit abrupt. He must be late for his momma's dinner, don't you think?"

*　　*　　*

As the twosome began silently rolling the lab carts away, Peters' brain was already in full organizational mode. First to the clean room, assess what is what, and then …

"Dr. Peters," Jonathan's excited voice interrupted, "don't you think we should go directly to the clean room to assess what all of this is?"

Startled by the near Vulcan-like mind-meld, Peters rapidly coming out of his own intellectual fog replied. "Yep, you're absolutely right Jonathan. Let's go directly to the clean room. We can then sort all of this stuff out in the morning."

Then he thought. *Roy, my boy, this Jonathan might be a bit green behind the ears, but he's alright. Alright indeed!*

* * *

"So John," Richards reiterated for the record, "do you still want Vesna to go solo?"

Sigh.

"No. I have to admit that you were right. Given the distances involved, the challenges of the trek in and out, no, I can't support such a solo adventure. There would be just too many variables in the works to chance a drop like that. Especially since what the two of you just went through near the border. What you brought back was representative enough."

Now frowning with a mix of interest and concern, "So precisely what do you mean by 'representative enough,' John?"

"Well Joseph, I mean that Dr. Roy Peters and his team out at Wright-Patterson have been one very busy analyzing your samples. As a result of their preliminary analysis, he has serious doubts about the nature of the meteor that created the Kamil Crater. While everyone assumed it was a standard iron-nickel meteor strike, he suspects something more, because many of the samples that you and Gregorieva gathered are not strictly composed of the usual and expected iron-nickel blend. Instead, about one fifth of the sample was composed of a high-tech alloy. I am told by Dr. Peters that it was manufactured and cannot be produced in Nature."

"What!"

"Yep, we have ourselves yet another potential watershed event, another mystery to solve. And that is only their preliminary read on the rocks. They are still hard at work on the big slab of stone that you found. And God only knows what that is."

"Damn."

"Joseph, the universe is a mighty big place. I suspect that out there we have many neighbors.

*   *   *

There is a famous quote attributed to Michelangelo, wherein he said, "I saw the angel in the marble and carved until I set him free." Four days straight Grisom and Peters carefully removed the heat fused and cracked limestone from around a rather peculiar object.

The pair looked much like goggled paleontologists in their hooded white jump suits, picking their way at a large fossilized brontosaurus femur. Instead of dental picks, they were using Dremel tools with a wide variety of abrasive tips, which rapidly chewed away at the limestone, sending tiny fragments all over the tiny and well lit lab room. They sat, hunched over as they were, as fine debris fans built up in the folds of their suits, on the floor, and their stainless steel work bench.

As they worked at removing the limestone layer that encased most of the object, they naturally discussed what they were dealing with. Yes, it was manufactured. No, it probably was not of terrestrial origin. As to what it was, well, that was nearly impossible to tell at this point. It would be like trying to understand a portion of a 1965 Corvette rear bumper, when you didn't know what a Corvette even looked like, or was. But that didn't stop the two scientists from speculating.

"Well Dr. Peters, I am just surprised that this fragment survived at all given the heat generated by the impact, much less the shock of the impact itself." Jonathan offered.

"Yeah, I've been noodling on that as well. In fact, I am willing to bet that what we are dealing with here is an unmanned probe that just failed, and consequently, piled in."

"How'd you come to that conclusion, Dr. Peters?"

"Well first off, it had to be massively heavy. This alloy is fifty percent iron. That's like nothing we use today as we are so weight conscious. Payload is king with us. Why? Because our propulsion systems are based on either a solid or liquid chemicals to provide thrust. On top of that, solids and liquids are heavy in and of themselves. That means that this object's propulsion system could not be based on a solid or chemical fuel like we currently use."

The veteran materials scientist paused to swap out a drill bit. "Nope, it's just too darn heavy, but it's definitely durable, and by the likes of that essay that we just ran, massively durable. So that suggests to me a gravitational propulsion system of some sort, maybe something that uses something exotic like dark matter for its fuel or maybe even harnessing gravity itself. Something that can take full advantage of all that iron, and that something to me means a gravity-based propulsion system."

After replacing yet another drill bit, Peters continued. "You know Jonathan, the composition of this fragment is turning out to be nothing like that of the Aten space craft. The alloys don't match worth a lick. What do you make of that?"

After allowing several moments of silence to pass, Jonathan finally found his tongue. "You know Doc, what you just said sounds, well, like this is a completely different design from top to bottom."

"And ..." the materials scientist pushed.

"Just maybe an entirely different group has been poking around in our solar system." The young scientist stopped to turn off his drill and stared directly into

Peters' eyes. "Actually, that thought sounds reasonable, given what we know, which isn't jack."

"Yep, I know that we don't know 'jack,' but in this business, you simply have to be able to think outside-of-the-box. Otherwise, you shouldn't be here. Period. And oh by the way, always remember that the universe is a very big place."

Jonathan couldn't agree more.

* * *

Roy Peters had a hunch after his brain-storming session with Jonathan in the lab, decided to run with it, and lifted his phone receiver.

"Maggie, could you please connect me with a Major Charles M. Perry, US Air Force? I believe he's out at Peterson AFB, Colorado Springs." He asked his secretary.

"I'd be happy to, Dr. Peters," as she pulled up the address book on her computer.

"Thanks so much."

Several minutes later, the materials scientist had the major on an encrypted line.

"Hello major, my name is Dr. Roy Peters out at Wright-Pat. How are you today?"

"Just fine, Dr. Peters, what can I do for you?"

"I need a surveillance satellite to be tasked over a meteor crater in southwestern Egypt. What I am looking for is another impact site or some kind of anomalous sign to the north of the impact site."

"Are you referring to the recently reported Kamil Crater, sir?"

"Why indeed I am major. I am trying to cover all the bases on this one. I have a high suspicion that a piece of the Kamil meteor calved and landed somewhere north of the primary impact site."

"Understood, sir. When do you want this to happen?"

"As soon as possible, Major Perry. Our hair is not on fire quite yet, but we're also trying to figure stuff out."

"Within the next three days, you'll be hearing from me."

"Thank you, major, I knew I could depend upon you. You folks in the Springs are the best. Do you need the crater's coordinates?"

"No, sir. I just pulled them up."

"See there? You're already on top of this."

"Thank you, sir. We're just the red-headed step-kids trying to keep up with you people out at Wright-Pat."

"Damnation, major, doesn't the crap ever stop?"

"No, sir. It never does." Perry said with a grin.

CHAPTER 20
More Observations

Kelly was at work bright and early the next day behind the her desk at the Philology Annex, numbly sorting through the day's mail—discarded the junk mail, unboxed newly arrived books, and paid the bills. She greeted visitors and addressed all the pressing correspondence of the day. Frankly, she yearned for some more excitement and began wondering, thinking, just how she could make that happen. Then it hit her squarely between the eyes—she remembered registering in thirteen academics and the exit of a fourteenth.

If someone entered from the gangway's secret entrance, then how could they exit through the front foyer? Wouldn't they have to exit through the same way they came in? Apparently not. So that means that there must be not only a secret conference room in this building, but also a way to get to it from the interior of the Philology Annex itself! But where would that secret entrance be?

Now energized with a brand new quest, Kelly began to methodically apply herself. Nosing about here and there, she decided that the entrance/exit to the secret conference room had to be on the first floor as she had never witnessed anyone using the staircase to the second and third floors. So, where could it be?

After canvassing the entire floor, only three options remained: the two bathrooms and a small coat closet. Banishing the bathrooms from her consideration, the small walk-in closet now received her full attention. As it was early winter, all of its seven coat hooks were full with patron's wraps, as was the shelf above, with an assortment of hats, backpacks, and the like. Even the umbrella stand had three in it. Everything was in its place.

Kelly was not entirely sold, however, that all was right with the world. So she got down on her hands and knees and began a close examination of the closet's polished floorboards and their beautifully matching woodwork trim. It was only then, and beneath a longish trench coat, that she found what she was looking for— two neat vertical breaks in the wall plates, each about three feet apart. They were so hard to see because they were cut using a forty-five degree, overlapping join. She now moved to inspect the wall itself. Any break in it was totally camouflaged by the decorative vertical wainscotings that ran from the floor to the ceiling.

Standing up and brushing off her knees, Kelly next figured that if indeed there was a hidden passageway at this spot, then a coat hook must trigger it. So removing the longish and oddly dusty trench coat from its antique brass fixture, she pulled down on it and nothing happened. Perplexed, she next twisted it to the left and it remained firm. But when the Minnesotan twisted it to the right, the fixture moved. When it did, she heard a subtle click. Daring, Kelly pushed and a doorway appeared that opened to a small room beneath the first floor's staircase.

On the room's only full wall was the frame of an elevator door and a call button panel. Daring again, she pushed the button and waited about fifteen seconds, until she heard the nearly silent elevator arrive from beneath her. The doors opened without a ding or bell. Daring yet a third time, Kelly, did not enter the elevator car. Instead she just poked her head in, looked around, and saw the interior control panel. It had no less than three buttons—Ground, One, and Two! *My God, there are two sub-basements to the Annex!* Retreating back to the coat room, she grasped the coat fixture, closed the doorway, and gave it a turn to the left, and was rewarded with that satisfying click. Replacing and rearranging the folds of the dusty trench coat as best she could, Kelly returned to her desk and sat down, her mind in a whirl.

*   *   *

At the security desk in the first sub-basement, Corporal Walker noted on his screen that the wardrobe entrance had been opened. Quickly checking over the day's schedule, the Texan wondered, who's arriving? Intrigued, he glanced up to his partitioned video monitor's screen and saw Ms. Kelly carrying a trench coat over her right arm. She then summoned the elevator, peeked in, and then rushed right out.

Lifting the telephone receiver from its cradle, he quietly waited while the automatic and encrypted connection was made.

"Cartwright. What's up corporal?"

"Sir, Ms. Kelly has just paid us an unauthorized visit. She's found the locking mechanism and opened the door in the coat wardrobe, entered its vestibule, and even looked inside the elevator cab."

"You're shitting me!"

"No sir. What are my orders?"

"Sit tight for now, Walker. Dr. Borov and I will have to discuss this development immediately. And Walker…"

"Yes sir."

"Good job."

"Thank you sir."

*   *   *

While Kelly was busy sending another message to her boss in Maryland about her latest discovery, Colonel Charles Cartwright, head of security, and Dr. Peter Borov, founder, chief investigator, manager, and cook and bottle washer for Horizon Pass and its adjunct facility in Chicago, the Philology Annex, settled down for a frank chat in the scientist's office deep underground.

"Well this week is turning out to be a real humdinger!" Cartwright exclaimed. "First, Dr. Young's e-mail at the university was hacked, and now this, our very own Ms. Kelly is making a royal nuisance of herself! It all just makes one wonder."

Only silence answered the vexed security chief as the slim runner Borov sat deeply in his office chair–thinking with slightly slit eyes.

"You know colonel, that e-mail break-in was inevitable given the times in which we live. Dr. Young is after all the Dean of Humanities, so I can easily imagine any number of scenarios for that theft. By the way, Mr. Lawson, our IT contact at the university, is currently addressing the issue with what he calls a 'patch.' I understand that it's not a permanent solution. That will have to do for the moment. Young tells me a more suitable solution will follow.

"But as for Ms. Kelly, I have to agree with you. I suspect that she was planted on us by someone who is very curious. If that is indeed the case, then Tuna do you want to alert that curious someone that we are on to them? Just like we were on to the Air Force's listening in on our early teleconferences before we encrypted them? No, I think not. That old adage that says something like, "It is best to know who your enemies are" seems appropriate here."

"Well, Dr. Borov, that's all well and good, but you pay me to provide security for both of these facilities.

Now you want me to look the other way on this documented breach?"

"Yes colonel, that's exactly what I want you to do. Let's leave Ms. Kelly alone for now. We'll just watch her watching us. As for the e-mail issue, now that's another thing entirely."

*   *   *

Meanwhile in Maryland, Kelly's supervisor Troy Sullivan and his boss Rick Black were having a discussion of their own about her latest find.

"So now our golden girl has found out that the Philology Annex has two sub-basement levels," Black stated reading from his laptop's screen, "accessible by a hidden elevator. How intriguing. My guess is that one of those levels is a meeting area and perhaps also where those teleconferences originate from. But as to the purpose of the second, Sully I think that we have another mystery on our hands."

"Maybe that's where their language training takes place," Sully offered.

"Blinking, "That's a damn good possibility, Sully."

"So what should we do about all of this?"

Holding his head in his hands as he leaned on his elbows over his desk blotter, Black said, "I think it is time that we take a look at Young's e-mail content, but just for the last six months. That should give us some idea of what's going on over there. And Sully, this is not a rush job. Have your team work as invisibly as possible. Leave no trace, no fingerprints, no footprints, absolutely nothing that someone can track or trace back to us."

"What about the search warrant?"

"Like I said Sully, no footprints."

"Gotcha."

*   *   *

"Okay guys, do you remember that rush job you did two days ago? The hacking of a university's e-mail server?" Seeing nodding heads all around. "Well now we have been tasked to retrieve a sample of Dr. Paul Young's e-mail content, but only from the last six months.

"But here's the kicker. Leave absolutely no trace. Absolutely zero. This isn't a rush job for quarters or school bragging rights anymore. It's all about stealth. Got that?"

Again, Sullivan received nods all around. Then a lone hand was raised.

"Sully, what about the content itself. Do you want it pristine for your eyes only, or, broken down and analyzed?"

"Pristine, Larry, I want it pristine and for my eyes only. Is that clear to everyone? No eyes on, period. Why? Because you guys are going in bare-assed and without a legal safety net."

Wide eyes looked at him, as they realized they were about to openly break the law.

No wonder Sully wants the take for his eyes only! They all had only one thought in mind—plausible deniability.

* * *

Two days later Sullivan had a thumb drive placed in his hand with six months of e-mail content from one Dr. Paul Young, Dean of Humanities. Staring down at the black plastic storage device, Sullivan wondered what sorts of secrets it contained. Thanking his team, he dismissed them, stuck the drive into the side of his laptop, and began to read. Rather quickly, the spook began to appreciate that only a handful of e-mail addresses pertained to the Philology Annex and one other location or facility, assiduously unnamed, but most likely Horizon Pass, New Mexico.

* * *

Another two days later and after one near all-nighter, Sullivan called his boss and asked for some scheduled time. "Yes sir, you'll want some quality time for this one."

When the appointed time arrived, Sullivan, uncharacteristically nervous, doubted himself. He couldn't bring himself to believe what just six month's worth of e-mail had just told him. Arriving at Black's office, he stopped, took a deep breath, knocked, and entered.

Just the sheer act of sitting down drove Sullivan crazy, because what he had to share wanted to make him stand up and pace about.

Black, a good judge of character and a close colleague of Sullivan's, immediately saw the four-o'clock shadow, the dark circles around haunted eyes, and an unusual twitchiness to his visitor.

"Okay," Black began, "spill it Sully. I can see that something's eating you up. By the way, you look like hell."

Ignoring his boss' pointed observation about his appearance, Sully began, "Well, sir, it's like this."

Whenever Sully addressed him as "sir," the former USAF officer knew that the subject under discussion was not good. Even worse, Sully could not even look his boss in the eye. He just stared at his hands and began to speak.

"Sir, we know, on the basis of our investigations, that the Philology Annex where Ms. Kelly is employed, and a place called Horizon Pass in New Mexico, are both funded by the same DOE black budget account.

"While the relationship between these two facilities remains foggy, it appears, based on Young's e-mails, they without any doubt work in concert. In fact, the Horizon Pass facility really appears to be calling all the shots. The man who is doing that is Peter Borov—a total ghost who doesn't exist anywhere in any database."

That fact elicited a surprised grunt from Black.

"As to what they do, together, is, well, pretty hard to swallow."

Sully paused and looked up into his boss' eyes for the first time. He then flatly stated.

"Sir, I believe they are in the time travel business."

To this Black frowned and shook his head. He even scratched his right ear.

"Whadda' mean Sully? They're travel agents?"

"No sir. Time, travel. As in H.G. Wells and the *Time Machine*. As in going back and forth in time."

"Really? How'd they do that?"

"Don't know sir. But apparently they have what they call a 'portable device.'"

"Okay, but where is this 'portable device' located?"

"I don't know sir. Perhaps it's stored at Horizon Pass, wherever the hell that is in New Mexico. Meanwhile, the Philology Annex seems to be a front for an extremely intense and cutting-edge form of language training. What kind and what for, I can only guess."

"So what's your guess, Sully?"

"Ancient languages."

"Jesus H. Christ," Black whispered.

*   *   *

It should be remembered that when Peter Borov first set foot on American soil, in March of 1942, he did so after over a two hundred day trek from the Soviet Union all the way to Switzerland. Soon after his arrival in the States, several interested parties wished to talk shop with him about their own ongoing project—CRYSTAL BALL. One of those interested parties was none other than Albert Einstein, the project's theoretical lead, based at the Institute for Advanced Studies at Princeton. That liaison occurred because a family friend had arranged for Borov's stay in Princeton. There, the young Borov and Einstein discussed quite a bit during the spring of that year.

The other interested party who wished to meet Borov was Vannevar Bush, an MIT graduate and government official of immense influence. As the head of the US Office of Scientific Research and Development (OSRD), Bush oversaw nearly all wartime military research and development. CRYSTAL BALL, one of Bush's pet projects, was an ambitious exercise of practical physics that sought to create high energy electro-magnetic fields around naval warships. These fields were so powerful they bent light, rendering a ship invisible, or so was the plan. It was believed at the time that Borov's own work might assist in this war-time effort.

But Bush could not be everywhere, so a fellow MIT engineer, Charles Gamble, became Borov's immediate supervisor and conduit to Bush, his influence, and access to OSRD's budget. So was Berov's temporal project interleafed under this organization's aegis, as was the Manhattan Project itself.

When Charles Gamble and Peter Borov first met, they were young, lean, and mean engineers. Gamble came by his credentials through his rigorous university training. Borov, on the other hand, was the product of a high-pressure university think-tank in St. Petersburg. Borov's approach reflected his quiet demeanor. He quite casually found solutions to impossible theoretical situations through the practical application of known technology. He made do. Needless to say, these two kindred spirits instantly hit it off, and in many respects, Borov's many later successes can be directly attributed to Gamble's unflagging support. In the vast morass and mire that was government bureaucracy, Gamble was Borov's front man, who in turn had Bush's ear.

Sadly, this happy team of two driven engineers ended in 1973, when Charlie Gamble died due to his congenitally weakened heart. Crushed, and now without his principal advocate, Borov struck out on his own. As luck would have it, the Russian quickly found a sympathetic ear within the Oak Ridge National Laboratory. The head of that facility, a man named Winston Smith, also an MIT graduate, knew Gamble personally and trusted him implicitly. So when Peter Borov made his introductory pitch for support, Smith just smiled and said, "Dr. Borov, if Charlie Gamble hitched his career to your wagon, then that is good enough for me." Then extending his hand, he continued. "By the way, my name's Winston, and I don't own any stock in those damn cigarettes neither. Welcome aboard." Henceforth after that conversation, Borov's black project funding was provided under the umbrella of the innocuous sounding Department of Materials Science.

As for Winston Smith, about twenty-five years Borov's junior, he was a passionate materials scientist, who, it is said, never encountered a metallic-ceramic alloy that he didn't like. This area of expertise he made his personal sandbox and as a result NASA came to him for suggestions on the composition of their rocket booster nozzles and later for the ablative tiles for NASA's space shuttles. An Italian F1 racing team once even approached him about light weight, low friction, ceramic engine parts. A men's clothing company came to him inquiring about high strength shirt buttons that wouldn't break or crack while at the cleaners. Even a beer distributor frankly asked him about ceramic molds for aluminum cans. The list went on and on.

Smith and Borov, unorthodox thinkers, peas from the same pod, faithful followers of country music, hit it off. Far more important, the former totally understood the criticality of what the latter had been tasked to do— to investigate and preserve our temporal reality. The pair had discussed the ramifications all too often, and had cringed at the many "what ifs." So when years later

Dr. Winston Smith of Tennessee got a phone call from a certain Colonel Richard Black, USAF retired, of Maryland, he knew precisely how to handle the inquiry.

"Colonel Black, respectfully sir, I am very sorry, but I cannot help you. Be advised, however, that there are some subjects that even you and your organization should: a) not know about, and b), if you do learn about them, then you should immediately forget everything and anything that you ever learned about them. Am I clear, sir?"

Strangely, that direct and concise reply from Dr. Smith, Black totally understood, and for a whole host of reasons, which explained what he did next.

*   *   *

"Sully, you know all that research that your team did on the Philology Annex and Horizon Pass?

Pause. Sigh.

"Yeah, that stuff. Well, I want you to purge it all."

Pause.

"I know that you can't 'purge' your team's memories, but I absolutely want every byte of data pertaining to that investigation erased.

"Yes, shred and burn the entire paper trail as well."

Pause.

"For the moment, yes, let's just keep her there. And, by the way, I want you to purge from her Z-Drive any and all information pertaining to this subject.

"Yep, that goes for all the paperwork as well."

Pause.

"Sully, let's just say that some things are best left alone. You read me?"

Pause.

"Yeah, it's just that sensitive. All I can say is that your speculations the other day were right on the money."

Pause.

"Sully, let me put it to you this way. You're standing in front of an airplane's turning prop. The motor's tachometer says that it's turning at three thousand RPM. Now, do you need to put your hand in its path to confirm the fact that the prop is turning?"

Pause.

"Yeah, let's let this dog lie."

CHAPTER 21
Some Interesting News

"I just got some interesting news Joseph." said Milson into his coffee cup as he washed down his last piece of apple pie at the university faculty club.

"Oh, what's that John?"

"Our friends at Wright-Patterson seemed to be really jazzed over what you and Gregorieva delivered to them. So excited in fact, that they tasked a satellite to do some snooping around and it came up with an unexpected result."

"Okay, and what's that 'unexpected result?'" Richards replied with a hopeful smile.

"Well, they have located what they believe is a rather large fragment some twenty-odd miles north of the crater that you and Vesna visited. And, they want us to retrieve it for analysis. Are you up to another adventure in paradise?"

Thinking a moment before he spoke, the younger Egyptologist finally said.

"Can Gregorieva come to?"

"Absolutely, I don't see any reason why not. I will be more than happy to request her presence from her minders in Moscow. By the way, Dr. Peters thinks this is more than just a fragment of a meteor, because he detected in the satellite imagery what he believes is evidence of a crash landing. Further, he said something about skid marks or a shallow trench."

*   *   *

Three weeks later the entire gang was at it again. Colonel Cartwright, predictably, was bitching a blue streak that he was sick and tired of being everybody's wet nurse. Then he railed on that this seemed too much like *déjà vu*. For myself, I was more than happy for any excuse to get out of Moscow.

Lieutenant Hassig was really raring to go. He was excited about getting another opportunity to fly his toy drone again, maybe get lucky, and shoot down another Sudanese Hind. He's such a dear.

On this go-round, Joey and I rode in on a MH-47F Chinook helicopter that the American Delta Force at Dashur was kind enough to loan us. With its two hot-shot pilots and gunners manning the 7.62 mini-guns we felt secure. The hold of this beast easily carried "Tuna" Cartwright's "school" of security personnel, along with the two of us. Further, I was told that the helicopter was a heavy, as in lift capacity, so that we could retrieve whatever Dr. Peters was so excited about. As it was, it still took us almost three hours of flight time to reach the precise GPS coordinates that Dr. Peters had provided us.

Flying practically due west from Abu Simbel Airport, we cruised across the now familiar blurred image of the southern Western Desert, but as we neared the target coordinates, a faint straight line could be seen. Clearly, it represented a gouge in the desert that was partially buried by centuries of drifting sand. This feature ran from the northwest to southeast and ended at our goal—a reddish-colored, rock outcropping.

Landing nearby, we quickly discovered that the outcropping was nothing of the sort, but rather was a partially buried stone object about the size of a VW bug, roughly oblong in shape. Frankly, it reminded me most of a large red granite sarcophagus of an Apis bull.

Armed with military trenching shovels, several large blue plastic containers, a large box of clear heavy-duty baggies, and black Sharpies to record what was what, Joey and I got to work. We cleared away the sand and rock from around the object, while Tuna's men fanned out to form a defensive parameter. Even Lieutenant Hassig had his drone up and flying overlook.

I never worked with a trenching shovel before, so Joey demonstrated the "doggie" method, as he so aptly put it. Now with the two of us digging and sweating away, the general outline of the stone object rather quickly came to light. It was a highly symmetrical, elongated, egg-shaped object with a remarkably smooth and extremely fine surface. Its color was that of a ruddy sandstone or red granite. Nowhere did I see any holes or ports, and no clear indications of a doorway or hatch.

Now standing before it, presumably nose on, it was beautifully crafted—its form classic, organic simplicity.

Suddenly very thirsty, we stopped and drank, per the numbers, our first liter of water under "mother hen" Cartwright's ever watchful eye. Then, Joey did something quite remarkable. He took a second liter of water and began wetting down the entire top half of the object's nose. And as he did so, a very fine line began to appear, which curved around, and eventually delineated a large oval outline.

I exclaimed, "How did you know to do that?"

With a smile, Joey said with a shrug. "It wasn't entirely my own idea. It was a trick I learned. Now we can tell Dr. Peters that we really got what we came for. So let's finish clearing away all this sand from the base, so that we can get the chopper's cargo netting around it."

About ten minutes into this seemingly mindless, necessary chore, I found my first bone. Seconds later, I let out a shriek as I found more, *many* more. As I was clearing the side that faced to the northeast, I was stunned to realize that I had stumbled upon what looked like hundreds of small animal bones. It was a veritable cemetery!

Joey, always thinking, had me collect the bones and put them into one of the large blue plastic tub containers. But before I was finished, I ran across some other bones, different ones, and what seemed to be a big and oddly-shaped skull. Not thinking much of it, I just continued to fill up both tubs to the brim with all the remains. Marking on the tub where its contents were found, we sealed it with some gray, you guessed it, duct tape, and finished the clearance.

Now with the cargo net secured around "the egg" as we came to call it, the helicopter crew winched it up the ramp and secured it within the cargo hold. From landing to takeoff, it had only taken some two and a half hours to retrieve Dr. Peters' "egg."

*　　*　　*

Some eight months after the second delivery to Wright-Patterson, a special government courier delivered Dr. Peters' preliminary report to Milson. This courier carefully inspected the Egyptologist's driver's license, faculty identification card, and credit card before he handed over the precious brown mailing envelope. Somewhat amused by all the formality, Milson's inner mirth quickly dissipated as soon as he read the title of its contents.

ALPHA CLASSIFIED MATERIALS

Kamil Crater and Secondary Impact Site.
Preliminary Report No.1.

Technical Analysis of the Artificial Feature,
Escape Capsule/Command Module,
& Osteological Analysis of the Impact Site's Remains

Copy Nr. 2 of 12.
Edited by Roy A. Peters, Ph.D.
Chief Investigator

ALPHA CLASSIFIED MATERIALS

PRELIMINARY TECHNICAL ANALYSIS
OF THE ARTIFICIAL FEATURE

Gebel Kamil. Lat. 22° 01 min. 06 sec. N
Long. 26° 05 min. 16 sec. E

Point 1. The material analysis of the imbedded artificial feature within the limestone matrix found within the East Uweinat Desert, Egypt, reveals a complex alloy made up of Fe, Si, Cu, Mg, Mn, Cr, Ti, Al, and Zn, with only trace amounts of C present. Remarkably, the principal alloy constituent was Fe (52.4%), while other metals made up the remainder. Unusual is the total absence of Ni in this alloy, which is a common constituent of iron meteoroids. In terrestrial terms, this alloy represents an extremely high-grade and durable material suitable, depending upon its temper and application, for anything, from a load-bearing structural member to an external surface.

Point 2. The purpose and function of the imbedded artificial feature is unknown. Its weight is 7.2 kg (15.84 lbs). Its preserved dimensions are 1.12 m (3.674 feet) long x 37 mm (1.456 inches) high x 17 mm (0.669 inches) thick. Full liberation of this alloy fragment from its limestone matrix failed to reveal any diagnostic features.

Interpretation. The use of high Fe content in terrestrial aviation alloys is unknown. While unusually strong, current propulsion technologies cannot provide sufficient thrust for an airframe constructed of such an alloy to achieve flight. Consequently, its presence suggests the use of a propulsion system that is not chemically based, but rather may be gravitational in its design and function.

Conclusion. The artificial feature is composed of a unique alloy. Its function is unknown due to its fragmentary nature. The closest terrestrial use for such a durable alloy would be in naval battleship construction and armor.

PRELIMINARY TECHNICAL ANALYSIS
OF THE ESCAPE CAPSULE/COMMAND MODULE

Point 1. The material analysis of the Escape Capsule/Command Module reveals that it shares affinities to the complex alloy of the artificial feature described above. However, in this instance, the extremely tough and durable outer skin or shell of the craft was made up of Fe, Si, Cr, Ti, and Zn, only. The principal alloy constituents were Fe and Ti, both at 44%, while the other metals made up the remainder. Again, the total absence of Ni in this alloy is to be noted. In terrestrial terms, this alloy represents an extremely high-grade and durable material suitable, depending upon its temper and application, for anything from a load-bearing structural member to an external surface.

Point 2. The weight of this module is 1548.6 kg (3,414 lbs), which given its gross dimensions of 2.499 m (8.2 ft) long x 1.249 m (4.1 ft) high x 1.493 m (4.9 ft) thick as measured from their maximum value, does not adequately describe its symmetrical ovoid shape. With its blunt nose and tapered tail, the hull is flattened or widened at its ventral side and tapers inwards towards its dorsal side (see attached views A-F). Given its widened or flattened ventral side, one wonders if that form was to either improve the craft's glide ratio or to provide it a stable base when at rest. Aerodynamic studies are underway to discover the craft's glide ratio, if any.

Conclusion. The purpose and function of this module has been surmised as either an escape capsule/command module, or perhaps both. Access into the craft's interior has yet to be achieved. Given that it successfully separated from the rest of its hull, which impacted some twenty-five miles to the south, argues strongly that this interpretation is a reasonable one.

PRELIMINARY OSTEOLOGICAL ANALYSIS
FROM THE IMPACT SITE

Lat. 22° 25 min. 16.85 sec. N.
Long. 26° 9 min. 14.43 sec. E.

Point 1. The osteological remains recovered from the NE side of the Impact Site are of two separate species.

Point 2. Eleven complete skeletons of *Canis aureus lupaster*, or golden jackal, were represented in the NE deposit of the Impact Site. Each individual was made up of 319 bones. All eleven individuals, seven females and four males, displayed mild malnutrition. Of the males, two were juveniles. None displayed any osteological trauma.

Point 3. A full (?) skeleton of an unknown species was

also represented in the NE deposit of the Impact Site.

a) ASSIGNMENT: Tentatively, the subject has been assigned to the Superfamily of *Hominoidae*, primarily based up its upright, bipedalism. The individual appears to have been made up of 214 bones, six more than an average *Homo sapien.*

b) GENDER: Undetermined.

c) CRANIAL DESCRIPTION: dolichocephalic, with protrusive features accentuated by the nasal structures and the prominence of overlapping beak-like incisors. A row of long, feather-like quills once protruded from the skull's sagittal crest, but are now partially evident. The slightly enlarged optical orbits suggest binocular vision with an extended peripheral range beyond 120 degrees. Cranial capacity was 2200 cc, with considerable expansion displayed in the frontal, parietal, and occipital regions.

d) DENTITION: Subject appears mature with sixteen fully erupted molars and four pre-molars. The frontal mandible and maxilla display two, overlapping beaks or shearing incisors.

d) STRUCTURE: Height of the individual was ca. 147-150 cm. General skeletal structure is endomorphic and extremely gracial in presentation. This individual possessed five fingers in addition to an opposable thumb, but only four toes, each with three joints. The center two toes were elongated. Long bone cross-sections are pneumatized, with criss-crossing internal struts or trusses for structural strength. Extensive air pockets within the bone matrix are strongly reminiscent of terrestrial avian species and may suggest a low gravity origin for the individual. The skeletal remains suffered considerable osteological trauma in the form of long bone shattering, no doubt due to animal gnawing.

Point 4. DNA analysis of the *Hominoidae*'s bone marrow proved inconclusive, as all of its long bones had been shattered and their contents either eaten or long-exposed to the elements.

Interpretation. The forensic opinion is that the subject, upon exiting its craft, was attacked, killed, and eaten by the above described golden jackals.

Conclusion. The forensic opinion is that the "kill site" of the subject occurred either at or near the NE deposit of the Impact Site. There, the jackals fed in the relative shade of the Escape Capsule/Command Module. Apparently, soon after their feed, the jackals died due to the adverse chemistry of the subject.

Upon finishing his reading of the preliminary report from Peters, Milson whispered to himself.

"My God, it's positive evidence of another ET landing! But this one appears to have been a total snafu from the very get-go. First, the total loss of the mother craft itself. Then the successful separation and crash landing by its pilot, who apparently survives, exits his life boat, but is then greeted by a hungry pack of jackals." *My dear God in heaven! What a way to go!*

CHAPTER 22
Pitch for a Drop

The start of a new semester typically was one of frenetic activity campus-wide. For Associate Professor Joseph Richards, however, his mind remained very much elsewhere. He just couldn't get out of his head the Kamil Crater's impact site, where truly brutal physical forces transformed the immediate area into a molten sea of yellow and green vitrified glass, inches deep. Perhaps it was just morbid curiosity, but the Egyptologist yearned to know that classic question— "What was it like?"

Fanciful and humorous thoughts danced in his head, sounding more like aerial traffic reports than anything else. "Interstate 294 is currently a real snarl due to a meteor impact near the Highway 55 interchange. Suggest rerouting via either Wolf or Joliet Roads."

Snapping back to the here and now, Richards decided to run the idea by his good friend, John Milson. He knew the man could inject some sound horse sense on the subject.

Lifting his phone, he dialed John's extension from memory, waited a few heartbeats, and was rewarded to hear Milson's phone begin to ring down the hallway.

"John Milson. How may I help you?"

"John, it's me. Do you have a few moments? I

would like to run a couple ideas by you."

"Well, Joseph, allow me a couple of minutes to clear my desk. I have this feeling that your 'couple of ideas' may take some time. How about fifteen?"

"Done. See you then. Bye."

Hanging up the phone, Richards then grabbed a clean sheet of paper and began to furiously scribble down his thoughts, organizing them as best he could, because he really didn't want to waste his colleague's time. Again, Richards chided himself. *Well, goofus, why didn't you think first, write second, and then call John?*

Richards then grabbed a second clean sheet, and began copying down in a clearer and more organized fashion what he wrote on the first. Almost finished with this second draft, he heard a knock on his doorpost. Looking up, there was Milson with a bemused look on his face.

"May I disturb you, Joseph?"

Now glancing at his watch, Richards saw that a full thirty minutes had passed.

"Christ! I'm so sorry John. I was just organizing my thoughts before I visited you. Grab a chair."

So the professor emeritus of Egyptology closed the office door, taking the only wooden chair that was available in his young colleague's office.

Sitting down and immediately crossing his legs, Milson began.

"So. Here I am. Speak."

And "speak" Richards did, explaining his thoughts in such a way as to persuade Milson to seriously consider the potential benefits of a purely sight-seeing deployment back into the late Eighteenth Dynasty. Pausing for breath, Milson just politely raised his right hand to pause his young friend.

"Joseph, all that memory enhancement therapy that Doc Allen has put you through must have triggered a psychic link of some kind, for ever since you and Gregorieva returned from that last escapade into the Western Desert, I have been thinking about precisely the same thing.

"You know Joseph, come to think of it, you and Gregorieva have never been deployed for purely scientific reasons. Instead, and you in particular, have been sent back consistently into the *somewhen* on missions of considerable violence and mayhem. Missions that you should not have survived, much less returned from.

"Consequently, I fully support such a scientific enterprise. I think it would be most instructive to witness not only the event itself, but also its immediate aftermath upon the Egyptian culture. After all, just look at what the entire Earth has been put through back on that September 29th—a double asteroid collision! We are still reeling from that near-miss, near-collision with our planet.

"Now, the only question that I have is one of duration. Are you talking about a few days or a few weeks? Regardless of what is finally approved, we both know that the insights gained will be extraordinary, perhaps even several historical and cultural details may be better explained.

"But as with all such adventures into the *somewhen*, this one too must be first proposed and discussed with all of our colleagues. After all, that is the way of the *RUTI*."

*   *   *

Two weeks later, a heavily encrypted teleconference took place, again courtesy of a handy US Air Force satellite hookup, and their ever-improving translation software. As before, the Air Force secretly allowed a select few from outside the teleconference to listen in. But this time, the ploy did not work, as their feeds were scrambled, making their viewing and listening useless. Surprised, angry, and finally questioning just what the USAF was up to, all they could do was shrug their shoulders. After all, they were just the hook up. How could the USAF predict that the users of their hardware and software had decided to further encrypt their signal's transmission?

The American panel in Chicago sat before their video camera in the first sub-basement of the Philology Annex. Professor Emeritus John Milson, Egyptologist, settled in on the camera's left. Dr. Paul Young, economist, and university dean, reigned supreme center stage. While on the right, sat Associate Professor Joseph Richards, Egyptologist, and currently the most experienced temporal field operative. All were seated behind a conference table. Richards, being that this was his first teleconference, kept nervously arranging and rearranging his notepad and pencil in a lame attempt at organizing his immediate universe.

Opposite the American panel the three heavy weights of the Russian Academy of Sciences lounged comfortably. Without question the youngest, Dr. Stefan Rosovec, was oriented on the camera's left. Academician Vasily Ostrogorsky had placed himself to the camera's right. Lastly Karlov Drazinzka, the Director of the ultra secret Special Projects Division, was seated directly dead center. Like their American colleagues, the three Russians also sat behind a conference table. When the appointed time arrived, the two monitors half a world apart suddenly sprang to life.

Seeing that they were live, Dr. Young, as had become customary, began the meeting with a broad smile and in his clipped, rehearsed British delivery said, "Welcome gentlemen. It's certainly good to see you again. I am Dr. Paul Young, Dean of Humanities. To my right is Dr. John Milson, Professor Emeritus of Egyptology at our Near Eastern Institute. And to my left is Dr. Joseph Richards, Egyptologist, also at the NEI, and of course, temporal field agent."

The American panel's introduction earned an eager look of genuine interest from the Russians, as this was

Richards' first appearance. To them, this suggested some sort of shake up in the American panel, or, perhaps even some sort of promotion for Richards.

So, thought Drazinzka, *they have decided to parade before us their young lion. How intriguing.*

Now gathering himself forward to his microphone, the Special Projects Director continued with the near-formulaic introduction process.

"Fellow Academicians, and of course Dr. Richards," he said with a nodding head of recognition to each.

While Richards did not know it, the Russian had properly singled him out with his opening words, as the term "academician," as understood by the Russians, was reserved only and solely for the most accomplished and seasoned of scholars. Clearly, in their world view, this youngster was considered neither.

"Indeed, it is very good to see you again as well." Continued Drazinzka. "As you already know, Academician Vasily Ostrogorsky, Director of the Institute for Theoretical Biology, is seated to my right. To my left, Dr. Stefan Rosovec, Director of the Advanced and Theoretical Technological Research Institute. I, of course, am Karlov Drazinzka, the director of a minor, subordinate division of the Russian Academy of Sciences.

"How may we be of service?"

Young and Milson, both surprised by the Russian's surprisingly deferential tone, glanced meaningfully to one another. Richards, oblivious, just stared squarely at the three Russians and tried to glean any information that he could.

"Thank you Dr. Drazinzka," Milson smoothly answered. "Our panel wishes to champion a purely scientific deployment back to the Eighteenth Dynasty, much like our first four calibration deployments that the late Major General Alexander Piankoff so ably conducted. Of course, as is stipulated in the *RUTI*, we all must first agree before such an undertaking should take place."

So the horse trading, posturing, hemming and hawing, began. But in the end, and after some fifty-three minutes of discussion, the deployment was given a green light. Throughout it all, Richards was amazed at all the arcane questions that were asked. Meanwhile his opposites in Moscow had watched Richards and his facial reactions very carefully.

After the teleconference's feed had been killed at their end, as well as the audio feed, only then did Drazinzka finally state what his colleagues had no doubt already surmised.

"That Richards fellow I find to be surprisingly young. Fit yes, that I would expect. But he's so damn young."

Ostrogorsky then interjected.

"And, my dear Karlov, didn't you notice that Milson spoke once again for the entire panel. Regarding Richards, I agree with you completely. And I am willing to bet that young pup probably was even ordered to keep his mouth shut."

Throughout all of this off-the-cuff, snap analysis, Rosovec had remained mum. Drazinzka, noting this, commented.

"Stefan, you have been strangely silent. Have you nothing to share?"

Sigh. *Should I or shouldn't I? Be a man Stefan!*

"Frankly, gentlemen, as formidable as both Young and Milson are, I believe Richards has the potential to eclipse them both. He is, after all, the one who saved our man Piankoff no less than three times. This is an undeniable fact. Recently, did he not bring back our new temporal agent from a sure suicide mission as well? And here he is, sitting before us. Silent and taking notes about *us*, instead of trading meaningless debating points."

*   *   *

So was it agreed upon that a dual deployment of Gregorieva and Richards would occur in the ninth regnal year of Tutankhamen's reign, the fourth month of the harvest season, on the twenty-eighth day—a full day prior to the reported meteoroid impact. It was also agreed that this scientific deployment was to be brief, no longer than two days in duration.

By the ninth year of his reign, the young boy king Tutankh*aten* had cannily changed his name to a more politically and religiously savvy one—Tutankh*amen*. Furthermore, he and the entire royal court of the eclipsed city of Akhetaten had moved back, lock, stock, and barrel, to the rejuvenated city of Thebes. Under the steady hand of Prince Horemheb and the pious fervor of the high priests of Amen Re, the city and its temples had arisen, phoenix-like, from their squalor, to become a fresh and revitalized urban center once again.

But politics, being what they are, had not been as rewarding for Prince Horemheb as he had expected. For an older and more politically astute rival by the name of Ay had successfully jostled the ambitious young prince into the background. Armed as he was with many high titles, such as "overseer of the horses of His Majesty," "fan bearer on the Right Side of the King," "Acting Scribe of the King," "beloved by the King," and most telling, "God's Father." Ay was a military man, who had garnered considerable clout within the royal court and held the ear of the young Tutankhamen as well. So the young Memphite prince did what all princes in-waiting must do. He bided his time.

As for the high priesthood of Amen Re, a position appointed by the crown, old Meryptah had adopted Joseph Richards as his son. His successor, Nebneteru, who worked so hard early on in the restoration of Theban temples and labored in concert with Prince Horemheb with the rebirth of Thebes, knew of Meryptah and his adopted son by name. But this was not the case with Nebneteru's successor Perennefer, who neither knew of Meryptah's many sacrifices under the heretic king Akhenaten, nor of his heroic acts in preserving the wealth of the Great Hidden One beneath his own temple.

By the time of Perennefer's ascension to the lofty station of First Prophet of Amen Re, Horemheb's career had moved on from administration to one of a more military nature. He openly formed around himself a loyal cadre of military officers. Now more concerned with potential Asiatic threats along Egypt's northeastern frontier, the once pressing importance of Theban civic affairs had been pushed far into the background.

So if Gregorieva and Richards were to gain access to the Karnak Temple for their astronomical observations, Horemheb's personal influence could not be brought to bear. Neither could the influence of his adopted father's name, as the current high priest was now twice removed from Meryptah's tenure. Instead, it would be essential that the pair make direct contact with this Perennefer in order to gain his trust and cooperation.

*   *   *

The two scientific panels specifically directed that every effort should be made to collect as much quantitative data as possible on the impact event. While the testimony of two enhanced eye witnesses was recognized as substantial, even more was required. Consequently, something had to be devised that could provide the required data. Good, old fashioned ingenuity needed to be tapped.

Needless to say, this peculiar requirement left the American panel scratching its collective head. So Dean Young convened a gathering of the Philology Annex's inner membership, some twenty-three scholars, who represented a wide range of disciplines. Their meeting was set at five in the evening. Per the usual, the Annex's secretary quietly took note of all the comings and goings. Their numbers surprised her.

"Thank you ladies and gentlemen for coming." began Dean Young.

"We have recently received authorization for another deployment. Its agenda is entirely scientific in nature. Our temporal agents are to witness the impact of a meteoroid in the southwestern desert of Egypt. While their eye witness subjective accounts will be very important, we wish to take this unprecedented opportunity to gather some quantitative and qualitative data as well. Since the *RUTI* does not allow for the intrusive introduction of technologies, our challenge is to come up with ways and means to record the impact event with locally available materials. So my dear friends, put on your thinking caps. We need your suggestions."

Not used to being active participants, there was initially a good amount of reticence in the sub-basement's conference room. One individual, however, a geologist named Michael Benjamin was not so easily intimidated.

"Dean Young, I have an idea. If past near-meteoroid misses and impacts can be used as a rule-of-thumb, then we need a simple means to measure seismic energy and displacement. I believe if we focus on these two parameters, then we should be able to reproduce them to some degree, in our laboratories."

At the end of the meeting, several primitive experiments were outlined that showed real promise. They could be readily set up in antiquity, observed, and then recreated in the present.

CHAPTER 23

The Hacker

The lot of a computer specialist is often one of cramped temporary spaces. In this case, the poor soul had been relegated to a seminar room located on the Niroo Research Institute campus, one of Iran's most innovative energy research centers. Located at the western end of Shahid Dadman Boulevard in Tehran's northwestern quadrant, the god-awful sulfur dioxide smog on that day obscured anyone on campus from seeing the city's skyline—much less its very distinctive Milad Tower.

While NRI is not exactly a household name, it is perhaps best known for the highly publicized disruption of its website by an Israeli hacker. This was why the specialist had been assigned to NRI, to plug the dam and retaliate in kind.

Hashem Shirazi was a roving member of an IT think-tank within Iran's Ministry of Intelligence and National Security, or SAVAMA, who had a long record of fixing porous firewalls. For him the NRI scandal represented only one embarrassment of many. But Shirazi thoroughly enjoyed serving up just-desserts to the opposition's hackers—the more devious the prank the better—be they Americans, Israelis, Russians, North Koreans, or Chinese. As a consequence, his online persona was called "the Velvet Hammer."

A creative and facile mind, the Iranian's superiors had many projects for him, lined up like train cars, all requiring his unique talents and expertise. But that didn't mean Shirazi had several "pet projects" on the backburner, waiting for that lull that never seemed to arrive in his work schedule.

One such "backburner project" that fascinated Shirazi had been the satellite encryption technology of the American Air Force. He had followed its development over the past six years, breaking in as soon as it was deployed—only to have the Americans shut him down just as quickly.

This sensitized the Iranian to his online footprint, his IP-origin, and even his favorite coding dodges. Shirazi, in essence, self-analyzed his online presence, and randomized his approaches to a problem. In the process, he discarded his persona as infantile. Online invisibility became paramount in order to avoid detection. This fundamental shift in thinking, this reinvention, occurred while Shirazi was only nineteen.

Two years later and after many heart-breaking failures, he had broken into a tantalizing twenty-three seconds of split-screen video from a USAF satellite. Oddly encrypted twice, Shirazi watched and listened in on a curious conversation in both English and Russian.

> "Then it is agreed," said an overweight and aging man sitting center in the right split of the screen, "regnal year nine, for a scientific deployment, duration of no more than two days."

"It is agreed," said a gray-haired man in the left screen split who sat in the center chair. "When might we expect your temporal agent for pre-deployment preparations?"

"How long does she require?" asked a younger-looking man with black hair in the right screen split.

"What is customary—eight weeks' time," Answered the gray-haired man in the left screen split.

With that, all three men in the right screen split nodded as one and their transmission ended. However, those in the left screen split had not terminated theirs. Instead, the three men turned to one another in animated conversation.

"Just who was the new one again on the left? The one with the wavy black hair?"

Then the transmission abruptly ended.

Shirazi had seen enough. While his English was fair, he needed someone to translate the Russian for him. But why were the two Great Satans' conversing so? That needed clarification. So Shirazi took his questions directly to someone who he knew would help him.

*   *   *

Dressed in black slacks, coat, and with a white, open-collared shirt, Aref Fardoust was the eldest son of Hussein Fardoust, the head of the SAVAMA, *Sazman-e*

Ettelaat Va Amniat Meli Iran, or the Organization of Intelligence and National Security of Iran. Aref, still in his twenties and with the plump face and heavy eye folds of his father, truly wanted to look the part of an intelligence officer in his neatly trimmed black beard. Even as a young agent, Aref showed promise, amazing instincts, and the needed ruthlessness, as he followed in his father's footsteps.

While Hussein had led the SAVAMA, his son Aref implemented many of his father's intelligence gathering directives, creatively, and with considerable success. In the process, Aref created his own following, based upon his sheer reputation for acquiring sensitive data. When it came to divining what the Great Northern Satan of Russia or the Great Western Satan of the US were up to, Aref would stop at nothing, and seemed even to revel in the oftentimes gory details. So, when a contemporary named Hashem Shirazi approached with his brief transcription from the USAF satellite's transmission, Aref eagerly met with him.

"So Shirazi, what do you have for me?" Aref queried his nervous visitor.

"I have a fragment of a United States Air Force video transmission from one of their satellites," Shirazi said, as he passed over a transcription of the conversation.

Aref grunted and then began to read. Finished, "This is all that you have?"

"Yes, minister."

"Shirazi, I am not a minister. In fact, we could be brothers of the same age. Call me Aref. Now, tell me about how you acquired this text?"

And the computer specialist did, even explaining the various layers of encryption.

"I see, Shirazi, but who are these people? Presumably, three Russians and three Americans?"

"Unknown Aref. But what is very interesting is that while the teleconferencing and simultaneously translating software were clearly written by the US Air Force, the overlaying security software was not. It is almost as if the US Air Force allowed these two panels to use their satellites, their teleconferencing software, and their translation software, but then was prevented from listening in on their conversations."

"And you figured out all of this from the coding?"

"Yes."

Aref frowned and added, "What is also odd, is that the US Air Force does not easily share its resources, its satellite time, or translation software. That makes this conversation one of considerable importance."

"Yes, Aref. My thoughts exactly."

"And what about the content of the conversation itself? What do you make of that?"

"That is difficult to say. It is clearly the tail-end of a deliberation of some sort, where a decision was agreed upon."

W.J. CHERF

Aref tapped at the transcription before him. "What is the meaning behind the phrase, 'your temporal agent for pre-deployment preparations'?"

"I have no idea, Aref. But both the English and Russian translations agree on that verbiage."

"Think Shirazi. What is a 'temporal agent'?" Aref continued to tap.

A thin sheen of sweat broke out on the computer specialist's brow. "On that Aref, I can only speculate."

"Then speculate."

"A time agent, as in a time traveler. They are discussing the deployment of time travelers, and one is a woman."

"By Allah's gray beard!" Aref murmured and then made a snap decision.

"Shirazi, I am retasking you to investigate this US satellite and its transmissions. I am also authorizing that one of our satellite disks is dedicated to listen in on this geosynchronous US satellite. What all of this means is no more house calls for you to fix someone's firewall. I want you on this 24/7. Is that clear?"

"Yes, sir." A dazed Shirazi said.

* * *

For the next four months Shirazi sat glued to his chair in his new cubical within the Ministry of Intelligence and National Security. With his laptop primed to record any and all transmissions from the USAF satellite, he

200

waited. In the meantime, he further refined his anti-encryption tools, and eagerly waited to use them. While he did manage to snag several transmissions from the satellite, their content was navigational gibberish—nothing like the previous teleconference.

After six-and-a-half-months of waiting and listening, Shirazi was again retasked back to his "house calls," the mysterious teleconference all but forgotten. But in the fullness of time, Shirazi's find would indeed be remembered, because he had left his monitoring protocol active.

CHAPTER 24
Regnal Year Nine

Temporal deployments require extensive preparation. Gregorieva and Richards began theirs' by submitting to the extensive physical and psychological examinations at Horizon Pass. Doc Allen, who administered these panels, intimately knew both of the temporal field agents quite literally inside and out. Both were deemed "fit as fiddles." However, the subject of Richards' post-drop syndrome was not mentioned. As Doc Allen remarked, "I cannot fix what I cannot see." Secretly, however, the red-haired physician from Oklahoma remained vigilant and cautiously optimistic. But if Richards again returned in bad shape, he would not hesitate to pull the proverbial plug on him.

Next on the list came the task of acquiring an all-over tan. This was dovetailed with a rigorous training schedule that included long jogs in the New Mexican desert that surrounded the secret facility. During these sojourns, only ancient Egyptian was spoken, and after the usual eight weeks, the deployment team was ready.

While Gregorieva and Richards were tuning up, other preparations were underway. Permits were sought through their contact at the Egyptian Supreme Council of Antiquities in order to gain access during the early morning hours to the Karnak Temple. Horizon Pass' very own and quite special Gulf Stream V needed inspection, pilots secured, and landing paperwork filed for the trans-Atlantic flight from Holloman AFB in Alamogordo, New Mexico, with a refueling stop in Gander, Newfoundland, and then on to the final destination of Luxor, Egypt. Finally, Colonel Cartwright and his security team arrived two days early in order to secure the drop zone within the temple and to make a special delivery. Only when all of these details, and a myriad more, were checked off the list, did Gregorieva and Richards board the eastbound Gulf Stream.

Upon landing in Luxor, a very old and familiar Chevy truck waited for them. Its driver, Colonel Cartwright, dressed in impeccable desert cammies, greeted them with his usual witty banter, as he had for all of their drops. Cartwright would not have it any other way. Besides, against all US Army regulations, the ragin' Cajun remained extremely superstitious.

"Okay you gadfly, cream-puff tourists! Grab your gear and load up. My wife's putting dinner on the table and I am no ways, no how, goin' to be late for that! And if I am, then there will be all hell to pay!"

Silently following the colonel's orders to the letter, Gregorieva and Richards piled into the truck's cab. The slim Russian taking the middle, on the hump, as had become her custom.

After a twenty-minute drive along paved and unimproved roads alike, the truck pulled to an all wheel-locked halt that caused a minor dust storm.

Waiting for it to pass, they exited the vehicle, secured their gear, and walked up to the friendly face of an Antiquities Service guard, who manned the rear gate access to the grounds of the Karnak Temple.

Sharing pleasantries with the guard in the local Egyptian dialect, the cyclone fenced gate swung open with a screech, and the three-some set foot on sacred ground. The local time was nine-thirty in the evening. As for the guard, he settled down once again in his shack and went back to sleep. For Gregorieva and Richards, it was close to show time.

*   *   *

It never failed to amaze Richards as the drop ring levitated between the four portable pylons. As the charge built in the four pylons with their powerful electromagnets, the air seemed to come alive. And in a sense, it had, in the form of static electricity. Mounted atop each pylon sat a horn-like device that pointed inwards towards the elevated ring. These were the ion-emitters, which somehow, some way, smoothed out the temporal ride going and returning.

Now dressed in their chosen attire and applied makeup, a white kilt for Richards and a white, one-shouldered dress and black braided wig for Gregorieva, all was as it should be. To the side of the four pylons, Cartwright's troopers had erected a neutral, non-conducting wooden scaffolding with a perch from which the pair could step off and drop through the temporal field contained within the levitating ring.

"How's the field strength, Corporal Gains?" Cartwright asked.

"Nominal, sir," came the quick reply.

"Confirm the calibration."

"18, January, 1323 BC, zero hundred hours, sir."

A grunt. Now looking at the pair of dressed and fully made-up agents. The colonel stated with quiet concern.

"Now that's a new date. It's a bit out of your sweet spot. Are you two sure that you're ready?"

Two silent nods were his answer.

"Okay people," Cartwright bellowed, "we're a go on this deployment. Corporal Johnson, give us a peek on the other side."

Stepping forward a tall soldier with a small hand-held screen attached to a long non-metallic fiber optic cable and lens carefully inserted the latter into the smooth grayish temporal field that had formed within the levitating ring. Twisting the cable between his thumb and forefinger Corporal Black surveyed "the other side."

"All clear Colonel, but its mighty cramped over there. There's not much room to land on, much less roll."

Richards noted that as the stress of a situation grew, Colonel Cartwright's Louisiana accent became more prominent.

"Whadda' ya' mean son?"

"It's just that the sanctuary is really full of stuff. It almost looks like my garage sir."

"Okay, did you-all hear dat'? Be careful now, hear?"

Standing atop the scaffolding's perch, the two agents looked down at the stationary levitating ring into the grey interior of its temporal field. Richards reached out and first dropped a leather neck pouch full of copper, silver and gold rings—their mad money, through the field. A faint ripple marked its passage. Next, Gregorieva, with her wig's braids standing out due to the van der Graff effect of the field, giggled, and then dropped with her knees bent as all good parachute jumpers should. Richards, waited ten heart beats, and did the same.

*　　*　　*

Passage through the temporal field felt like a cross between slippery silk sheets and an oil bath. Gregorieva just loved the experience. Landing squarely on the balls of her feet, she rolled effortlessly to her right and almost knocked over a heavily gilded offering stand in the process. Reaching up to steady the golden object from crashing over, she then heard Richards' landing thump. Turning, Richards didn't move at first. He just quietly moaned in the ancient Egyptian tongue.

"Ahhh, I'm upside down ... again ..."

One of the strange phenomena about the temporal device was that males who passed through it suffered from a malady called post-drop syndrome, which caused some sort of temporary disorientation that quickly passed. But at this very moment, Richards was in sad shape.

"My brother, I am here. Try to clear your head." Gregorieva said while supporting him.

Then, after some thirty seconds, Richards' head did.

"Sister, I am well. We must go."

As Richards, still a tad bit disoriented, began to rise, Gregorieva grabbed him by the shoulders and whispered into his ear.

"Be still my brother. Look around you."

In truth, it was good the Russian did what she did as the sanctuary was literally cluttered to the walls with offerings in gold and silver everywhere. Their landing point, before the life-sized golden image of Amen Re, represented the terminus of a narrow path that led from the sanctuary's massive cedar wood door leaves.

Now with widening eyes, Richards expressed the obvious.

"By the gods! So this is what the sanctuary is supposed to look like. I would never have guessed that such wealth could be packed within such a small space."

"Never before?" Gregorieva asked.

"No. But that makes sense. For all of my visits had

been during that dark time of the one-who-should-not-be-named.

"But enough of such talk, we must leave this most sacred place."

As they approached the two massive cedar door leaves of the sanctuary, Richards did so with concern. First, he gently tested their ability to swing with a gentle push. They had barely moved.

"It is as I suspected. The old and stretched ropes of the warning gongs have been replaced. We will have to go forth most carefully my sister."

With infinite care, Richards, ever so slightly, began to simultaneously push open one door leaf and pull on the other. After some moments of strenuous effort, and with a gap of some eight inches, Gregorieva slithered her way through. Then, Richards thrust one of his muscular thighs between the open leaves and then paused to get a breather. Having gathered himself, he slowly began to inch his way into the ever-expanding gap. And then he was through! But he still had to slowly close the leaves, which took another intense effort. Now dripping wet from exertion and nerves, the pair made their way through the semi-darkness of the temple, guided by the evening oil lamps, to their favorite side exit behind the statue of the lion goddess Sekmet.

Now out of the temple proper and under the open heavens, they worked their way through the many warrens of the Karnak Temple. They passed many new magazines and workshops by before exiting the sacred grounds through a massively rebuilt mud brick gateway.

"Maatkare, I twice almost got lost while we made our way through the magazines. There has been much rebuilding and construction taking place since we have last visited."

Their walk to the household of Prince Horemheb was a good two miles distant. Once there, they had planned on crashing in one of his unused guest rooms. Unsaid was the hope that one might be available. Even though the prince had adopted Richards as his half-brother, the prince still entertained. The time spent en route to the prince's estate went by quickly, as the travelers yet again discussed the extraordinary clarity of the star field above them.

Their entry into Horemheb's estate, silent as it was, disturbed the reigning house cat, which ran off. Finding an empty guest room, each found their own sleeping frame, immediately lay down and went to sleep, exhausted, totally spent.

The house cat was not the only one who had detected their stealthy entrance into the noble's estate. Nesi, the head houseman had. But even though it had been almost ten years since Maatkare and Mayneken had visited the prince's household, he remembered how they once before had made their surprise appearance, and in this same fashion. So he waited outside the room until the first snore was made. Then, he quickly peeked in. Immediately Nesi saw Mayneken's heavily scarred back in the dim lamplight that he carried, smiled in positive recognition and with considerable relief, and left to return to his wife's side.

As far as the temporal agents were concerned, dawn arrived far too soon. Groggy, they arose, partook of their morning rituals, and presented themselves in the kitchen. There, peeling some onions and garlic, sat Nesi, all smiles. With a slight bow of the head, he said.

"Good morning noble Mayneken and Maatkare. It has been many inundations since I last saw you. I must apologize for my prince, as he is in the north fighting the Bedouins of the Western Desert. By the time of Hapi's annual blessing, he should return. But I have prattled on enough. Please, sit at the table, and refresh yourselves!

"When I told my wife of your arrival, she got up early this morning and prepared the honeyed sweet breads that you so enjoy, noble Mayneken." Nesi added conspiratorially with a gap-toothed grin. "She never seems to want to make them for me anymore."

After a hearty meal of cheese, dried fish, fresh sweet breads, and some fried onions and garlic, Richards, ever true to form, was the first to belch.

Smiling even more broadly, Nesi just dipped his head in acceptance on the high compliment and continued on with his kitchen chores.

Feeling that the time was right, Richards asked the head houseman about the health of the high priest

Nebneteru, knowing that the man had already passed on.

"Oh, noble Mayneken! Haven't you heard? The most blessed Nebneteru went West two inundations ago!" Nesi replied with emotion. "He was such a righteous priest, generous to anyone in need. Frankly, I truly miss his visits to this household."

"He came often?" Gregorieva inquired.

"Oh yes, noble Maatkare. He and my prince often counseled each other on many matters concerning Thebes and its rebuilding. Many matters regarding the return of the royal court as well." And with that Nesi, suddenly reticent, returned to his onion peeling.

CHAPTER 25
Perfect Pitch

The nearly 2400 pound escape pod rested securely on its wheeled cart, itself a modified ammunition dolly, complete with a convenient tow bar. It was a practical solution for a practical need.

As Roy Peters stood before the extraterrestrial artifact, his mind began to turn on just that thought. Whatever triggered the hatch mechanism on this pod had to be practical. That meant something obvious to the materials science expert, some simple method that would be fool-proof in times of extremis and convenient in normal use.

Okay Roy, so what do we know? What has experience told us?

Well, it turned out that the Aten's hanger in Middle Egypt opened and closed using a simple FM frequency. The Aten space craft's hatch was triggered by the vocalization of a specific ancient Egyptian phrase. In both instances, an alien civilization and culture had thought it natural enough to construct their locking mechanisms around a single sound frequency, or a set pattern of them. So Roy pulled a small pad of Sticky Notes out of his pocket and began to take down some ideas.

Well Roy-boy, what do I need to test that hypothesis, what sound will trigger the opening of the pod? Well, for one, a wide-band transmitter and a set of damn versatile speakers, maybe even several sets, that are capable of producing sound, both audible and not. Then we'll need some kind of animation program that can methodically tune from frequency to frequency and broadcast that frequency on a twenty-four hour basis at ten second intervals. That should work out to, let's see, about one hundred and thirty-eight days to complete, and that's only for the immediately audible range. Frequency selection will be based upon whole integer values measured in Hertz, between twenty through twenty thousand.

Next, Roy-boy we'll need a video camera, connected to a motion sensor, both to record the opening of the pod and to record which frequency triggered it. Some sort of feedback loop will be necessary to stop the animation program when and if the hatch opens.

Now for the big question, who do I know that can rig up such an experiment? I think I'll call in the audio and robotics managers. They'll know what to do.

* * *

Two days later the escape pod and its cradle had been encased within a large anechoic chamber, its walls covered with acoustic damping tiles for sound absorption. Surrounding the pod were no less than four composite speakers and one tiny video camera. At precisely four in the afternoon, on a Friday, the experiment began, starting with a 20 Hz tone for ten seconds.

On that next Monday afternoon, at precisely 2:01 pm, Roy Peter's computer chimed with an urgent e-mail notice. Opening it, the materials scientist read.

440 Hz: Musical A above middle C
(See attachment)

WHOOPIE SURPRISE!
CONGRATULATIONS ROY!

Truly over the moon excited, Roy couldn't get the .jpg attachment open quickly enough. But when it *finally* did, it depicted the anechoic chamber, with the pod's hatch yawning open like the mouth of a barracuda.

"Oh my God," Roy whispered, "the hatch, seat, and fuselage hinge together in unison so that there is no need for a ladder! You would just have to step over the cockpit's sill and you'd be on the ground."

How clever! I'll just bet those flight engineers will go gaga over that setup!

*   *   *

With the successful opening of the escape pod, Roy Peters was once again in business and there were a million things to organize and prioritize. While it seemed like only days ago, the calendar said that a full three months had already passed. But what a full three months of investigation it had been, full of discovery, wonder, and yes, even a moment of absolute panic.

Early on, Roy, ever curious and adventurous, provided perhaps the greatest moment of drama, when he gently sat down into the escape pod's cockpit seat for the first time. At first nothing happened, but as the scientist began to wiggle around while he looked at this doohickey and that, the seat subtly shifted and conformed to his body, gripping him in a comfortable embrace. Then, the articulated pod, seat, and hatch cover began to move, retract, and close as one, clam shell-like.

Yelping like a pinched school girl, Peters could not get out of his form-fitting seat, and suddenly found himself captured within the pod. But once so encased, it wasn't the dark dungeon that he had expected. Instead, the interior had taken on a restful and calming golden hue, and looking about, Peters could *see* all around him, as his colleagues scrambled outside this way and that at his obvious distress.

But Peters' initial surprise was now transformed into absolute wonder, as practically every surface of the entire interior had come to life. Not in the form of flat screens and dials, but with glowing light surfaces and outlined shapes that had appeared where they were not previously.

Those must be buttons, a now very cautious Peters thought, who purposefully tucked his hands under his armpits and consequently out of harm's way.

I'll be damned if I touch one!

And then, just as suddenly, the interior's panel instrumentation disappeared, its golden colored lighting faded, and his ability to see all around the pod vanished. Once again he felt his cockpit seat move forward and down, its gripping flower petal-like bolsters relaxed their grip, the opening crack of the raising hatch and lowering nose of the craft allowed the harsh external lighting of the laboratory to flow in. His colleagues, in a panic, had triggered the opening tone, but for Peters, now strangely saddened, his magical carnival ride had just ended.

Now pummeled with many shouts from his concerned colleagues, Peters just silently indicated his condition with a thumbs-up signal.

"People," he began, "we have a lot to do. What I just experienced, and what I want each and every one of you to experience, is this cockpit, its seat, its sensor system, and its surface instrumentation. And by the way, this hatch, from the inside, is not as opaque as it seems. In fact, from where I am sitting, the entire pod seemed transparent. That's how good the surface sensor system is."

Shaking his head in astounded wonderment. "Now I just hope that we don't run down the battery on this thing, while we investigate all of its bells and whistles."

Days passed and one of Roy's Boys, an aircraft designer, accidentally pushed against an edge of a flat surface within the pod's cockpit. Actually, he had excitedly over-gripped the right side cockpit sill as he gaped in wonder at the interior. The result of that indiscretion was the discovery that all the panels of the entire interior were designed to be easily removed like a take-apart toy. Each and every pliant and textured surface was attached with ingeniously crafted pressure sensitive attachment points. And once out of the way, what was revealed was a dizzying array of technology that was guaranteed to take years to appreciate, much less duplicate, adapt, and make use of.

The exposed technology presented Roy's team with the wonder of beautiful crystalline circuitry, diagnostic sensor arrays embedded in the pod's entire fuselage, a harnessless, full-body, force field restraint system, and a gravimetric-magnetic propulsion system that completely canceled out the notion that flight required light weight materials to do so. The spin-offs seemed endless and endless.

* * *

"I do not trust the Americans. Yes, they come to us with their requests for a temporal insertion. Yes, they invite our temporal agent to participate. But beyond that, we hear nothing," Karlov Drazinzka emphasized with a tight fist.

"I fully appreciate what you are saying, my good friend. However, they do pass on their information in a timely manner. Just look at all the data alone from the Aten space craft project," Vasily Ostrogorsky pointed out.

"And consider this, Karlov," the young Stefan Rosovec added, "They invited our scientists to help them analyze the Aten space craft at their high-security facility at Wright-Patterson. They did not have to do that. Yet, they did, and I believe out of a spirit of cooperation."

Drazinzka's face took on the color of a ripe beet. "The Americans have this bizarre expression, 'a come to Jesus moment.' It is time that I shared the results of my deepest and darkest suspicions with you. Let us not forget the testimony of Gregorieva following her participation in the Americans' visit to the meteor crater and one other nearby site in the Egyptian desert."

"And?" Ostrogorsky prodded.

"They recovered considerable evidence from the primary impact site. What Gregorieva could not possibly tell us was that the primary impact was not that of a meteor, but rather the crash site of an extraterrestrial vehicle."

"What sort of evidence?" Rosovec eagerly asked.

Now leaning forward against the conference table of the secure chamber, "That they found from the primary craft a lone structural element at the crater." The head of special projects then raised his finger in emphasis. "But elsewhere, they recovered, with our Gregorieva present, and without the Egyptian government's knowledge or permission I might add, what most likely was an escape pod. How did I surmise that? When Gregorieva described Richards pouring water across the stone-like slab. When he did that, a seam was revealed. Now, have either of you heard anything about that?"

Two heads shook as one.

"I didn't think so. Now my dear colleagues, how should we proceed?" he asked with open hands and a devilish smile.

"We confront them with this news, directly." Rosovec blurted out, as if betrayed by an errant lover.

A stone-faced Drazinzka looked the man in the eye, "And what of my sources you dolt! The Americans would go on a house-cleaning mission the likes of which we haven't seen since the Cold War. No, I am sorry, that is not how to proceed."

"Perhaps Karlov, we should sit back and wait to see what the Americans *do* wish to share," Ostrogorsky opined. "That Karly, would preserve your confirming sources, which in the interim we can continue to listen to."

Drazinzka nodded once, staring off into the distance, "We need to establish a time limit on the Americans, however. I would fully expect that an escape pod would have much to offer in terms of technology transfer. The reverse engineering might take decades to fully appreciate. Frankly, gentlemen, I will not see the fruit of this stolen artifact. But you will."

Drazinzka pointed accusingly at Rosovec. "How does that make you feel Stefan? All warm and fuzzy?"

Rosovec sat back and slitted his eyes in thought. "Perhaps I should pay a visit to Wright-Patterson. Dr. Roy Peters is a reasonable man."

"And I would lose all my internal sources!" Drazinzka pounded on the conference table. "The Americans are not stupid!"

"No, you are correct. They are not, but they are gullible," the youngest member of the triumvirate said.

"I still do not like this approach," Drazinzka firmly stated with a head shake.

Now leaning forward, "Karlov let me try." Rosovec said with his open hands. "It could blunder into another scientific exchange like the Aten space craft. And if it does, then our nation will not be left behind technologically. We will instead work with the material at hand, real-time, instead of from reports, photos, and descriptions."

Drazinzka sighed and pursed his lips in disagreement.

"Why don't I go," Ostrogorsky cheerfully said. "I'm a biologist. They still have the Aten pilot's remains. I could legitimately make a request for a visit on that basis alone. Then, once there, perhaps I could perhaps work some magic."

"Vasily, when was the last time you visited America?" Drazinzka said with dramatic concern.

"Never."

Again with that devilish smile, "Then your visit would be perfect!"

*   *   *

Later that very afternoon, Professor Dr. Vasily Ostrogorsky crafted an e-mail to Dr. Roy Peters.

> To: Dr. R. Peters, Director, Materials Technology Department, Wright-Patterson AFB, Dayton, Ohio, United States
>
> Greetings Dr. Peters:
>
> My colleague Dr. Stefan Rosovec made mention today of your hospitality, both to him and our fellow scientists, that you so generously extended during a past joint-scientific endeavor.
>
> I sincerely hope that I, a biologist, might make a similar request to personally see, and perhaps examine, the remains of a certain pilot.
>
> I eagerly await your reply.
>
> Sincerely yours,
>
> Vasily Ostrogorsky, Academician & Director, Institute of Theoretical Biology

*   *   *

Roy Peters' e-mail chimed. Glancing up from his paperwork, the materials scientist saw the odd address and put down his mechanical pencil. *Well, Roy-boy, that's a first—an e-mail from someone in Moscow that I only know by name.*

The man carefully read, and reread the brief missive and then sat back in thought.

Okay, he's a big-wig theoretical biologist. I get that. But didn't we already send him a full report on the Aten pilot's remains? Why now all the interest to visit?

Then it dawned on Peters'. *They must know we recovered something and now are giving us a convenient pretext to fess up.*

Peters scratched his head, rubbed at the back of his neck, and lifted his phone.

"Yes, Dr. Peters?" his secretary answered.

"Would you be so kind and get a hold of Professor John Milson for me? And when you do, make sure that the call is on an encrypted line. Be sure to tell him of that fact as well."

"Right away Dr. Peters."

Three minutes later, Peters' phone rang.

"Dr. Peters, Professor Milson is waiting on the line."

"Thank you, Maggie. Let the man through."

After a brief pause with a background hiss and pop, "John, is that you?"

"Indeed it is Roy. To what do I deserve the pleasure?" the emeritus Egyptologist asked.

"I'm calling you because I need your advice. I just got an e-mail from Moscow, John, from a gentleman named Ostrogorsky, their director of the Institute of Theoretical Biology. In it, he made a request to visit us here at Wright-Patterson. What's your read on him? I've never met the man."

"That's difficult to say Roy. I have never personally met with the man. What I can say is that Ostrogorsky is one of the three you sent the final Aten report to. That should tell you something."

"Yeah, that's what I remember as well. But what's bugging me is the timing of his request for a visit, especially given how we're so busy right now."

"Yes Roy, that thought did come to mind. What is the security status of your current project?"

"Can't talk about that."

"I thought so. Sorry for asking. Well, from my humble point-of-view, I think he's worthy of at least a tour. You might also want to think about forming a joint-team on your project, using the Aten effort as a precedent. Other than that, I am quite sure that arrangements can be made at your end."

"Understood. I just wanted to get your read on this, John. By the way, how's your health? I've been hearing some rumors on my end."

"Thank you for your concern Roy. I truly appreciate it. The long and the short of it is simply this—I am fighting."

"Well John, you're in my prayers."

As Milson hung up the phone, he wondered just how much the Russians knew about the current project.

That made the man nervous. Yes, Wright-Patterson may have a leak, but what then about the secure status of their teleconferencing software and satellite?

*   *   *

Later that evening and only after a long discussion with multiple security officers representing several concerns, Peters wrote an e-mail response that outlined a two-week window of availability for the Russian, four months out. Even so, the Hoosier didn't like treating the man so coolly and rigidly. It went contrary to his natural sense of hospitality. On top of that, he never could get a straight answer from the security pukes about letting the Russian in on the "current" project—the escape pod. In the end, Peters decided that he would make that call based upon what security had harped upon, Ostrogorsky's demeanor, and his gut.

CHAPTER 26

The fy-*snake*

Richards, not one to allow an uncomfortable moment to hang too long, probed a bit deeper with Horemheb's estate manager Nesi.

"So with Nebneteru enshrined in the West, what about his successor?"

At the question, Nesi's face contorted into a frown, for clearly he had been trying to avoid the subject.

"Noble Mayneken, I do not know the man."

The onion peeling became more furious.

"Do you know his name?"

"Noble Mayneken, it is Perennefer," the head houseman softly replied.

Silence.

"Nesi," Richards began, "I trust your heart fully and you have our bond not to speak of this subject again. However, just who is this Perennefer?"

The onion peeling stopped and Nesi turned towards his seated guests.

"Noble Mayneken and Maatkare, he is not a priest, much less a high priest of the Great Hidden One. He is a soldier imposter. He is one of the foul one's minions. He is as dangerous as a *fy*-snake!" And with that the man returned to his onions.

Never before had either Richards or Gregorieva heard an Egyptian describe another in such a way. To call a priest an imposter was damning enough. But then to be described "as dangerous as a *fy*-snake"—a sand viper, that was beyond the pale, for the horned viper only dealt death with its poison—a creature aggressive and silent in its attack. A demon *fy*-snake even inhabited the netherworld and threatened the evening journey of Re himself.

"Thank you Nesi for speaking with your heart." Richards softly said. "We will heed your wise counsel."

*   *   *

Promising to return for the evening meal, Richards and Gregorieva left Nesi with his onions, and walked back to the sacred compound of the Great Hidden One, Amen Re. Their purpose was to meet this Perennefer and to seek his permission to stargaze from his temple's rooftop.

As they walked, now in the daylight, both marveled at the marked changes to the city. The flowing wells, the pools filled with Nile perch, the endless flower beds, the fig trees groaning with ripe fruit, and everywhere it seemed, the fresh application of whitewash on the mud brick houses. Even the streets had their central drains capped in stone in an effort to prevent the smell of their noxious contents from escaping. As for the people themselves, they were well fed, boisterous, and of good cheer. Children, always a society's litmus test, were everywhere, getting underfoot, and generally being playful nuisances.

But beyond updating their memories of the town, the two temporal agents also discussed a certain message that had been delivered to the sanctuary two days prior, a message, in the form of a prophecy, that the first prophet of Amen Re no doubt would have by now received. The wily Piankoff had performed that trick once before with great success. Richards, once his assistant, believed that the strategy was worth a repeat.

As the pair neared the gate to the sacred compound, the one that they had passed through before, they now saw two young *wab*-priests with stout staves now standing guard within its shade. Unspoken between the visitors was the question—where were they early this morning?

Richards, as usual, took the lead on this encounter, while Gregorieva remained faithfully at his right side. At precisely six feet before their goal, the priests extended their staves to form an X, effectively barring their passage. Stopping and noting this, Richards made a snap decision.

"Good morning most honorable priests," Richards stated with his best command voice.

"I am Mayneken, *sem*-priest of the god Ptah of the Great White Wall. This is my sister Maatkare, priestess of the same. We have journeyed far. We wish an audience with the High Priest of the Great Hidden One, Perennefer."

While Richards' chiseled torso indeed commanded

their attention, it was Gregorieva's sultry poise that really confounded them.

The one on the right, the taller by maybe two fingers, first slitted his eyes for a menacing effect, and only then spoke.

"This is the Great Temple of the Hidden One. You, *sem*-priest of the lowly god Ptah, have no business here. Go away!" he said with a dismissive flick of his head.

Then Gregorieva, took a step forward, and directly addressed the priest on the left, ignoring his rude colleague.

"Dearest priest, my brother and I wish audience with your all-powerful high priest. Yes, we are just a priest and a priestess from a humble village, far to the north, but we are also very appreciative ones as well."

This come-on created a clear split decision between the two priests. Silent eye flicks, a nod of affirmation from the one on the left, a head shake of negation from the one on the right. In short, Gregorieva had achieved gridlock. Then she suggested.

"Perhaps one of you should go to the household of your all-powerful high priest, to discover if he indeed is already awaiting our arrival?"

Gridlock solved, the priest on the left turned on his heel and briskly strode off into the compound, while his more aggressive twin now repositioned himself squarely in the center of the gate's entrance.

At this point, Richards looked over to his partner and whispered.

"I certainly hope that the good high priest is in-residence, and that he received our specially delivered missive. Otherwise, we might be waiting out here for quite some time."

To this uncharacteristically negative outlook from her partner, Gregorieva merely stated. "If it comes to force, we can take them."

Surprised by her lecherous grin, the American's hopes buoyed. And not thirty seconds later, from within the compound returned the messenger priest, but he was not alone. For accompanying him were four serious looking soldiers with their ox-hide shields, a spear each, and wearing a sheathed dagger at the hip.

Winded, the messenger priest said. "Most noble ones (wheeze), the First Prophet awaits you (wheeze). These soldiers will escort you to his household."

And so with a mixture of pleasure at the discomfiture of the one guardian *wab*-priest and caution at the presence of the soldiers, the Russian and the American allowed themselves to be escorted.

"En route," Gregorieva whispered.

"I now fully appreciate what Nesi was referring to. I am willing to wager that those priests were just soldiers poising as *wab*-priests."

"I have to agree. The military flavor is quite apparent."

Moments later, they arrived before the once modest household of the high priest of Amen Re, one that both knew well from previous visits. They were, however, immediately struck by all the construction that had taken place. Easily, the structure had been enlarged three-fold, the entrance way's portico lengthened, six more pillars added, and that was only what they could see. Who knew what the once modest interior of Meryptah's home now looked like?

Two tall and burly *Medjay* warriors barred all access through the surrounding low wall that encircled the now meager grounds and its encroaching, enlarged central structure, stopping all further progress. The four soldiers lead Richards and Gregorieva up to these blue-black Nubian guards, stopped, and then said absolutely nothing.

The American stared sourly at the *Medjay* before him, expressed his impatience by placing his hands on his hips, and continued to glare at their clear obstruction. It was a stand-off as the pair stood there in the building heat of the sun.

Meanwhile the Russian looked her warrior up and down, and then noticed a swelling in the front of his white kilt. Smiling at it, she then looked him in the eye and licked her lips, slowly, which caused him to shuffle his feet. Then, a loud voice announced from the shadows of the portico.

"*Medjay!* Let them pass. The First Prophet wills it!"

Approaching the three steps that led to the coolness of the portico's shade, that same voice ordered, now localized within that blessed shadow between the last two pillars, "Halt! That's far enough. Enjoy the warmth of Re's radiance a few moments longer. The First Prophet is not ready to receive you as yet."

At this point, Richards looked at Gregorieva and Gregorieva looked at Richards in total, utter, surprise, and in the American's case, growing anger. Using his best command voice, Richards bellowed back.

"So, shadowy one, he who dares not reveal himself to the glorious radiance of Re, how dare you not show proper respect and hospitality to a *sem*-priest and priestess of the god Ptah of the Great White Wall!"

The American's challenge rang off of the portico's walls and surely carried as far as the household's interior. Without question, the two *Medjay* heard the challenge, if not most of the immediate neighborhood.

The hidden figure, surprised at the force of the rebuke, staggered slightly back, and so now the Russian joined in on the feeding frenzy saying, "Indeed, my brother, look how frightened he seems. Hiding like rabbit in the reeds, while a falcon circles."

During this exchange, both agents clearly heard chuckles of mirth from the two *Medjay* behind them.

Silence. And then the figure turned and scampered into the estate.

Richards smiled and said.

"Rabbit indeed my sister."

Then a second figure appeared who also remained in the cool darkness, but with a deeper and more resonant voice, quietly stated.

"Who dares to bellow like an ox before my household?"

Richards quickly retorted. "My apologies great one. I and my sister wish an audience with the First Prophet of the Great Hidden One. Clearly by your household's impoliteness and total lack of respect and hospitality, we were mistakenly escorted to the incorrect household. Again, my apologies great one, we shall leave you in peace."

And with that, Richards gently took Gregorieva's arm and turned to leave, purposefully exposing his well muscled back and its magnificent scarring to the second figure.

At this point, the hidden high priest of Amen Re beheld before him a vision that exactly matched the words of the recently received prophecy.

> First Prophet of My House
> You shall meet a priest and priestess pairing
> Brother and sister
> She breathtakingly beautiful
> He heroically scarred
> They seek but a trifle
> Grant it and your office shall prosper
> Do not
> And I will turn My back upon you
> As they did you.

Taken aback by the uncanny correlation between

the prophecy and what his own eyes told him, the high priest called out. "No, it is my apology I offer, most noble *sem*-priest and priestess.

"Please, stop. Be welcome within my humble household. For within its cool walls refreshment awaits."

Richards and Gregorieva, now looking back over their shoulders, and briefly at each other, shared a knowing look. Then, slowly they returned, mounted the three steps of the portico, and entered its soothing shade.

*   *   *

The high priest of Amen Re wielded raw power and influence during the late Eighteenth Dynasty. If there was ever any notion of a nationalistic spirit in the ancient world, then it can be attributed to this once regional god of Thebes. Egypt had found itself divided during what modern scholars call the Second Intermediate Period. It was a time of decentralization where the south was overseen by local warlords and Nubia, and the north controlled by an amorphous and disjointed power called the Hyksos. During this time, Thebes and its surrounding territories were on their own. This situation, this disunity of the sacred Two Lands, was vinegar in the mouths of the Thebans, who wished to reunite Egypt and return the Two Lands to their former glory. So, during the historically shadowy late Seventeenth Dynasty, the Theban revolt began with campaigns into the north that culminated with the establishment of the Eighteenth Dynasty. The divine totem that ensured this early victory was the patron god of Thebes, the Great Hidden One, Amen Re. As a result, the power and influence of that god continued to grow throughout the history of the dynasty, excepting of course, the bizarre interlude of Akhenaten.

But with the re-establishment of the Theban god's supremacy during the reign of Tutankhamen, a whiplash-like, brutal reaction occurred across the reunited Two Lands against all trace of that heretic king's memory. Make no mistake, the Theban god Amen Re reaped the vast material benefits thereof. And with that massive infusion of wealth, as Egypt became an empire, came untold power and influence that was personally managed by the god's First Prophet, the god's high priest. In importance, influence, and sheer clout, the First Prophet of Amen Re equaled, if not surpassed that of the later Vatican pontiff.

*   *   *

It was obvious to Gregorieva and Richards—from the tart smell of the fresh plaster alone, that much had changed within the interior of the high priest's abode. Escorted to the dining area, they filed around a low groaning board surrounded by soft cushions filled with duck and goose feathers. Gregorieva sat opposite

Richards with Perennefer at the table's head.

With their eyes now fully adjusted to the interior, what they saw was a tall man for an Egyptian, mid-twenties, fit, with broad shoulders and well-muscled arms. That he was once a soldier was clear.

For the Russian, unconsciously reverting to her Directorate training, Gregorieva ignored all of that and focused instead on the longish, well-proportioned head, his straight nose, and above all, his eyes, which even as he mouthed a traditional greeting, had failed to do so.

Yes, my dear Nesi, she thought, *you were absolutely right in your assessment. A* fy-*snake he is.*

As for the American, he saw in football terms the build of a defensive safety, quick and powerful. But he too was unnerved by the shallowness of the man's greeting.

"So," the high priest began, "you both must be thirsty, for I certainly am. Ramose! Bring us your coolest beer. Two jars worth," he offhandedly commanded to the house servant.

With that task executed, he then returned his attention to his guests.

"Welcome to my humble household. I am Perennefer. What is your desire?"

And with that opening Richards began.

"Thank you, Great One for your hospitality. I am Mayneken, *sem*-priest of Ptah of the Great White Wall. This is my sister, Maatkare, priestess of the same. We are students of the heavens. We seek your permission to study the sky this evening and the next from an advantageous high place within your great temple. We have been told that you have such a place, where your own priests study the heavens. This is all that we seek."

*   *   *

Listening to this muscle-bound priest and his bewitching sister, Perennefer could not help but again recall the words of the prophecy. "They seek but a trifle. Grant it and your office shall prosper." And in so doing, he remembered its warning as well if he didn't. So, as was his nature, Perennefer decided to probe for more information before he granted what truly was "a trifle." So for the moment, he totally ignored the granting of the simple request.

*   *   *

"Mayneken—that name seems familiar to me. Why is that so?"

Richards, immediately recognizing the evasion, decided to pile it on high and thick, like a well-made and steaming hot pastrami sandwich on rye.

"Great One, it is indeed entirely possible that you have heard of my name, as I am the adopted son of the Osiris Meryptah, himself First Prophet of Amen Re, who labored to preserve this very temple and its wealth during the dark time of the heretic. It was I who arranged for my father's final place in the West, within the sacred precinct of Prince Horemheb's own family tomb near sacred Mennefer. This was made possible by the prince himself, who caused the tomb to be built, as he is my adopted younger brother. Finally, it could be also as I was the personal ambassador of the Lady of the Two Lands, Neferiti. So, indeed, it is very possible that you have heard of my name."

Having finished with his resume, the widened eyes of their host was most telling, but to Perennefer's credit, he did recover quickly. Now turning to Gregorieva, the high priest asked, more out of politeness than anything else.

"And you my lady?"

"I too wish to thank you, oh Great One, for your hospitality."

And as the beer was being poured, both Richards and Gregorieva respectively paused for the traditional first toast by their host. And Perennefer did not disappoint.

"May this cool beer so shared refresh our most noble guests. May their pursuits come to fruition. And may the Great Hidden One triumph over all of Egypt's enemies."

And all drank, deeply, Richards perhaps overly so, as he had totally drained his cup. Putting down it down, the American paused, burped mightily, and added.

"Great One! That was most delicious! May I have another?"

Blinking with surprise, the high priest could only

say the obvious as he looked into his still half-full cup.

"Why most certainly Mayneken. Ramose! More beer."

Not to be forgotten, Gregorieva then continued.

"As I was saying, Great One, I am Mayneken's sister and assistant in all things. As for my name, my mother chose it as it was the name most favored by the blessed Osiris Hatshepsut."

Now finished, Gregorieva nursed her beer, as its thick, *Weissbier*-like flavor did not agree with her. Yes, the natural carbonation was pleasant, but the heavy grain flavor was not of her liking. Still and all, she was enjoying Richards' clearly juvenile fraternity approach, and wondered if this little gathering would develop into an all out chugging contest. Then, the Russian got her answer as Perennefer threw back the remainder of his beer.

My, my, Professor Richards. You sly devil! She thought.

"So," a now overly grinning Richards began, "Great One. I wish to make no offense, but you possess the look of a powerful warrior to me. Or, am I mistaken?"

Smiling again with those cold snake-like eyes, the high priest responded.

"Your eyes do not lie, Mayneken. I have proudly served as the Master of the Chariots of the Horus Squadron. My commander was the most Noble Ay."

"Ah ha! I knew it. Those strong arms of yours must

pull only the most powerful of bows! Am I right?"

Now smiling with genuine pleasure for the first time. "Indeed, Mayneken. My arrows can pierce a solid copper ox hide!"

And Richards rewarded that macho detail with open-mouthed wonder, much to Perennefer's pleasure. Gregorieva, near-gagging at Richards' fawning display, remained silent and stole another sip of her beer to hide her smile.

After four more rounds and much boasting, Mayneken was finally asked of their much softened-up host, just what he and his sister were up to with their "star gazing."

"Great One, it is simple. We wish to compare the position of several of the gods as they traverse the belly of Nut. Why you say? Because I believe their location in Mennefer to be different than that in most sacred Thebes. You might well ask, what is the point of that? Well, if the positions of these gods are indeed different, then that means that the Two Lands lie upon not a flat plain, but are instead part of a vast, circular ball."

Now it was Perennefer's turn to gape in total disbelief. As for Gregorieva, she had to stifle her shock at Richards' proposition, as it was a clear violation of the *RUTI*.

"The Two Lands are only 'part of a vast, round ball?' Are you mad Mayneken? Is this what the priests of Ptah ponder? Such insane things?"

"Perhaps. But mathematics would support such an

apparently mad thought *if* indeed the positions of the gods in the sky are different. This is precisely why we are here, Great One. To find out."

CHAPTER 27
Sharing the Wealth

Instances of collaboration between scholars in the humanities, while a much-lauded virtue in academe, in reality, tended to be an extremely *rara avis*. On the other hand, such teamwork consistently was the norm in the hard sciences, where ten or more collaborating minds often appeared as the authors of a research publication.

Why was this so?

The humanities graduate student experience, while a rigorous road, was a lonely one—not to be taken by the faint of heart. Highly competitive graduate-level seminars have been accurately characterized as voracious shark tanks, where the establishment of a professor's notice encouraged cannibalism. As a consequence, enterprising graduate students have been known to remove key library resources from their usual shelving and then hoard them elsewhere. To discourage such tactics, seminar resources many times were placed in library reserve collections, where they could not so easily wander. This crucible, the graduate seminar, is believed by many inhabitants of the Ivory Tower to be where true scholarship is attained, and where the wheat was separated from the chaff. Nothing could be further from the truth.

In actual fact, such seminars in the humanities

often imprinted upon young, impressionable, and creative minds the utter nonsense and institutional biases that their professors espoused. Evidence of this transformation can be seen in the adopted use of expensive and finicky fountain pens, wire-rimmed glasses, exotic sounding accents, speech patterns, and bizarre and overly clever vocabulary choices. All were pure pretentious drivel.

Once past the seminar, next came the dissertation, where an appropriate topic must be first negotiated and then championed. Along the way, several sympathetic professors must be recruited, who will review the project through its many rewrites and ultimately affix their stamp of approval. This lengthy process oftentimes consumed years and held up potentially blossoming careers for a host of totally unnecessary reasons.

Meanwhile, during the writing of the dissertation, the candidate must market themselves to the world and somehow, someway, make an impression. The best way to do so was to publish an article or two in recognized, juried, academic journals. While a clear statement of academic professionalism and a powerful indication of future promise, care must be exercised because one's dissertation advisors might somehow perceive such intellectual industry in a negative light, or worse, as a personal threat. Either way, such publications slow the dissertation's progress.

Not everyone, however, can intellectually pull off

this feat *and* write their dissertation at the same time, and so they must resort to other means. This can lead to a whole host of overly pedantic gestures that can be best compared to the mating display of a peacock. The most common avenues available to graduate students, which are encouraged by their professors, included the delivery of papers on exceedingly narrow and obscure topics at conferences of purported note, and the writing of hyper-critical and scathing book reviews. All of this nonsense is done in the attempt to establish one's intellectual credibility, in place of actual publications, which actually do.

If an individual's dissertation is completed and approved, then they are confronted with the academic market where one is poked and prodded like a side of beef. Those early publications are now gold as are any influential liaisons that have been established at the many academic conferences. Their sole purpose is to acquire face-to-face interviews, where the eager and job-hungry candidate now must transform themselves into a formless social chameleon.

The curious double-edged blade of academic interviews and their resultant campus invitations is that if the candidate is strong, then their *curriculum vitae* is placed on the A-pile. But if that individual is too strong, then their intellectual powers might intimidate a member of the hiring department's committee.

In short, the academic hiring process in the humanities is fraught with funky encounters, chance, intrigue, and disappointment. Without question, it is a very delicate dance that does not end until the individual is granted full-tenure. It is then, and only then, that a scholar can finally be themselves. The problem is, however, that the four to seven year period prior to the granting of tenure, the last vestiges of individuality are usually crushed. In the end, the successful survivor of this grueling gauntlet is usually a spineless paragon of mediocrity. It is any wonder that the humanities suffer so?

*   *   *

John Milson, however, was far and away beyond these petty considerations. Not only was he an established and well-respected scholar in the field of Egyptology, he was emeritus as well. As he gazed upon his translation of the NEI's unpublished papyrus, he didn't think twice about not sharing his fresh and unpublished research with his Bavarian colleague von Staufen. He selflessly realized that together, their two papyri needed to stand side-by-side, as only then did they together provide a unique perspective on the creation of the Kamil Crater. To that end, Milson sent an e-mail to von Staufen with the original text and his translation as an attachment.

*   *   *

Four months later, Ostrogorsky struggled to deplane

down the narrow stairs of his Russian commuter jet. Human joints at the age of eighty-one sometimes thought ill of such maneuvers. Yet, nothing was going to stop the Russian. In his mind, receiving permission to land upon a Wright-Patterson airstrip represented an unimaginable privilege for this survivor of the Cold War.

How things have changed, Vasily. Here I am stepping down upon one of America's most secure places. He thought as he gazed out his window. *And only a black sedan greets me, without a military presence in sight. Simply remarkable.*

However, the Russian was wrong, for two men exited from the sedan. One, obviously a civilian, wore a sports jacket, tie, and tan slacks. Youthful looking, the man's hair was cut short. His lean and lanky look resembled that of a runner. The other, obviously military, was dressed in the blues of a high-ranking United States Air Force officer. Oddly, neither of these relatively fit youngsters made any attempt to assist the aged Russian down the aircraft's stairs.

Once on the ground, however, the three men shared stiff and formal handshakes of greeting, while a fourth, Ostrogorsky's personal aide, provided translation. The Russian presented himself proudly in his British Savile Row gray pin-striped wool suit, which matched well his thinning head of hair. Ostrogorsky instantly, however, regretted his choice, now standing in the sunny and humid Ohio weather.

With those formalities out of the way and their baggage transferred to the vehicle's trunk, they were whisked away, while a bright orange fuel truck pulled up to the aircraft.

"Academician Ostrogorsky, do you wish to be taken to your quarters to freshen up first before I take you on a tour of the facilities?" Roy Peters asked from the right side of the rear seat. Between him and the Russian academic sat his translator.

"Yes. That would be pleasant."

"Okay then. When should I come by and pick you up? It's about one-thirty in the afternoon right now."

After some discussion between the Russians, "Please pick us up at four pm."

"May I suggest that you put on lighter, less formal attire? Perhaps a casual cotton outfit? A good portion of the tour will be conducted outside and today is warm."

"Thank you for the suggestion," was the processed reply.

*　　*　　*

"What do you think of him?" Colonel "Wild Bill" Riggens asked the materials scientist, while they sat killing time in his office. A veteran of some twenty years at Wright-Patterson, Riggens read people like a book, but he was always curious about other people's impressions. He found them valuable, even teachable moments.

"In profile, Ostrogorsky's portly profile reminded me of a certain Hollywood movie director. Other than that, the man is old, very old, and looks to be painfully arthritic. He's not the movie star that his colleague Rosovec is, but his eyes are sharp. They miss nothing." The Hoosier said with conviction.

"Really?" the security officer said from the comfort of Peters' visitor chair, as his eyes twinkled and danced with interest. "Give me an example, Dr. Peters."

"Certainly," the materials scientist obliged, "I watched him as he totally inventoried the car's interior in a flash. Then, he glued his nose to the window as we drove around the base."

"Huh. Couldn't see all that from the front seat."

"And his personal assistant," Peters added, "the translator, is the same—a human video recorder. I wouldn't be surprised one bit if they both have photographic memories."

"You beginning to regret putting on this dog and pony show, Dr. Peters?" Riggens asked with a smile.

"No, not at all. It's just Ostrogorsky is my first contact with a Cold War dinosaur. To him, we are the enemy and have always been the enemy. I fully expect him to take every opportunity to exploit his visit."

"Okay, I buy that. So how are you going to handle him?"

"Like a long-lost uncle or perhaps even better, a grandfather, with lots of respect and humor, salted with extreme caution."

"I see. Do you want us to plant a bug on him? Perhaps listen in on their conversations?"

"No. That's not my style colonel. And if such a bug was discovered, it would ruin everything."

A single nod.

"Understood. So where will you begin the tour?"

"With a quick visit to Hanger P, then on to the life sciences nerds. They have prepared an exhibit for the theoretical biologist. Besides, they can better answer his questions than I."

"Then where?"

"We'll see. It all depends on him and my gut. At the very least I want his read on the escape pod pilot's remains. I think they will fascinate him. After that, then perhaps a quick peek at the pod, closed of course."

"Are you sure that you want to do that?"

"Yes, I am. I suspect its organic shape will cause the man to reveal more than he wants to."

"What about me? Do you want me tagging along?"

"No Bill, sorry, but I don't think so. My read is that less is more with this man. Remember: he's a Cold War survivor who expects to be watched. My hope is that out in the open he relaxes."

"Is that your famous gut speaking Roy?"

"Yes it is. I have a feeling that with less pressure on, he'll have to fill it in with something."

To this the colonel just rolled his eyes. "Roy, how long have we known each other?"

"I don't know, twenty-odd years?"

"Twenty-four."

"And Bill, did we have any issues while those Russian research scientists were here helping us with the Aten spacecraft?"

"None."

"And didn't several of them find jobs here in the States?"

"Yes they did, at Cal Tech and MIT."

"There you have it."

"Roy, you're not trying to turn this Russian too?"

"Nope. He's hard core through and through. Therefore, I can't do that. But nothing's stopping me from making him feel welcome and comfortable."

*   *   *

To Ostrogorsky's absolute delight, his host Dr. Peters picked them up from their quarters in an extended electric golf cart. He had only seen the contraption on television. The Russian also brightened when he saw that the previous officer was nowhere in sight. But when he saw that the American had removed his coat and tie and wore his shirt collar open with the sleeves rolled up, Ostrogorsky began to relax.

Meanwhile the Russians had clearly received Peter's suggestion. Both had changed into cotton slacks and brightly colored, bloused button-down shirts.

Once everyone was settled in the golf cart, the American materials scientist zoomed his guests around seemingly without a care in the warm and sunny afternoon air. The pale blue sky was marred only with a handful of fluffy clouds. The scene reminded the Russian of his *dacha* on the shore of the Black Sea. Indeed, they had dressed for it.

With Peters at the wheel, Ostrogorsky hung on while his assistant sat in the back. Both were astounded as they breezed by an active flight line, the air filled with the distinctive reek of half-burned aviation fuel and the screech of turbine engines. This was also the Russians' first view of the base's functioning military personnel, specifically several mother-hen maintenance crews dressed in their bright yellow one-piece flight suits.

Ostrogorsky said something to his assistant, who then tapped Peters' shoulder.

"Why are they all dressed in yellow?"

"High-visibility. We have a lot of fog here."

Both Russians just nodded in understanding without the benefit of any translation. This Peters noticed.

Continuing on, they then passed numerous hangars, while their driver took a serpentine path turning here and there among them. Ostrogorsky wondered how he didn't get lost in the maze.

Peters finally stopped before one hangar with a large letter "P" painted in white upon its wide doors. He turned to his passengers. "Academician Ostrogorsky, please notice the fresh construction repairs to this hangar's roof." The materials scientist pointed out. "This is where the Aten space craft used to be located, that is before *they* took it back."

Following the translation of that statement, the Russian asked through his assistant, "The Aten went through the roof, Dr. Peters?"

"Yes, Academician Ostrogorsky. The owners of it either used a tractor beam of some kind or had powered up the craft remotely. We're not sure which, just that they made quite a mess doing so."

While Peters spoke, he took note of the Russian's intense ice-blue eyes. What Peters saw he had already suspected—Ostrogorsky understood every word he said. The real question was—could he speak as well.

Waiting patiently for the faux-translation process to complete, Peters then added, "Now we will go to the Life Sciences Building. I told my people you are coming. They are prepared to show you everything we have concerning the Aten's pilot." And off the trio went, but not before Peters again registered that quick glint of understanding from the Russian's eyes.

* * *

Their final destination was a drab and care-worn two-storey building of yellowed brick—just like the rest of the low government buildings around them. Coming to a halt, Dr. Peters turned to the Russian and quietly said, "Academician Ostrogorsky, what I am about to show you is extremely sensitive material, in fact so sensitive, that I must insist your assistant remains behind."

While Peters waited patiently for the faux-translation process to once again to take its course, he found himself smiling with amusement at the Russian's feigned outburst of confusion.

"Dr. Peters, without my assistant I cannot function! What is the meaning of this! This restriction is quite irregular," his translator said.

"Take it or leave it, Academician Ostrogorsky. Either he stays and waits here, or you go home. By the way, my first name is Roy," he said extending his hand. "What's yours?"

After a good two minutes of intense discussion in Russian, Ostrogorsky finally asked, and in a thick British accent, "Dr. Peters, how did you know I understand English?"

"Easy. Those intelligent eyes of yours gave you away. Besides, you asked about the yellow flight suits and your assistant failed to translate my answer. Let's face it, I could clearly tell you think this entire translation charade is far too cumbersome. You're a bright man used to communicating rapidly. And your assistant is not cleared by my government to see what lies beyond those doors. So what is your decision? He stays or you both go home?"

The Russian squinted his eyes in thought, pursed his lips, and looked back as his assistant, "Yuri, my good friend, stay with the cart. I will not be long."

With that answer, Peters removed two plastic water bottles from the golf cart's forward shelf and handed them to Yuri.

* * *

Once inside the building's entrance, both men were presented with lanyards and empty plastic pouches hanging from them. The pair then had their photos taken, followed by the ritualistic signing of disclosure documents.

"Ah, Dr. Peters … Roy … what did I just sign?"

"One bad-ass governmental disclosure agreement. If you tell anyone about what you're about to see, then your first born-child is forfeit," Peters deadpanned.

"Truly?" the Russian asked an amused expression.

"Vasily, you don't have a first-born child do you?"

"Was that your attempt at a phenomenon called humor?"

"Yes it was. Terrible wasn't it?"

"No, it was quite Russian." The man grinned for the first time. "By the way, when did you first make your assessment of my language skills?"

"In the car, on the way to your quarters."

"That quickly?"

A shrug. "Does it really matter?"

"I suppose not."

"Good, because my people have a lot to show you and even more questions to ask."

"Questions for me?"

"Yes Vasily. Aren't you a theoretical biologist?"

"Indeed I am."

*   *   *

"Roy, what am I now looking at?" Ostrogorsky said with some confusion while looking into the sealed environment. Several ports with rubber-like gloves provided access to the stainless steel cabinets' contents.

"The skeletal evidence of our newest visitor, Vasily."

"What! Skeletal remains? Your biologists just got through briefing me on the Aten pilot, who had no apparent skeleton—just a cartilaginous framework of some kind—much like a skate or shark."

"That is correct, Vasily. These remains our recovery team recently found near an egg-shaped craft that we will next visit. It's stored over in Hanger P. Be advised, however, that I have broken about every rule in the book just to show you these bones."

The Russian crossed his arms in thought. "So, Roy, we now have hard evidence of two extraterrestrial species visiting our planet?"

A simple nod. "And extraordinarily different ones, Vasily."

A grunt, "Any DNA?"

"I'm told no results as yet. The life sciences' team have been extremely cagey on that subject. It seems that they don't believe we will be able to recover any, due to the long exposure of the remains in the desert."

The Russian, gazing into the specimen cabinet, noted, "Roy, are those feathers?"

"They certainly appear to be so."

*   *   *

During his flight back to Moscow, Ostrogorsky found himself typing his recollections furiously into his laptop. Stopping briefly to allow a numbness in his left hand to pass, he asked Yuri Amur, his first choice to succeed him as the Director of the Institute of Theoretical Biology, "What did you think of Dr. Peters?"

"That is a difficult question, academician. I was not allowed as much time with him as you were."

"Yes, yes, I know, but what is your impression of the man? You know you will have to deal with him in the future after I retire."

A deep sigh, "I found him to be a very clever and sneaky American. I feel that he played us well."

Smiling, "Indeed he did, Yuri, but he was a fair man. He showed me much that he didn't have to. And as a result, together we have arranged for another joint investigation of another alien spacecraft and its pilot."

"What!"

"And that makes the American a generous man as well. My biggest concern is that the *Rodina* will lose several more of our best minds to this country's universities."

"Yes. That will happen again if Academician Rosovec again is so generous with his travel visas."

"My question to you Yuri, is will you do the same? Will you also grant your best and brightest theoretical biologists such freedoms?"

At this Amur paused to think. "Yes, I will. Not to please you, but to grant the *Rodina* the opportunity to enjoy such a nurturing exchange. After all, I have to think about my successor as well."

"Well stated Yuri. If there is anything that I have learned during my long career, it is always best to embrace the long term first, and to quietly endure any short term bumps in the road."

CHAPTER 28

The Astronomers

Mankind's fascination with the heavens is an old one. Given the ancient Egyptian's insatiable interest in their environment, that included the intense observation of the grand star field above their heads. Their fair land's cloudless skies invited such curiosity, while overly gawking at the Milky Way could easily put a crick in the neck.

As a consequence, early on the Egyptians tracked the cyclical appearance of certain stars, along with the track of the moon's movements across the sky goddess Nut's belly. Such observations, all duly noted and recorded, eventually founded the basis of the ancient Egyptians understanding of basic celestial mechanics. They found certain stars made highly predictable appearances, from which blocks of time could be conveniently organized and calculated. Thoughts about cyclical periods were entertained, and the establishment of a highly accurate calendar of 365 days was the result.

Fueling this intense interest in the stars and their movements, nearly every major temple possessed their own astronomical observation deck and a priestly faculty, who were specifically tasked to watch and record the procession of the heavens. As recordkeeping was a major part of this scientific activity, promising scribes were recruited from the temple schools for this nocturnal enterprise. While some succeeded, others just fell asleep.

*   *   *

Sebekmose, a stooped and heavily wrinkled man of fifty-one inundations, knew that his time was fast approaching. Like a mature date palm that had for so many seasons produced a fine harvest, the aged *sem*-priest and chief astronomer of Amen-Re knew that it was time.

Old by Egyptian standards, Sebekmose's eyesight had nonetheless remained as keen as a falcon's. A short man of powerful intellect, the venerable priest was a patient teacher, who now was in search of a young scribe of promise, perhaps even his successor.

From the scribal pool he chose a candidate assistant, someone who the astronomer hoped was trainable, who would perhaps share in his scholarly passion as well. The selected candidate assistant named Seneb, unlike the others, was two years older than the rest. Further, Sebekmose believed him to be two years wiser as well, because the young one had recently arrived among the many from that city to the north, Akhetaten, that was no more.

From all indications, the lad was bright, enthusiastic, and clearly the best among his scribal peers. He came from a modest, yet remarkably successful family. His father was an architect and sculptor, a man named Nakhti. Sebekmose's only reservation was that he hoped that he had chosen wisely, for his successor had to be patient, diligent, and exacting of eye. He needed to be a careful thinker, methodical in his recording, but a dreamer as well. Clearly, an odd collection of characteristics to master and encourage.

*   *   *

As chance would have it, the astronomical observation platform at the Karnak Temple was actually the flat roofline of the Pylon of Osiris Thutmose I. At the time the pylon was the tallest structure in all of Thebes and its lofty roof had not been dedicated to any other activity. So this vast rectangular space, oriented as it was on a north-south axis, was deemed a perfect place from which to observe the immortal and unchangeable ones.

To aid in this most worthy of undertakings, upon the pylon's limestone roof three separate circles had been precisely carved along its length, one at the north end of the roof, one in the center, and the last at the south. Sebekmose favored the central circle.

Each circle was six royal cubits in diameter, or a bit over ten feet. Each circle was then divided into thirty-six radii, and the gap between each of the radii was further subdivided into ten equal units along the outer diameter.

In the center of each observation circle was conveniently positioned a wooden surveyor's frame for sighting, which smoothly swiveled on a socketed post, well-greased with animal fat. Also provided were a basket full of large, flat pottery shards and a beer juglet full of charcoal sticks. At the sighting frame's central post was another juglet, this time filled with water and a linen rag. Such provisions were made for the recording of sightings, as was a filled oil lamp with a fresh wick, because one was not expected to write in the dark. Although on some nights the evening's brightness was such that the lamp was not even required. This evening was such a night.

On any given evening with a clear sky, which in Thebes was practically every night, small teams of priestly astronomers and their scribal assistants could be found busying themselves at their assigned observation circle. One manned the sighting frame, while another marked the observation along the circle's diameter with a pottery shard. A third took notes about the observation upon one of the handy potshards.

*   *   *

On this particular evening, for some inescapable reason, Sebekmose could not believe how peaceful it was, sitting at this great height, above all of Thebes. The usual post-sundown braying of donkeys had come and gone. Even the flocks of birds were at peace. The entire river seemed to slumber. A gentle and cooling breeze tickled across the astronomer's shaved scalp.

But then that peaceful moment of reflection was rudely broken, when his priestly colleagues at the northern end of the pylon began to noisily and excitedly point towards the northwestern quadrant of the heavens.

Frankly, the seasoned astronomer didn't see the glowing spec at first. But as he pivoted the sturdy sighting frame around to the general direction, as had his neighbors, he then quickly saw what all the excitement was about. A glowing dot in the sky had appeared that he did not recognize. Add to that, the speck appeared to be getting bigger by the moment!

"Assistant, mark that eternal one's location with a shard along our observation circle. Quickly now!"

The young scribe did so, as he already had several of the handy markers on hand. Pleased at seeing such anticipation, the astronomer smiled, and then added. "Assistant, note its color. I see white. Confirm."

"It is confirmed," the scribal assistant dutifully answered, as he made a quick note of the star's color on the marker shard with the charcoal stick that he had held at the ready between his teeth.

Mere moments later, as the astronomer continued to sight along the frame he excitedly announced. "The star has moved! Mark it so."

"Done," his scribal assistant stated, as he placed another shard upon the outer edge of the observation circle, this time a full ten units south from the first.

"Master astronomer Sebekmose," the scribal assistant formally noted with some astonishment, "the star has moved a full ten units across Nut's belly. What does that mean? And," he continued with curiosity, "is it just my imagination or has the star begun to appear longer?"

"No, my sharp-eyed falcon," Sebekmose said with considerable pride for the young man, "you are not imagining it. It is beginning to form a tail like that of a flaming arrow shot into the sky. Small, but a tail has formed nonetheless. Even now I am beginning to see a yellowish tinge to it."

"Agreed. I will make a note of it," replied the scribal assistant.

"And my sharp-eyed falcon, the movement of the star across a full ten units of the heavens means that it is no longer fixed in the sky; rather, it is moving quite fast, much faster than any of pharaoh's swiftest chariots.

"And in this particular case, my assistant, we are witnessing an exceedingly rare event, one that I have never seen before in my lifetime. Although, tomorrow I will take you to the *per ankh*, our temple's archives, and show you two scrolls that describe precisely what we are now witnessing."

"Assistant! The star has moved yet again! Mark it so!"

"Done."

And so this truncated, nearly coded conversation continued on, falling into an easy rhythm of communication between the observer and recorder. Sebekmose, who had drilled the youth in the correct procedures and tasks to be performed during just such a momentous event, smiled inwardly at the seamlessness of their mutual cooperation.

This young man truly has promise.

Meanwhile, with their equally excited neighbors to the north and south, the team of Sebekmose and Seneb tracked the ever-growing star and its ever-lengthening tail, until its path was sighted as being squarely due west of Thebes. All during this celestial sojourn the scribal assistant had dutifully placed shards along the circle's diameter, and in so doing, recorded the precise track of the star's progress across Nut's belly, the lengthening of its tail, and even its changing coloration.

"Mark another shard to the south my assistant."

"Done."

Silence.

"It continues to move so swiftly across the heavens…," the chief astronomer murmured more to himself than for Seneb's ears.

"Mark another shard to the south my assistant."

"Done. Note now its color Master Sebekmose—a white head with a yellow to red tail."

"Agreed. Excellent observation Seneb! Record it so," the seasoned astronomer said as he refused to remove his eye from the sighting frame, as he was so entranced by its rapid passage through the heavenly ether.

"Mark one more shard … Oh, by the gods no!" The astronomer cried out as the slowly descending star had touched the earth, and when it did so, had caused a brighter than bright explosion of light over the horizon.

Looking down upon his last marker shard and not at the heavens, Seneb noted two things. The last sighting was squarely to the southwest of the extreme glare. It reminded him of dancing before a large fire, or the early morning beams of Re's first appearance, when one could cast extremely long and distinct shadows. Even having looked away, the assistant was glad that he was on his hands and knees as the after-imagining of the event was painful in the extreme. It was only then that he heard the Sebekmose's low moan.

"Seneb, I am blind."

Rushing to him, the assistant supported the master astronomer's slumping form and said. "Keep your eyes closed Master Sebekmose! Let your tears heal thyself. That is what my mother has always said. Be assured that I am here to support you no matter what."

Glancing off to his right and left, the scribal assistant saw that all three priests at the northern observation point were doubled over in obvious pain. Oddly, the priest and priestess at the southern circle were not in such distress. Looking back down to the old astronomer in his arms, the scribal assistant saw that he was furiously blinking his eyes.

"What do you see Master Sebekmose?"

"Stars, blobs of light! Seneb, I am not blind! Just temporarily so! Thank the gods!"

Then Sebekmose took a deep, sobbing sigh as he, still in great pain, rested his eyes and continued to lean upon his scribal assistant's shoulder.

"Oh Seneb! That was so close. I could not bear to lose my sight. That, and my intellect, are the only things that I still possess."

After some twenty minutes, with the old astronomer still being gently supported in the arms of his young scribal assistant, much of Thebes was now awake and curious as to what had just happened, as many of them habitually slept on their rooftops in order to better enjoy the cool evening breezes.

Sometime after the impact, came a great peal of thunder, temporarily and painfully deafening all. It was as if the cloudless sky was being rent from end to end. But even worse, was the later arrival of a several earth movements, which shook Thebes to its very foundations. Cracks and fissures appeared everywhere and in great profusion, even atop the pylon.

In the gentle light of their oil lamp the astronomer, with his still sore and tearing eyes, carefully summarized on several pottery shards the fallen star's remarkable events, while his assistant collected all the marking shards, cleaning off those with notations with the dampened linen rag, and then placed them back into their basket for reuse.

CHAPTER 29
Celestial Murder

Early that evening, just after a delicious evening meal at Horemheb's estate, and still sporting slight hangovers, Gregorieva and Richards were escorted by a *wab*-priest up to the enormous rectangular roof of the Fourth Pylon of Thutmose I. There, they discovered that they were not alone, as three other priests were busying themselves at the northern end of the massive gateway, with two others in the center.

Noting this, Gregorieva asked the escort. "Who are they? What are they doing?"

"Oh them? The same as you priestess. Those are our temple's stargazers. They're up here all the time, but gazing at what I am not certain. They are an odd collection, who sleep during the day and work at night. Regardless, this is your place, here, at this end. Be mindful that you don't fall off during the night. And, here is your fire," the priest said as he passed to Gregorieva a small lit oil lamp. Then they were left on their own, to their own devices, under a slowly darkening sky that promised to be absolutely stunning.

Placing down all of their burdens, the two temporal agents then noted that "their place" on the pylon's limestone roof was deeply inscribed with a broad circle evenly divided into radii, with each gap between the radii further subdivided. In the center of their observation circle a wooden surveyor's frame was positioned, which swiveled on a socketed post. They found next to the frame's post a handy basket full of large pottery shards and a small cup of charcoal sticks, along with another oil lamp with a fresh wick.

They began by laying out their experimental materials that they had purchased in the marketplace in preparation for the coming event—a jar of drinking water, a wide serving bowl that Gregorieva had etched with horizontal lines on its interior to record its volumetric content by the cup, and three cups, two for drinking and one for the serving bowl.

Having filled their indexed crater to its brim with six cups of water, they declared themselves ready for the coming event as they sat down facing the northwest.

Gregorieva could not believe how peaceful it was just sitting, at this height, high above all of Thebes. As a gentle breeze caressed and soothed her face, she imagined herself a falcon, effortlessly gliding on the high thermals.

Then that blissful image was rudely broken when their colleagues on the northern end began to noisily and excitedly point towards the northwestern quadrant of the heavens.

Frankly, neither Gregorieva nor Richards saw the glowing speck at first. But Gregorieva swung their sighting frame into that direction in imitation of their two neighbors, and quickly spotted a glowing dot that was getting bigger by the second.

"Mayneken! I see it!" she said excitedly. "I see it!"

"Mayneken, it appears white in color."

"Understood," he answered and made a note in hieroglyphs on a shard, transforming it into an *ostrakon*: a shard used for note taking.

As Maatkare continued to sight along the frame she announced.

"The star is clearly heading south Mayneken."

"Mayneken. Is it my imagination or is the star beginning to appear longer?"

"No, my sister, you are not imagining it. It is beginning to form a tail. Small, but a tail nonetheless. I now am beginning to see a yellowish tinge to it."

"Agreed."

"I am making a note of that as well."

The Russian and the American, as with their very animated fellow astronomers, tracked and noted the ever-growing star and its ever-lengthening tail until it was squarely due west of Thebes.

"How long have we been tracking this star?" Gregorieva inquired.

"Some four hundred and eighty seconds."

Silence.

"Tracking time please?"

"Now five hundred and ten seconds."

"Note its color my sister. A white head with a yellow to red tail."

"Agreed," she said as the Russian suddenly ducked her head away from the sighting frame.

"Close your eyes, Mayneken!"

She exclaimed as the slowly descending star touched the earth over the horizon in a glaring explosion of light.

With his head down while taking notes, the impact reminded Richards of a very prolonged photo flash that exposed the world with extremely harsh and distinct shadows. Even to him, so warned, the after-imagining was painful.

Then, glancing off to his right, he saw that both of the other teams of priests were on their knees, hands to their faces, in excruciating pain. As for Gregorieva, she was marveling at the over-the-horizon afterglow of the impact.

After some moments, Gregorieva said, "My brother, do you remember the time to impact?"

"Six hundred and twelve seconds my sister. Just a bit over ten minutes. I will make a note of it."

"The teacher in me wants to make a rough calculation. I count that the immortal one touched the land about ten times the swiftness of a bird's call."

"By the gods!"

"Indeed."

"Mayneken, we must now prepare our notes, and record our calculations, for much more is about to happen," Gregorieva said with a nervousness that betrayed and simultaneously conveyed her fear.

Thirty-eight minutes after the impact, the sonic boom arrived. It was as if an F-22 had just passed overhead.

But even worse, were the succession of tremors, which shook Thebes to its very foundations. But the only fact that Gregorieva and Richards cared about was limestone pavement around their serving bowl, which had been darkened by the bowl's entire contents.

As Richards carefully recorded on several of the *ostraka* the event's pertinent data, Gregorieva noted the lamp light of a silent crowd of some twenty to thirty who were seen moving quite rapidly down that most sacred road that connected the two Theban temple complexes—Karnak to the north with Luxor to the south. As the crowd neared, the temporal agents saw that a much-bloodied figure was being stretchered between six individuals in what looked like a common sun awning. Curious, they descended from their place atop the pylon with their handful of precious ostraka.

Now standing at the bottom of the staircase and in full view of the crowd, it became clear from their demeanor that the limp fallen one was of high station, and in actual fact, was the young king, Tutankhamen himself.

Following this fast moving throng, was a lone figure carrying a burden, a very bloody one. Stepping now from the shadow of the pylon's doorway, Richards asked, "Honorable priest, what is that you're carrying?"

Stopping with a great sigh, the priest placed the bloody and jagged stone on the ground before him, only then did he wipe off his sweaty brow.

"A stone from Amen Re's own harem temple," the priest said, while he bent over panting with his hands on his knees.

"The king was inspecting the day's progress on his wall decorations within the Great Colonnade when the trembling of the ground began. First, the workmen's scaffolding fell to the ground. Then, the two foremost pillars of the great hall cracked and fell. This god-forsaken stone that I carry fell as well and struck the king in the head, shoulder, and chest."

Stunned, Richards went to one knee and examined the gory stone, turned it over, and in the process discovered a smoothed side. And there, in the broken, but fresh carving he clearly read the glyphs—Amen Re. Now turning the inscribed side of the stone towards the priest, the Egyptologist declared.

"Here is the name of the culprit who struck down the king! The Great Hidden One himself!"

At this revelation, the weary priest ran off, forgetting his bloody burden, kicking up rooster-tails of sand with his sandals. His exhaustion was forgotten and replaced with the full-force of fearful superstition.

"What you just said was cruel, Mayneken." Maatkare chided with a sly smile.

"Perhaps, but just imagine my sister, the rumors that it will create?" Richards replied with a devilish

271

grin. "Imagine the vengeful righteousness of the Amen Re priesthood regarding the memory of the Amarna family."

"By the gods, Mayneken, you have just triggered that backlash and dashed to bits everything that the young king tried to mend!"

"That may be, my sister. That may be."

*   *   *

As one might imagine, the departure of the two temporal agents that night via the Karnak temple's innermost sanctuary should have gone completely undetected, for the sacred complex was entirely focused upon their recently fallen king. But as the old adage goes: "Familiarity breeds contempt." What should have been a none-issue turned into a white-knuckled event, because of the meteor-induced tremor, which shook Thebes. The Temple of Amen Re also was affected by it but in more subtle ways. The blocks that held the alarm gong mechanism shifted, making their ropes tighter.

*   *   *

Mayneken strained against the heavy cedar wood leaves paneled in gold that granted access to the god's inner-most sanctuary. The problem was that the edging on the leaves' exterior had been reworked during the temple's restoration, while those on the interior remained more graspable. Instead of gently working first one side and then the other, the temporal agent now had to work with both simultaneously and therein lay the difficulty. The tautened ropes attached to the hammers of the warning gongs were poised to strike at any sudden mistake.

With a grunt, Mayneken again succeeded in slipping his thick thigh into the gap between the door leaves. With a well-earned sigh, he relaxed as the alarm mechanism ever so slightly eased as well—strangely tighter than he had remembered.

"Maatkare, enter first," he nearly wheezed out from the effort. His head, torso, arms, and hands dripping with sweat.

Again, the lithe and flexible Russian managed to wriggle herself through, only slightly disturbing the hard-earned access. Then, she reached back through, for the all-important *ostraka* that she had left at the entrance.

Winded, but fast-recovering, and perhaps a bit too eager, Mayneken made his move. He slid through the opening with his slicked trunk, but too rapidly. Realizing his mistake, he used his right arm to block the closing breach, but not quickly enough.

*   *   *

Amidst all the chaos surrounding the young king's death, and the many preparations launched in such an event, a single peal rang of a warning gong. Deep and resonant like the mournful bellow of a gored ox, no one could mistake it within the temple.

At first, the single tolling caused more confusion than an immediate call to investigate, for its vibrant sound had never been heard before. But Perennefer, the high priest of Amen Re and former chariot commander all too familiar with moments of crisis, quickly assessed the situation. "Neferankh," Perennefer ordered his second in command—the Second Prophet of Amen Re, "see to that warning sound!"

Off ran the unarmed priest not knowing precisely what to do if he indeed found something amiss, while words like "abomination" and "heresy" rang in his head.

*   *   *

Meanwhile, breathless, the two temporal agents awaited the appearance of a brilliant white disk to appear about six to seven feet above them.

"I just hope for this one time Cartwright fires up the Disk of the Horizon early," Mayneken tensely whispered. "For as soon as it forms, I will signal them, and you are going out first with the data. Understood?"

Maatkare nodded once, clutching the *ostraka* to her breast.

At that very moment, the half-darkness of the inner-most sanctuary of the Great Hidden One vanished before the presence of a blinding light. Once fully-formed, Mayneken jumped as high as he could and extended his tightly fisted arm through it to signal their retrieval.

*   *   *

"Jesus H. Christ!" Colonel Cartwright roared, "They didn't even give us a chance to reconnoiter with the optic probe! Men, swing that crane and rope over right quick! Something's up! I can feel it in my bones!"

As directed, the wooden beam creaked as it swung into position above the hovering drop-ring. An old hand-made hemp rope tied with a noose at its end disappeared into the silver-colored temporal field.

*   *   *

Neferankh arrived at the massive and heavily gilded doors of the inner-most sanctuary only to marvel at the brilliantly narrow beam of light that pierced the near-darkness of the sanctuary's outer alcove. Daring to pass his hand through it caused shadows of such sharpness that he was amazed. At best it reminded him of Re's first appearance upon the horizon. Then a thought occurred to him. *Did Re appear so every evening during his sojourn through the Underworld?*

*   *   *

Per their agreement, Gregorieva was pulled out of the drop-ring first. Four of Cartwright's men pulled mightily on the rope and its pulley and the light Russian practically rocketed out of the floating ring.

Before she was swung wind and deposited on the ground, Gregorieva encouraged the men. "Hurry, hurry! Forget about me! Get Joey out—fast!" the Russian ordered in panic as several soldiers tried to unnecessarily assist her to the ground outside the portable temporal device.

*　　*　　*

But something had to have caused the sanctuary's alarm to ring, Neferankh finally decided. Exceedingly blinding light or no, his sense of responsibility, and also curiosity, overcame his natural fear of the unknown. And with both of his powerful shoulders, he pushed hard on the door leaves and entered the inner-most Holy-of-Holies just as the brightness winked out.

With his eyes seeing spots and the deafening sound of the warning gongs clanging, several of them this time, Neferankh became disoriented. Approaching the life-sized image of the Great Hidden One, the priest averted his eyes in self-conscious reverence while he recovered. Glancing about, he found nothing amiss. The glittering offerings, the burning oil lamps, and incense burners were unmoved and in their place. All that was missing was that strange and wondrous light.

*　*　*

"So how did it go?" Cartwright quizzed the adrenaline–buzzed Richards once the portable temporal device was shut down.

"I slipped on the sanctuary's door leaves and sounded off an alarm." Raising his arms and shaking his head. "Colonel, I was covered in sweat. Other than that, the meteor impact was spectacular. Those pottery shards that Vesna are carrying have all the data on them."

Now glancing over to Gregorieva, "So what's your story missy?"

"The beer was delicious and plentiful."

"Damnation! You people know how to party!"

*　*　*

Returning with their precious cache of *ostraka*, the debriefings at Horizon Pass went swiftly and soon Richards and Gregorieva were returned to their respective home bases, one in New Mexico, the other in Moscow. Sadly, Gregorieva had to look forward to enduring another debriefing at the hands of her colleagues.

The data that the temporal agents had brought back was swiftly translated and passed on to the technical and scientific experts in Chicago and Moscow for their evaluation. After many simulations, their best estimates placed the impact at around two miles per second, or better than ten times the speed of sound. Meanwhile, the aftershocks recorded in ancient Thebes were judged between 6.0 to 6.9 on the Richter Scale. To paraphrase a knowledgeable source that range would produce,

> Damage ... to a moderate number of well-built structures. Poorly designed structures receive moderate to severe damage. Such tremors are felt in wider areas, up to hundreds of miles/kilometers from the epicenter.

Perhaps the greatest tidbit to come out of the deployment was the surprise revelation concerning Tutankhamen's death. Paradoxically, the truth would have to remain a tightly held secret. But for Richards and Milson, they at least knew what the truth of the matter was. No, the young king wasn't murdered by an assassin's blow to the back of the head. No, he wasn't killed by a rampaging hippopotamus. No, he didn't die in battle by being run over by a chariot. As for the rest of the imaginative and oftentimes convoluted scenarios that scholars liked to spin, they could all be discarded in the dustbin labeled—fiction.

In the final analysis, however, who would have guessed that the conscientious young king preferred to inspect his pious additions to the Luxor Temple in the cool of the evening? Who would have believed that the youngster Tutankhaten accompanied his father on his inspections of the many monumental boundary *stelae* in the Amarna region? And during those inspections, who would have imagined that the young boy-prince had befriended a common stone cutter named Nakhti, who in turn had gladly shared the tricks of his trade with the young lad? And finally, who would have ever dreamed that the young king, who had acquired such a keen eye for proportion and space, would have chosen to access his artisans' progress from the harsh glare of an oil lamp's light?

Epilogue

Ay, the clear choice to succeed Tutankhamen, swiftly took charge of the royal crisis. He set into motion the process of arranging for the teenager's embalming and the acquisition of a tomb in that Most Select Places—the Valley of the Kings. This Ay had to do, for in actual fact, Tutankhamen had not even started his own tomb's construction. But regardless, a place for him had to be found. Ay quickly found that one such place was available, which could be made ready for the king's burial within the eighty or so days of his embalming.

His plan for Tutankhamen's burial was as unorthodox as it was fitting. After all, his mother Nefertiti, who had succeeded her heretic husband as Pharaoh Ankhkheperure Neferneferuaten, already resided within a substantial royal tomb within the Valley of the Kings. Ay's plan was to simply partition off a portion of Nefertiti's tomb, quickly decorate it as appropriate, and rob that which was needed from Nefertiti's burial to complete it. The last significant member of the heretic's family was finally put to rest, son with mother, together for eternity.

Ay's solution was pure brilliance. It also solved many courtly problems on several levels. When the boy-king was buried in his tiny tomb, Ay officiated, and days thereafter was crowned as pharaoh of the Two Lands.

*   *   *

While sitting on a crash cart in Horizon Pass' infirmary, Doc Allen finished thoroughly inspecting this young patient.

"Well, no breaks, no parasites, no bumps or bruises. Good for you," Doc Allen concluded with a slap on Richards' back.

Then the temporal agent poised a question for Doc Allen. "Doc, I've been thinking."

"Sure Joey. Shoot," the congenial Oklahoman invited with a smile.

"It's about this post-drop syndrome stuff."

"Yes …" the physician said now frowning with his hands on hips in anticipation of what might come next.

"Have you noticed I never seem to get PDS on the way back, but only on my arrival to the *somewhen*? And that Vesna never seems to be affected by the transit like I am?"

"Now those are interesting observations son," the physician said while crossing his arms across his chest.

"Why do you think that's so?"

"Well, it might have something to do with how many times you have dropped. The Soap Bubble's characteristics have changed over the past several years. On the other hand, the symptoms you experience may be because you're male and she's female. Then again, it could be the time itself that you're originally from. There's lots of pollution here that you don't experience back in the somewhen. In short, Joey, I don't have a definitive answer for you," Doc Allen said thoughtfully.

"Anyways, I'll take this up with Dr. Borov first thing. He might have some insights into the matter."

*   *   *

Imam Farhad Kurasan, the brother-in-law of the Grand Ayatollah of Iran, would not take "no" for an answer.

"*Imam*, please, allow me to drive," his driver pleaded.

Furious and turning beet red, "I can drive. I have a certificate!"

"Indeed *imam*, you do, but it is not a certified license. It is just a learning permit to do so," his driver tried to explain.

"If those whores in Saudi Arabia can now sit behind the wheel, then so can I! Now, Eshan, hand over the keys!"

"May I sit next to you in case you may have any questions?"

"Certainly, I'm not a fool!"

Fortunately, the vehicle that the *imam* was about to drive away was four-door Peugeot—an automatic. To Eshan's great relief, Kurasan settled himself in, adjusted the rear-view mirror, and clipped in his seatbelt. He turned the key and the motor sprung to life.

Revving it, Kurasan smiled to his driver, "This is pleasurable." And off they went into the snarl that is

Tehran's traffic. Within the first three minutes, Eshan thought that he would surely die, yet his student-driver seemed to possess the needed reflexes.

During the fourth minute, however, while rounding a curve too briskly, a pedestrian stepped out into traffic just as the light turned red. While Kurasan hit the brakes, his speed carried into the man who ended up on the hood and caving in the windshield. Blood was everywhere. The pedestrian looked like a rag doll.

Eshan covered his mouth with both hands in shock at the sight. Kurasan froze behind the wheel with his foot still plastered on the brake pedal. Both men were covered in chunked safety glass. Only a brief moan could be heard from the pedestrian, the left side of his head crushed like a ripe melon.

Finally, Eshan reached over and turned off the engine as a shouting crowd formed around the scene.

"*Imam*, get out of the car and I will take your place. You cannot be seen as the driver when the authorities arrive."

"Yes," was all that Kurasan could manage.

*   *   *

Hashem Shirazi was absolutely ecstatic. His monitoring program had just sent him a message that a recording 106 minutes and 37 seconds long had been retrieved from the US Air Force's satellite. Now all he had to do was get back to his cube at the Ministry of Intelligence and National Security and break it down with his laptop's hacking tools.

Walking with a new-found sense of purpose and vindication, Shirazi stepped off the curb just as the light turned in his favor. He heard the roaring of squealing tires, looked to his left in horror, and that was all he remembered.

His precious laptop flew as well, landing squarely on one edge, tumbled, as its frame and screen shattered against the curbing. Damaged but recoverable, the hard drive was crushed by the tires of the emergency ambulance that arrived minutes later.

Shirazi and his laptop died during those moments as did his dream of hacking a full US satellite feed. However, Iran would hack again—not of a satellite's teleconference, but of Horizon Pass' database.

THE EVIDENCE

2010. Gebel Kamil. *Meteoritical Bulletin*, **MAPS 45 1530-1551.**

> **Gebel Kamil.** 22°01'06" N, 26°05'16" E
> East Uweinat Desert, Egypt
> Found: 19 February 2009
> Classification: Iron meteorite (ungrouped)

History: A total of about 1600 kg of iron meteorite shrapnel (thousands of pieces), ranging in mass from < 1 to 35,000 g, plus a single 83 kg individual completely covered with well-developed regmaglypts, was found in and around the 45 m diameter Kamil impact crater by an Italian-Egyptian geophysical team in February 2009 and February 2010. Approximately 800 kg of the total mass observed in the field (the regmaglypted individual inclusive) was recovered. The Kamil crater was identified by V. De Michele, former curator of the Natural History Museum in Milan, Italy. The geophysical survey was carried out within the framework of the "2009 Italian-Egyptian Year of Science and Technology."

Physical characteristics: A 634 g type specimen, measuring 88 x 70 x 55 mm, is flattened and jagged shrapnel with a rough, dark-brown external surface. The surface originally sitting in the desert soil shows some oxy-hydroxides due to terrestrial weathering.

Petrography: (M. D'Orazio *DST-PI*; Luigi Folco, *MNA-SI*). Etched sections show an ataxitic structure interrupted on a cm-scale by crystals of schreibersite, troilite, and daubreelite enveloped in swathing kamacite. Kamacite spindles (20 ± 5 µm wide) nucleated on tiny schreibersite crystals. The spindles form small aligned clusters and are rimmed by taenite. The matrix is a duplex plessite made of approximately the same proportion of kamacite and taenite lamellae (1-5 µm in thickness) arranged in a micro-Widmanstätten pattern. Many sections show, particularly close to the external surface, shear dislocations offsetting the plessitic matrix and the crystals of the accessory phases by several millimeters.

Classification: (M. D'Orazio, *DST-PI*; Luigi Folco, *MNA-SI*) Iron meteorite (ungrouped), Ni-rich ataxite, extensive shear deformation and low weathering.

Specimens: Type specimens of approximately 15 kg and one section at *MNA-SI*; approximately 5 kg at *DST-PI*. Main mass of the recovered specimens at Egyptian Geological Museum (Mineral Resources Authority), Cairo, Egypt.

July 22, 2010. The Kamil Crater in Egypt.
Sciencexpress **Vol. 10, 1126, page 1.**

Impact craters up to a few hundred meters in diameter are common structures of solid surfaces of planetary bodies in the Solar

System. Statistics predicts that impacts producing small craters on Earth occur on decadal to secular time scales. However, small craters are rare on Earth because they are rapidly eroded, and the few identified so far [15 <300 m in diameter out of 176 craters up to 300 km in diameter] have lost most of their primary features.

We report the detection of a rayed impact crater 45 m in diameter on a Cretaceous sandstone target in southern Egypt. The ejecta rays highlight the exceptional freshness of the structure. The crater was identified by V. De Michele during a Google Earth survey and named Kamil Crater after the nearby Gebel Kamil. A geophysical expedition undertaken (SOM) in February 2010 revealed that the crater is bowl-shaped and has an upraised rim typical of simple craters. The true crater floor depth is 16 m and is overlain by a ~6 m-thick crater-fill material. Morphometric parameters agree with those predicted by models for a transient crater generated by an iron meteorite 1.3 m in diameter (equivalent to 9.1×10^3 kg) impacting at a velocity of 3.5 kms^{-1}, assuming an average meteoroid entry velocity and entry angle of 18 km sec^{-1} and 45°, respectively.

Centimeter-scale masses of scoriaceous impact melt glass (fig. S3) occur in and close to the crater, and indicate local shock pressures >60 GPa. We identified 5178 iron meteorite specimens totaling ~1.71 tons in the crater and surrounding area during systematic searches (SOM). They consist of <34 kg shrapnel produced by the explosion of the impactor upon hypervelocity collision with the target, except one individual fragment of 83 kg. This indicates that the Kamil Crater was generated by an impactor that landed nearly intact without substantial fragmentation in the atmosphere. The meteorite is classified as an ungrouped Ni-rich ataxite. Magnetic anomaly data show no evidence of buried meteorites larger than some tens of centimeters. Based on systematic meteorite searches, the estimated total mass of the impactor is of the order of 5-10 x 10^3 kg, corresponding to a pre-atmospheric mass of ~20-40 x 10^3 kg. According to geophysical models (2, 7), iron masses <3 x 10^6 kg normally fragment upon impact with the Earth's atmosphere, thereby reducing the energy of the impact at the Earth's surface. The present statistics, which include the recently discovered Whitecourt Crater and the Kamil Crater, suggest however that ~35% of the iron meteorites in the above mass range are not disrupted in the atmosphere.

The Kamil Crater in Egypt was found by V. De Michele in 2009 using Google Earth. An article in Science Express today announced the results of a 2010 expedition to the site. The site is indeed an impact crater, 45 meters in diameter and 16 meters deep, created by an iron meteorite 1.3 meters in diameter. Over 5,000 meteorite fragments were identified, totaling 1.7 tons! Owing to the existence of ejecta rays, the crater is estimated as being only a few thousands of years old.

November 2012. Geological and Geophysical Investigation of Kamil Crater, Egypt. *The Meteoritical Society* 47 (11) 1842-1868.

We detail the Kamil crater (Egypt) structure and refine the impact scenario, based on the geological and geophysical data collected during our first expedition in February 2010. Kamil Crater is a model for terrestrial small-scale hypervelocity impact craters. It is an exceptionally well-preserved, simple crater with a diameter of 45 m, depth of 10 m, and rayed pattern of bright ejecta. It occurs in a simple geological context: flat, rocky desert surface, and target rocks comprising sub-horizontally layered sandstones. The high depth-to-diameter ratio of the transient crater, its concave, yet asymmetric, bottom, and the fact that Kamil Crater is not part of a crater field, confirm that it formed by the impact of a single iron mass (or a tight cluster of fragments) that fragmented upon hypervelocity impact with the ground. The crater's shape and asymmetries in ejecta and shrapnel distributions indicate a direction of incidence from the NW and an impact angle of approximately 30 to 45°. Based on this mass value plus that of shrapnel >10 g identified earlier on the surface during systematic search, the new estimate of the minimum projectile mass is approximately 5 ton.

April 19, 2013. Iron from the Sky: the Potential Influence of Meteorites on ancient Egyptian Culture. The Royal Society A. London.

The Kamil Crater, as reported in the journal *Science* (2010), was formed by a hyper-velocity impact of a solid iron meteorite. The remarkably fresh bedrock ejecta from the crater, indicating a relatively recent date, covered prehistoric remains nearby, which were abandoned around 5000 BC. This would infer that the meteor impact occurred sometime after that period. The presenter of this lecture, Dr. Diane Johnson, noted that the establishment of the neologism for "iron from the sky," dates from the end of the 18th and beginning of the 19th Dynasties, in the neighborhood of 1300 BC. Johnson reasoned that the origin of such a neologism must have been established because of some famous, memorable, if not dramatic event. Johnson then speculated that the meteorite impact, which formed the Kamil Crater, may have indeed provided that event.

August 17, 2013. Microscopic Impactor Debris in the Soil around Kamil Crater (Egypt): Implications for the Impact Scenario. *75th Annual Meteoritical Society Meeting*, Cairns, Australia

The Kamil Crater is a 45-m-diameter simple crater recently discovered in SW Egypt. It was produced by the hypervelocity impact of the Gebel Kamil iron meteorite on layered sandstones. Due to its very young age (probably <5000 yr) and the dry climatic conditions in the Sahara, it is exceptionally well-preserved with a pristine crater structure, rayed pattern of bright ejecta, various types of shock metamorphosed and impact melt rocks, and a nearly intact assemblage of fragments of the projectile that exploded into thousands of shrapnel upon impact. In order to study the nature, mass and geographic distribution of microscopic impact debris associated with the iron impactor, we analyzed the magnetic extract of soil samples systematically collected around the crater during the February 2010 Italian-Egyptian geophysical expedition. The study has implications for the definition of the impact trajectory and for the estimation of the impactor mass.

The < 5 mm magnetic extract of the soil was sampled at incremental distances along eight radial traverses (45° apart) extending for up to 1.3 km from the crater rim. Each sample was obtained from a 30 x 30 x 5 cm soil volume. A total of 44 samples were collected. Aliquots of 10 representative samples collected in all directions within 200 m of the crater rim were washed in deionized water and subsequently dry-sieved and weighed prior to petrographic investigation.

The magnetic extract is generally dominated by magnetite or Ti-magnetite bearing lithic fragments belonging to the Precambrian crystalline basement. The latter outcrops are some hundreds of meters due NW of the crater. Particles typically several 100s of μm in size of Fe-Ni-rich (13-16 and 1-5 wt%, respectively) siliceous, vesicular impact melt glass testify to some melting of the projectile and occur in all samples around the crater with a significantly higher abundance in the SE sector. They have varied globular shapes, although many are spheroids. They often show delicate micro-structures in relief on the external surface such as glass filaments projecting from vesicles, micro-bubbles and irregular masses of P-Ni-Fe-rich melts resembling splashed schreibersite melt droplets. With the exception of rare stony cosmic spherules (mainly Barred-Olivine type; Ni = 0.4 ±) no other Ni bearing particles were found.

The high concentration of microscopic impact melt particles due SE of the crater is consistent with previous conclusions that Kamil Crater was formed by an oblique impact from the NW quadrant. The preservation of the delicate microstructures on the external surfaces of the impact melt particles is consistent with the young age of the crater. Ni-bearing material in the soil around the crater is essentially Gebel Kamil debris and can be used to quantify the impactor mass.

Based on their calculations, the team thinks that a 4.2-foot-wide (1.3-meter-wide) solid iron meteor weighing 2,267 to 4,535 pounds (5,000 to 10,000 kilograms) smashed into the desert – at speeds exceeding 2.1 miles (3.5 kilometers) a second.

October 24, 2013. Meteor brightens skies over city. *The Denver Post* 121 No.116 2A.

A large shooting star over Denver dazzled many Wednesday night and prompted calls and e-mails to the media. The meteor streaked across the sky a little before 9:30 p.m.

North American Aerospace Defense Command officials told The Denver Post that the shooting star was a remnant of the annual Orionids' meteor shower, which is winding down after starting on Oct. 21.

November 7, 2013. Russian meteor shows risk is bigger than scientists thought. *The Denver Post* 121 No.130 14A.

Scientists studying the terrifying meteor that exploded without warning over a Russian city last winter say the threat of space rocks smashing into Earth is bigger than they thought.

Meteors about the size of the one that streaked through the sky at 42,000 mph and burst over Chelyabinsk in February – and ones even larger and more dangerous – are probably four to five times more likely to hit the planet than scientists thought before the fireball, according to three studies published Wednesday in the journals Nature and Science.

Until Chelyabinsk, NASA had looked only for space rocks about 100 feet wide and bigger, figuring there was little danger below that.

This meteor was only 62 feet across but burst with the force of about 40 Hiroshima-type atom bombs, scientists say. It's shock-wave shattered thousands of windows, and its flash temporarily blinded 70 people and caused dozens of skin-peeling sunburns just after dawn in icy Russia. More than 1,600 people were injured.

January 2014. Did the Kamil Meteoroid contribute to the downfall of the Old Kingdom? *The Ostracon* **24 (2013) 12-20.**

The area of the explosion was inhabited during different prehistoric periods (or during historical times), as remains of human settlements are found close to the crater. There is no clear evidence that the event happened while the settlements were occupied in the region. The event was surely of catastrophic effect on the region as a whole, nonetheless. The shock-waves burned all living creatures in a wide region surrounding the epicenter of the explosion.

January 2015. Kamil Crater (Egypt) a natural laboratory to study shock metamorphism and impact melting. *Meteorite Time Magazine.*

Kamil is a simple crater of only 45 m in diameter. It was generated by the hypervelocity impact of the Gebel Kamil iron meteorite into sandstone rocks of the Cretaceous Gilf Kebir Formation. On the basis of archeological evidence, the impact occurred likely < 5000 years ago.

EGYPTIAN PRIESTS & PRIESTHOODS

The burden of performing the ritual functions for each god fell to the Egyptian priesthoods during the New Kingdom (1567-1085 BC). It was they who performed these myriad of acts on their king's behalf, which freed up his everyday existence.

Ritual acts required temples and resources that priestly bureaucracies managed for each god's estate. Just as naturally, priestly hierarchies developed in order to apportion the many tasks associated with the care and maintenance of a specific deity. At the top of this priestly ranking stood those who served the god directly in place of the king. These were the high priests, literally "the first servant of the god," who in some instances was supported by the "second," "third," and "fourth servant of the god." In contrast to these highly-placed priests, the vast majority of Egyptian priests, who shouldered the day-to-day temple duties, were the common priests, the *wab*-priests, literally "the cleaners."

This is not to say that specialty priesthoods did not exist, for they did, especially for those devoted to mummification and the necropolis. But one class of priests, the *sem*-priests, appears to connote a ranking of importance unto their own. While certainly not as powerful as high priests nor as lowly as *wab*-priests, the *sem*-priests were those associated with special cultic activities and even the royal palace itself.

While an old resource, the two volume work by Hermann Kees, *Das Priestertum im Ägyptischen Staat vom Neuen Reich bis zur Spätzeit*, (Leiden, 1953) and his *Indices und Nachträge*, (Leiden, 1958), remains the best place to begin the study of the high priesthoods of New Kingdom Egypt and later.

Sadly, English readers do not have such a resource. Instead, one must patch together disparate citations, which are often fragmentary and contradictory. A thorough-going overview of the history and development of the Egyptian priesthoods has yet to be written.

The Vocalization of Ancient Egyptian

The fact of the matter is simply this—the ancient Egyptian language is a very dead one. Its sound values have been long lost. The closest linguistic cousin, Coptic, is itself a dead language, but at least one that included vowels within its script. On this shirt-tailed basis, philologists have compared the vocabularies of the two languages and have constructed a "scientific" vocalization scheme *that approximate* what the Egyptian language might have sounded like.

Even if the assigned sound values are accurate, their quality remains as uncertain as their emphasis—or where the accent falls on a particular word. But it does not end there. Strong evidence suggests the existence of regional dialectics during any given dynasty.

To add more fuel to the fire, different vocalization schemes have been championed by the various schools of Egyptology, be they American, British, French, Italian or German. Consequently, the vocalization of ancient Egyptian is more a matter of one's cultural preference than anything else. In short, just what the language really sounded like during any given time period and region is totally up for grabs.

With the above caveats and considerations in mind, the author suggests the following sound values for the ancient Egyptian names that appear in this book.

Akhenaten – Pharaoh of Egypt: *ach-en-aten*

Amen Re – Chief divinity of Thebes: *a-men-ra*

Heketemankh – Astronomer and scribe of the Temple of Amen Re: *hechet-emm-anch*

Horemheb – Prince of Memphis: *hor-em-heb*

Mayneken – *Sem*-priest of Ptah: *may-necken*

Meryptah – High priest of Amen Re and adopted father of the *sem*-priest Mayneken: *mary-p-taah*

Memnefer – Egyptian capital of the Old Kingdom: *mem-nefer*

Nebamen – Vizier of Upper Egypt: *neb-a-men*

Nebkheperure – Tutankhamen's Golden Name: *neb-kheper-oo-ra*

Nebneteru – High priest of Amen Re: *neb-neter-oo*

Neferankh – Second high priest of Amen Re: *neffer-anch*

Nekhti – Stonecutter, sculptor, and second architect: *nech-ty*

Nesi – Chief houseman of Prince Horemheb's Theban estate: *nesy*

Parennefer – High priest of Amun Re: *pa-ren-nefer*

Ptah – Chief god of Memnefer: *p-taah*

Sebekmose – Astronomer and *sem*-priest of Amen Re: *seb-ek-mosy*

Sekemka – goat herder: *seck-em-kaa*

Sekemkare – Middle Kindom Pharaoh: *seck-em-kaa-ra*

Sekmet – Lion goddess of war: *seck-met*

Sobekptah – Commander of Fifty: *sobeck-p-taah*

Tutankhamen – Pharaoh of Egypt: *toot-anch-a-men*

Tutankhaten – Pharaoh of Egypt: *toot-anch-aten*

ABOUT THE AUTHOR

For W.J. Cherf, this is his last book of The Manuscripts of the Richards' Trust series. After a "sabbatical" into the realm of magical urban fantasy and paranormal archaeology, it was good to return to the facts and bedrock of historical science fiction.

Cherf is no novice to either archaeology or the ancient world, having excavated in Israel and Greece, along with extensive travel throughout the length of Egypt. Ask him sometime about what a sunrise looks like from atop the Great Pyramid. Or for that matter, walking ancient roads and surveying precarious mountain fortifications in Central Greece. Even better, inquire about a certain Fourth of July celebration atop Tel Beer Sheva in Israel.

As to why Cherf writes in his retirement years, he says, "I always wanted to write a book without footnotes." While this is surely true and is an oblique reference to his treadmill "publish or perish" days in academe, more than that drives the man. On more than one occasion, Cherf has said he has all of these stories in his head, which bedevil him until freed upon the world. In the end, you decide.

For free chapters of Cherf's works, not to mention a handy source for the latest and greatest in Egyptology, go to www.wjcherf.com. Cherf always says, "Sample before you buy." For reviews, go to www.amazon.com and search under "w.j. cherf." If you like this book, review it there. That's how authors find out if they still have the right stuff, straight from their readers.